MIRROR TARGET

An Urban Assassin Novel

by Austin S. Camacho

Cover Designed by: GinnefineArt.com

ISBN: 978-1972046005 - PAPERBACK
ISBN: 978-1972046012 - EPUB

Published by:
Audecyn Books, LLC
Upper Marlboro, MD USA

MIRROR TARGET
An Urban Assassin Novel

Chapter 1

There had already been fourteen homicides in Washington DC that month. Skye was about to add one more to that list.

The problem with tar roofs is that they get so hot during the day that even at twilight the stuff sticks to your clothes if you lie there for more than a few minutes. Not that it mattered. She planned to toss that black vinyl jacket and those black jeans in the trash as soon as she got home.

He was a couple of blocks from Blow Pierce Elementary School, his hunting grounds. And she was just a couple blocks from him, looking down at him with nothing in her line of sight between them. Neighbors here would mind their business and the nearest cops were more than a mile away. She held a firm grip on assassin's rule number eleven: own the geography.

Skye watched the target walking toward her. Mother Nature was being kind, giving her a moderate, breeze-free autumn day with just enough cloud cover to cut the fading sun's glare. She lay prone with her left hand feeling the warmth of the roof, palm down between the legs of the rifle's bipod. She slowed her breathing, snugged her rifle to her shoulder, and considered how this tall, lanky Haitian man had come into her sights.

Everybody knew Roberto "Bobby" Auguste molested those little boys. He was smart and he was careful, very likeable and a very good liar, but hell, he did it. And when that one child disappeared, well, things got crazy. No one ever found the body, but that one good cop did find the kill site. He found what most people would call undeniable evidence. Too bad he found it without a warrant. In Skye's mind, the illegal search and seizure law was a case of two wrongs making another wrong in what she laughingly called the criminal justice system. She thought the system itself was criminal.

The search was illegal, but would the cop be charged with a crime? Of course not. But Bobby Auguste wasn't charged either, since the evidence – proof of his ugly crimes – couldn't be used in court. Not the hair, not the disgusting selfies, nothing. Kind of a fucked up view of justice if you asked her. But that was what people paid her for. To un-fuck it.

This piece of 19th Street was on a pretty steep hill. The roofs of the bland row houses looked like a flight of stairs some giant might use on his way down into The District. Auguste stopped in front of one of those houses, two block away on the other side of the street. Another man trotted down the steps of the stoop to greet him. They were laughing and chatting like old friends.

This guy has friends?

Then the newcomer looked around a bit and produced an envelope. He grinned when he opened it and pulled out a couple of five by seven size photos. Skye would bet they were child porn. For a while molesters did all their trading online, but law enforcement had gotten so good at tracking and trapping them electronically that some had reverted to sharing hard copies because it was safer. And here these two were, standing there in broad daylight, trading pictures like baseball cards. The newcomer, shorter and not as dark as Auguste, was probably just as evil. And right then he was blocking her view. It would be easy to take them both down. Easy, and probably a community service.

But he wasn't the job. Skye breathed slowly, embracing her patience. Then the newcomer stepped to the side. Auguste was facing her. She had a perfect sight picture.

"Goodbye, boys," she whispered. She pressed her cheek hard against the buttstock. She stopped breathing. She eased her index finger back, slowly increasing the pressure against the trigger until the rifle pressed back against her shoulder, the suppressor made its coughing sound, and in her telescopic sight Auguste's crotch disappeared.

He screamed but at that distance it was a silent movie to her, just as he could not have heard her silenced shot. He fell forward and slammed down on the sidewalk, his head thrown back, mouth wide. Auguste's friend stared down at him, eyes wide, his face a mask of horror and fear. Pictures spilled from his hands, scattering around Auguste, some sticking to the blood spreading in all directions. The standing man looked around, then dashed down the street. He was probably screaming too.

Skye was already sliding three and a half feet of rifle into a case holding a portable folding tent canopy, the kind people set up at street festivals. The case had two wheels at the bottom, making it easy to roll even with the rifle's extra twelve pounds. She could take her time getting the case to the ground floor. The job was done.

At the request of the client Auguste did not get an instant death, but Skye knew he would bleed out inside of three minutes. Shattered pubis and ischium bones aside, there was now a gaping wound where his reproductive gear used to be. Her bullet had gouged out enough of his inner thighs to tear the iliac veins and arteries on both sides. And it was a good bet that even if somebody wanted to help this asshole, no one was going to try to apply direct pressure to that wound.

Inside, the building smelled like fried chicken and spilled beer. Three flights of stairs later, Skye pulled the blue cloth tube out onto the stoop and down sandstone steps to the sidewalk. She figured nobody in this neighborhood would notice a single black woman, average height and weight wearing long dreadlocks decorated with colorful beads. She was rolling her case up hill to the north when the ambulance passed her with sirens blaring. Would the first responders laugh, or even wonder about the dead man's condition? She imagined someone saying something like, "It was certainly personal," like they do on TV.

She turned left at the corner walking toward the thin sliver of sun just about to drop over the horizon. A black Honda Accord was parked halfway up the block. As she approached it, the trunk popped open, and the driver climbed out. He was dark with a quick smile and looked a bit like comedian actor Chris Rock. He reached into the trunk and pulled a latch that allowed him to lower the left half of the back seat. Skye lifted the canopy tent and slid it into the trunk until it touched the driver's seat. The driver slammed the lid shut.

"Thanks, Mo," Skye said. He nodded and returned to the driver's seat. Sky got into the back seat on the other side. She relaxed back into the corner as they pulled away from the curb.

"Do I want to know what you were doing with that thing?" Mo asked.

"Probably not."

"Well, I know there ain't been no street fairs around here since that Taste of DC thing," Mo said. "Got some damned good barbecue that day, but I don't think cooking is your thing anyway."

Skye chuckled, pulling off her wig, revealing her own short, cropped hair. "You getting to be one nosey-assed Uber driver. After that crap out at East Potomac Park I'd have thought you'd be glad to just get me where I need to go. Right now, how about you just get me to the storage area to drop this thing off, then carry me home. Can you do that please?"

"I guess," Mo said, "If you promise not to be dragging no more dead bodies into my car."

"I ain't promising you shit, nigga," Skye said with a loud laugh. "But you know I do my best to keep you separate from my business."

"Whatever that is," Mo mumbled. Skye wasn't sure how much Mo knew or had guessed about her profession. He had seen enough to conclude she was an undercover government agent, a freelance spy or maybe a gang shot caller. Or he might have guessed the truth. But for his safety she kept him in the dark as much as possible and she paid him enough to moderate his curiosity.

She did wonder what he would think about tomorrow's return trip to this neighborhood. It would be the first time she had asked him to take her to church.

Chapter 2

Skye didn't really get the whole AME Zion Church designation. The African part she got, since she had never seen a white person go into one. But she had seen Methodist Churches and Episcopal churches, and they looked very different. Bigger. Fancier. Like they were trying to impress God. The church she was standing in front of didn't look like it was trying to impress anybody.

There were four AME Zion churches in the District, and this was the newest. It occupied a modest building you might drive right past if not for the signage. As usual she had asked Mo to drop her off a couple of blocks away. Walking toward the sunset, almost exactly twenty-four hours after Bobby Auguste's shock neutering, Skye wondered if she looked okay. Would jeans and combat boots, a pullover and denim jacket be acceptable to church folks? Maybe not but considering what these church folks had asked her to do, It could be that standards were lower than she expected. How would she know. Neither her birth parents nor her adoptive father had ever taken her to church.

The skinny black girl at the door wore a dark dress and white pumps. When she spotted Skye she showed a nervous smile, like a person might wear if they were about to pick up something they knew was hot and might burn their hand.

"Evening," Skye said.

"Welcome, sister," the girl replied. "They all downstairs. Careful on the steps." She led Skye inside and down a narrow flight to a wide finished basement. The two rows of long tables covered with white tablecloths were set up like church pews with an aisle down the middle. Skye imagined these paneled walls and folding tables had seen more fried chicken dinners and Sunday school classes than business meetings. But this was business and the last part of what she was hired for.

Six women sat at two of the tables. All wore black dresses and white pumps, the apparent uniform of this informal team. It wasn't hard to determine which two of the women were the mothers of two others. Regardless of age their faces were uniformly grim, a couple looking embarrassed. All eyes were on Skye as she entered the room, the anticipation thicker than the worn beige carpet beneath their feet.

"Welcome Sister Skye!" The woman who broke the silence, seated separately from the others, was taller and lighter than Skye with a more robust figure. She sprang to her feet and rushed forward with a bright, embracing smile.

"Chalondra," Skye said, accepting the outstretched hand and the intense shake it brought. There was a beat of silence, as if Chalondra expected Skye to say more. Her smile dropped, then returned full force, perhaps to show she accepted the lead role.

"Well, we're all here. These are the ladies who asked me to contact you. We all just got back this morning from the trip, what we called the Auguste Farewell Cruise. You know, so we can prove none of us was in town when he… well when you… well, anyway, shall I introduce…?"

"No need," Skye said, raising a palm to quiet Chalondra. "I don't need to know no names and they already know all they need to know about me." Still standing, she turned to address the others. "And I know what I need to know about you. The mothers and, I'm guessing the grandmothers of the little boys who was molested and, in Chalondra's case, murdered by Bobby Auguste."

Tears welled up in the eyes of women whose children were damaged in ways they themselves could not even grasp. But they had their children home to nurture and care for. Chalondra, whose child never came home, had no tears. She was still running on hate. Well, it was closure time, but Skye wasn't quite sure how to proceed. The light in the sanctuary was too bright for this. The air was too fresh. These women were too soft. She should have practiced something.

"I know I agreed to report back to all of y'all. That was part of the contract. But I don't know how to say this, I mean, in God's house and all."

One of the mothers stood. "You just speak plain, sister. We ain't none of us saints."

Chalondra stepped back to stand beside one of the tables. Skye took a deep breath, and focused on her, the gang leader, the person who had the heart to find and hire her. Then she shrugged and pretended it was easy.

"Okay. I followed him long enough to get a pattern down. I set up on a roof not too far from here and watched for him. Not the first day or the second cause he's not all that consistent. When I caught him in my sights, he was trading pictures with another guy."

"And?" Chalondra said.

"And I blew his balls off with a heavy caliber rifle round. The .338 Magnum is a high-powered, long-range cartridge military snipers use. He knew he was shot, and he knew where and it would have hurt like hell. Took him three or four minutes to die. He had time to think about all the shit he done and who would have wanted him gone. The other guy ran off as soon as Auguste fell so he died alone."

Four of the women burst into tears. Skye thought they looked like tears of joy. One of the women muttered, "Praise the Lord." Chalondra nodded, then shook her head, then nodded again. What did that mean?

"So, it's over," one of the older women said, getting to her feet.

"It is," Skye said. "And you should be in the clear. Y'all was smart to get out of town while I did my work. Maybe not so smart to be all together but you got something in common so it'll work if you can all keep your mouth shut about me. I don't think the cops will push too hard to solve this one. They won't admit it, but a lot of them will see it as a civic duty thing. Good for the community, and like that."

Chalondra stepped forward again, shaking Skye's hand more softly than before. "Thank you. That was what they needed. Now they going home. Then you and me can finish our business."

The women rose and walked single file toward the door, led by the biggest of them who was also the oldest. Skye stepped aside to let them pass. The first woman stopped, turned and pulled Skye into a fierce, intense embrace that might have cracked a lesser woman's ribs.

"God bless you sister," the woman said, just loud enough to hear.

"Don't. Don't do that," Skye said, struggling to free herself. "And don't say that. I don't deserve it. I'm not the kind of girl you want to know."

The second woman also embraced her and whispered, "You the kind of woman I want my little girl to be."

To Skye's awkward surprise each of the women hugged her on the way out and mumbled, "Bless you child" or "Thank you" or some variation of one or the other. Moments later Skye stood stunned, staring at Chalondra who was now sitting on one of the long tables.

"Thank you, Sister Skye," Chalondra said. "Time to settle up, right? Now they all gone, we need to talk about your fee."

Here it comes, Skye thought. More negotiations. When this woman first came to her, broken down and pleading, it was clear she and her little group couldn't possibly afford the services Skye provided. But, so righteous was their need that Skye eventually agreed to payment over time, assassination on an installment plan. Now that the deed was done, was Chalondra going to try to tell her it was too much? And if they didn't pay, what then? Skye wasn't sure what she was prepared to do about it. All that flew through her head in a couple of seconds but her spoken response was terse.

"We had a deal." She crossed her arms.

Chalondra nodded and pulled a black leather purse from under the table. Her smile spoke of some secret she was bursting to share.

"I know we did. And you held up your end perfectly, right down to coming in tonight to give us all the word in person. I really do appreciate that. But I thought we could maybe change it up and pay you in a lump sum."

Skye rolled her eyes. "What, you want a discount? Auguste, he all the way dead, not ten percent off dead."

"I know," Chalondra said. "And I want to pay you off. Right now." She pushed the black Coach bag across the table toward Skye.

"Bitch, I told you the day we met I don't roll out of bed for less than twenty large."

"And that's what's in the bag, smartass."

Skye's eyes narrowed. She stepped forward and opened the purse. She found two stacks of bills wrapped in mustard colored banknote bands. She pulled one out and flipped through it.

"Is this for real?"

"Two hundred Benjamins," Chalondra said. "The pocketbook is my gift."

"Y'all steal the collection money or something?"

The thought made laughter bubble up out of Chalondra. "Shit, girl, that would have taken a couple years. I ain't never seen this much cash in one place before. It was a donation, kind of."

"Kind of?"

Chalondra nodded, facing Skye in the aisle between the tables. Her face became hard and serious, and Skye detected a hint of fear.

"I don't know how, but the man who made this anonymous donation knew about you," Chalondra said. "He knew what we hired you to do. He said he'd keep our secret and even pay your fee. And he said there's this much again for us four mothers to split if I'd do him a favor."

"Damn. What kind of favor is worth that kind of cash?"

"He wants to meet you," Chalondra said. "Seems like he's got a similar job for you but he's not sure how best to make contact. I wouldn't tell him how we found you, and I sure wouldn't let him ambush you here. So, he asked me to tell you he wanted to meet you. That way it was up to you. If you wanted to meet him, you'd contact him."

"Good looking out, girl," Skye said. "I can blow him off if it sounds shady. But if I do take a meeting, you girls all get paid."

"Yeah, and we can all use it."

"Who the hell's got that kind of money to throw around?" Skye wondered aloud. In response, Chalondra handed her a plain white business card. Embossed black lettering said, "Eric Gagnon Enterprises" along with a phone number and an email address. Skye was pretty sure she'd heard that name before or read it in the Washington Post's business section. Was this someone she should meet with? How did this wealthy businessman find out about her? And who would such a legitimate sounding man want killed.

Chapter 3

Jayla Johnson's patients often surprised her, none more than Skye who was a very special client.

"So? You like it?" Skye asked. She stood in front of Jayla's desk showing off her new Coach purse. The psychotherapist leaned back in her plush leather chair fighting to temper her smile. Jayla owned a bag just like this one, but it looked so incongruous slung on her patient's shoulder. It was suited for carry with the little black dress and three-inch heels, not the black jeans, tight tee shirt, combat boots and denim jacket that seemed to be Skye's comfort clothes.

Beyond that, Skye had the broad shoulders, flat stomach and small breasts you might associate with a body builder or a gymnast. Only her substantial hips and thick thighs stood against that judgement, but the fact that she wore no jewelry and there was no hint of perfume, solidified the body builder image. There was nothing girlie about this girl, as Jayla had long since realized.

"It's certainly a nice one," Jayla said. "This was a gift from a grateful client?"

"Yep," Skye said, turning once and dropping onto the chaise facing the desk. "See? It's not always cold, hard business. Maybe I should work with women more often."

Jayla jotted a few words in her notebook, the newest in a series devoted to Skye. She thought she was finally coming to understand this very unique patient. In the literature much was known about the minds of serial killers, angels of mercy, "Death Wish" style crusaders and mob hitmen. Skye, in Jayla's judgement, was none of these things. And there was nothing in the literature about those rare individuals who made assassination their profession. Skye was different from those others in one very important way. Despite her rigidly structured professional behavior, she had to know on some level that there was something broken inside. Otherwise, she wouldn't be sitting in Jayla's office every week. The décor - floors, carpet and furniture - was soft tans to keep agitated patients relaxed. Jayla thought this one might be more at home in a harsher setting.

Skye's smile was relaxed, contented. Her post-mission look. "What, no questions today?" she asked. "You're usually full of them."

"Wanted to give you a chance to share whatever was on your mind," Jayla replied. "Did you want me to guess? I'm thinking you're responsible for Roberto Auguste."

Bullseye. Skye's eyes flared and she sat forward. "I'm impressed. As many niggas get smoked in this city every week you picked out my work? Good thing you ain't a cop."

"It's not that hard," Jayla said. "Since I've been working with you, I read the paper a little differently, especially the crime reports. Yes, there's a lot of violent crime in The District these days, too much of it black on black crime, but you do things with a certain style, and your victims tend to fit a certain profile."

"Victims?" Skye snapped to her feet. "That nigga wasn't no victim. Them little boys he was fucking with, *they* the victims."

"Calm down," Jayla said. "I'm not judging you. Perhaps target would be a better word. Or your assignment."

"That's good," Skye said. "The clients gave me an assignment and were happy with the outcome." She waved her black leather trophy again.

"But not your typical clients," Jayla said. "And you said clients, plural. Parents of the little boy who was killed?"

"Actually, four families got together for this one."

"I see," Jayla said, writing again. "Based on what the news reports said this man was accused of, I understand why local families would want to take action. But I know the school the murdered child attended. Not the best neighborhood. I'm surprised that even together four families there could afford your fee."

"Well, they couldn't." Skye's eyes slid to the right and down. A new expression for Jayla. Was Skye embarrassed? Jayla waited, knowing that often opening up was a challenge for this patient. When Skye looked back at her, her eyes were hooded and her tone apologetic.

"What happened was, when the dead boy's mother approached me, she was real emotional and I thought she deserved my services. After all, the cop who fucked things up, he was trying to help, but as it was, the cops would never be able to get this guy. Anyway, I kind of agreed to do a monthly installment kind of thing." For Jayla, this was a whole new side of Skye. Not defiant or prideful. She sounded ashamed. Jayla knew she needed to step carefully.

"I think I understand. Are you perhaps regretting that choice for some reason? Was it uncomfortable?"

Skye looked up and her lips curled in the familiar smirk she used to deflect. "You probably think it was the right thing to do. Don't you?"

"You know what I think doesn't matter."

"You God damned skippy," Skye said. "You don't know shit about this. There's a right way and a wrong way, and sometimes…" the smirk phased into an arrogant smile. "Anyways, it don't matter. When it came time to settle up, they came up with the cash. And they even gave me a reference. Possible new client. I ain't checked him out yet. You ever heard of this guy Eric Gagnon?"

Jayla sat forward and laid her notebook down. "Wait, *the* Eric Gagnon? Media mogul Eric Gagnon?"

Skye stood long enough to hand Jayla the business card. She recognized the four trademarks, one in each corner of the card. Making the connection between this man and Skye left her both excited and chilled.

"So you know this guy, huh?"

Jayla shook her head in wonder. How could Skye be so worldly, so knowledgeable about so many things and still have these cultural blank spaces?

"Skye, this man is one of the most powerful people in the business world. He's Canadian, but now has dual citizenship in the U.S. His media empire spans three continents. He owns major newspapers, radio stations, television networks. Not stations, networks. And movie studios. That's not to mention the telecommunications assets."

"So he's rich," Skye said.

"Rich."

"How rich?"

"Way rich."

"How many commas?" Skye asked.

"Commas?" It took Jayla a moment to understand the question. Then she stopped to picture a dollar sign with numbers behind it. "Oh, I see. Three."

Skye nodded. "So, billions, with a B. And he ain't a sheikh or a prince or nothing. Interesting. Wonder who he would want pushed over the ledge."

"So do I," Jayla said. She was aware that Skye's moral compass pointed well wide of true north, but she worked by a set of rigid guidelines that substituted for the sense of right and wrong that directs most people.

"Skye, you've told me quite a bit about your business, after the fact of course."

"That's on you," Skye said. "Something about you having to report it to somebody if you knew I was getting ready to punch somebody's ticket."

"Yes, if I knew who and that it was a real plan." Even following those rules, Jayla knew she'd probably lose her license if anyone found out how much she did know. "Still, from what you have told me I don't believe you've accepted work in the past to just eliminate business rivals. This could open the way for a new avenue of discussion for us."

Skye heaved a deep sigh and stood, indicating the session would end a little early. That happened sometimes when she got bored. "Doc, you don't know me no better than that? No matter the money, you know the assassin's number one rule. The bastard's got to deserve it."

A swift elevator ride later Skye stepped out onto Connecticut Avenue and turned north toward Dupont Circle. The wide sidewalk was clogged with pedestrians walking like they had someplace to be. In Washington DC, rush hour wasn't just about cars.

Skye almost always met with Jayla after normal business hours. Today she had gone in just after the receptionist left at five. but at six o'clock the sun would hang onto the edge of the horizon for another hour. She walked through daggers of brightness at each cross street. They flash-heated the left side of her body for as long as it took to cross the street, but she was well distracted dodging the steady flow of walkers, bikers, and those crazy scooter things people rented but never truly learned how to use right.

It felt like dinner time, and there were lots of good places to eat right around Dupont Circle. Skye wasn't very hungry, but she figured she'd stop in to one and have a bite. By the time she finished she could continue her walk home, a mile or so due West, without having her eyes burned out by solar radiation.

She was just passing Café Citron, a good choice if she was in the mood for Mexican. They called it Latin food, but she knew what it was. Or she could swing through Un Je Ne

Sais Quoi... and just have dessert for diner. If she waited and hooked left on P Street she'd pass Pizzeria Paradiso, Emissary, Bagels Etc, Soho Tea and The Fireplace within a few blocks.

And that was when she noticed him six or seven yards behind her. A tall white guy with thick black hair and aviator sunglasses, broad shoulders and narrow hips. Gray suit and running shoes. He walked with a military gait and people headed in the other direction seemed to flow around him.

Checking back through her visual memory she realized he had been back there since she left Jayla's office. Maybe too long to be a coincidence. More to the point, he kept the distance pretty constant. When she stopped, he stopped. When she looked right at him he looked away. Most guys stared back at her. Some would smile.

Not quite trusting her instincts yet, Skye walked on into the Circle, crossing two streets against the light, raising a chorus of car horns and at least one profane outburst. She ignored the rude comments, focused on reaching P Street. A glance over her shoulder told her that she had not lost her follower in the traffic.

The sun, a red ball dead ahead, made her turn her eyes down to the wide brick sidewalk, moving forward a little more slowly. Who the hell would want to track her? DC's finest had never connected her to any of her work. Auguste sure didn't have any friends smart enough to find her or brave enough to try to do anything about it. She was the hunter, not anybody's prey.

She slowed in front of the gray brick building that housed Second Story Books and joined two women who were browsing through the line of wooden racks. The book racks lined the wall for almost half the block. She picked up some coffee table volume but was really watching her pursuer in the reflection of the three-sided storefront window. She grinned when her man stopped to examine the architecture.

A smart tail would have kept walking and passed her. He was no pro, and it appeared that he did not know she spotted him. On the quieter west-bound street it was also clear that he was alone. Did he have a death wish? Or maybe he didn't know who he was following. That was okay. She figured it was time to let him know.

Right past the bookstore was a little pizza joint, a place Skye wouldn't consider with Paradiso right across the street. But between that and the basement taco place was a narrow alley. When Skye came even with it, she side stepped and dashed down the alley, brushing the trash cans on the way. Halfway through the block the alley opened onto a small parking area, probably reserved for the employees of local businesses. She hopped left, crouched behind the nearest car, and waited.

It took gray suit three more minutes to emerge from the alley. He looked around, muttered a profanity, and stalked toward the street. When he was halfway there Skye gripped his hair and pressed her boot dagger against his neck.

"Don't be stupid," Skye said.

He froze and held his hands up, palms forward. The universal posture of surrender. He couldn't see the hand forged and ground stainless steel blade she held against his carotid artery. But his reaction told her he felt the edge and knew any resistance would bring a swift death, and that was enough. She backed him up until she could hop up on the hood of a Dodge. She was seated comfortably while he was bent backwards with just enough balance to keep standing. Too awkward a position to do much of anything.

"Can we talk?" he asked in a low, calm voice. To Skye's surprise she sensed no fear in the man.

"My questions, your answers," Skye said close into his ear. "You know me?"

"You go by Skye."

"Right. So who the fuck are you?"

"Isaac Thomas," he said. "Call me Ike. Look if we stay this way much longer, I'll lose my balance and you could accidentally slit my throat."

"Yeah, that would suck, huh?" Skye said. "Why you following me?"

"Mr. Gagnon asked me to talk to you."

Chapter 4

To Skye's left the street remained well lit. The building she faced bathed the parking lot in ever deepening darkness, but she knew their privacy wouldn't last and this was no place to drop a body. Too close to home.

Ike said. "Look, you ever hear that old saying about killing the messenger?"

"Yeah," Skye said. The boy had balls, she had to give him that. "It kind of depends on whether the messenger is armed."

"Paddle holster on the right,' Ike said. "Would you like me to…"

"I'll get it," she said. Skye transferred her knife to her left hand, making sure he could still feel the steel against his skin. She pressed her knees into his back and reached down with her right to feel for the holster inside his waistband. As she yanked the pistol free, she pulled the knife away from him and pushed him forward. He quickly spun to face her but kept his hands forward. Skye aimed the gun at Ike but pulled it in to rest against her thigh.

"Nice piece for a messenger," Skye said. "Me, I ain't big enough to carry a Colt Commander in my pants."

"Did you think I was just excited to see you?"

Despite herself, Skye chuckled. In the corner of her eye, she saw a couple start into the parking lot, stare at her, and back away. The lengthening shadows would make identification impossible, but this was still too public for her tastes. She needed to end this.

"All right, smartass, what's the message?"

Ike lowered his hands but maintained eye contact. "First, Mr. Gagnon wanted me to assure him that you're all he heard you were. I can check that box. Then he wanted me to set a time and location for a meeting. He hopes to contract your professional services. He knows you're selective and he thinks a face-to-face meeting would be most appropriate."

In her peripheral vision Skye spotted another couple starting into the parking lot. They stared at her and her captive and backed out. She wouldn't have much privacy for long and she wanted to continue this conversation. If this Ike guy was telling the truth, he was no threat to her, and her instinct was to trust him, for now.

"Hey, you hungry?"

Ike looked surprised, but only for a second. Then he shrugged. "I could eat."

"Come on," she said, hopping down from the car. "Tacos sound good. There's that little joint we just passed on P Street." She jerked her head toward the alley, indicating that he should lead. She walked close behind.

Halfway down the dark alley Ike said, "Can I have my gun back?"

"Sure." She dropped the magazine and racked the slide back. A .45 caliber shell flew out and bounced off the wall to her right. She pocketed the magazine, grabbed Ike's right sleeve and pressed the gun into his hand. He got it into his holster before they reached the street.

Once on the sidewalk it was only a few steps down to Tiki Taco, a narrow noisy place with a counter and stools along one side wall and a real jukebox. It was close and bright and busy, the kind of place where Skye felt safe. They moved toward the one empty table. Ike started to sit facing the door but when Skye tugged his sleeve he sighed and surrendered the seat to her.

"Kind of surprised you'd hold my own gun on me," Ike said. "What if it wasn't cocked and locked? What if I didn't maintain it and it would misfire?"

"Yeah, not my usual move," Skye said, "but as it turned out I judged you right."

"I'll take that as a compliment," Ike said. He picked up a menu. "Wait. Poke bowls?"

"It's kind of a Hawaiian taco place," Skye said. "Me, I always get the same thing, but they got a pretty wild mix of stuff."

"Maybe I should follow your lead then."

They ordered and waited until a stack of kalbi beef tacos stood between them before they returned to business.

"Not that this isn't pleasant," Ike said, "but the boss, Mr. Gagnon, tasked me with establishing a time and place for the two of you to meet. He's in town for the next three days. He has offices here but didn't know if you wanted to talk on his turf or not."

Skye crunched down on a taco, chewed, swallowed, then asked, "What's the mission? I don't get involved with business rivalries and shit. I'm kind of picky about the work I do."

"Mr. Gagnon will want to discuss the details with you himself," Ike said. "But I did a lot of the background checking, and I can assure you that this would fit your normal mission profile."

Skye's eyebrows spiked. How the hell could they know that? She had to admit she was intrigued, both by the possible assignment and by the messenger.

"What if I listen to Gagnon's rap and I don't want the work?"

Ike smiled. He wiped his hands on a napkin and pulled an envelope from his inside jacket pocket. He placed the envelope on the table and slid it toward Skye. "Five K just for taking the meeting. For your time."

Skye laid three fingers on the envelope and slid it back toward Ike. "Not yet. I don't know him. I know you. Will you be there?"

"Yes, ma'am," he said. "I'm Mr. Gagnon's personal security."

She nodded. "You wanted me to see you behind me."

"I'd have been real disappointed if you didn't."

"And you carry that piece cocked and locked in your pants," she said. "You know if you fell wrong that could ruin your whole day."

"I don't fall."

She sat her last taco down and locked eyes with him. "You was a SEAL."

"Yep," he said. Then paused, holding her eyes for a few seconds. He blinked first, then said, "Okay, you're not going to ask me. I'll tell you anyway. I knew Master Chief Maddox."

Skye swallowed and slid the envelope back toward herself. "Pick me up tomorrow morning at ten. I'll be in Dupont Circle Park."

Chapter 5

Skye stood relaxed in a light, misty drizzle on the circular marble rim surrounding the fountain at the center of Dupont Circle. The fountain claimed it replaced a statue of Rear Admiral Samuel Francis Dupont, whoever he was. Skye didn't know why the marble men and woman at the center were holding a giant bowl over their heads. There was no water running so it didn't even qualify as a fountain. But she liked the park surrounding it for what it represented: a core of serenity surrounded by chaos. She sometimes saw herself that way.

At nine fifty-eight she walked away from the statue and down the sidewalk that bisected the circular park. She passed the benches that embraced the park and ten steps later she was at the curb watching Massachusetts Avenue traffic race past her while drivers jockeyed for position to leave the traffic circle at their chosen street, one of the eight spokes of that peaceful wheel.

As she reached the street, a gray Ford Bronco slid to a stop, raising a hail of horn blasts from other drivers. Skye yanked the back door open and hopped in behind the man she had met the day before, the man who looked like a white version of Papa Maddox. Papa took her in at the start of her senior year of High School, after her real parents abandoned her. But even though Skye took his last name she hardly ever used it, certainly not on anything official. So how did Ike know her connection to him? Her curiosity was enough to make her want to consider taking a job that would have her working with Ike.

They exchanged good mornings and Ike circled the park once more before breaking free down 19th Street, a one-way business lane, one side of which seemed perpetually under construction. Jackhammers and tall cranes serenaded them for half a dozen blocks until Ike turned right and drove two blocks down L Street and down a ramp into the parking garage under a block-long, glass-fronted office building.

They exchanged no small talk during the ride. At the elevator Ike looked her up and down hard. He looked like he wanted to say something but didn't know how. Did he think she was in the same black jeans, combat boots and denim jacket she wore yesterday? Did he notice her star-shaped belt buckle? Did he think her soft gray Henley was too tight?

When the doors slid open Ike waved her in first. Inside he stood beside her, hands clasped in front of him, looking straight ahead.

"You strapped?" he asked.

"Of course."

He nodded. "I don't want to have to pat you down."

Ahh, he had to know what she was carrying, but was reluctant to ask. Skye appreciated being treated with respect. "There's a .380 auto at my back in my waistband. Got a one handed folder in my pocket. Couple more blades on me."

As the elevator doors opened again, Ike said, "And the belt buckle. That comes off?"

"Yeah."

Now Ike looked at her. "Thanks."

"You want them?"

"Nah. I'm good. Just needed to know before we went in the boss' office."

Ike led the way and kept walking, but Skye stopped after three steps to take it all in. The space was huge and not at all what she pictured when she thought "office." White walls, floor and ceiling made it feel even bigger. Over there was a full-size refrigerator, a coffee machine, microwave and a sink. Through that alcove she saw a meeting table with eight leather chairs around it. Ike had stopped at what looked like a family room setup. Full size brown leather sofa and two modern styled armchairs grouped around a wooden coffee table under a halo light. As she finally fixed on the only other person in the room, the man on the sofa stood and held out his right hand.

"This must be Skye," he said in a slight French accent. He was average in height and weight, yet this opulent setting didn't dwarf him. He had to be in his eighties, but he generated an energy that made him feel much younger. Small hand movements were quick and confident, even aggressive. He had a full shock of sandy hair and a smile so spirited and dynamic it made you return it. His suit fit like it was made for him. It probably was. She approached and took his hand, startled by the power of his grip.

"Skye, this is Eric Gagnon" Ike said.

"Well done, Ike," Gagnon said. Then to Skye, "The eyes reveal so much. Yours tell me you are the person who can do what must be done."

When Skye raised a questioning eyebrow, he said, "You can kill the killer."

Chapter 6

Skye settled into one of the chairs. Ike took the other. A trim blonde woman in a business suit appeared with a tray and poured coffee for them. She knew how Gagnon and Ike wanted theirs. She offered Skye cream and every kind of sugar and sweetener there is. Skye declined them all. Gagnon said, "Thank you, Daisy." The woman smiled and clicked away on businesslike heels. Skye sipped the strong black brew, more relaxed than she thought she should be.

"Why the smirk?" Ike asked.

"Hey, you know you've made it when a white girl brings you coffee and you ain't even on a plane." Then she turned to Gagnon. "Okay, what you got?"

Gagnon actually slapped his thigh. "Oh my. You are a joy. But to answer your question, what I have is a business proposition. One of my covert employees is in danger. I'm dispatching Ike here to recover him, and I'd like you to accompany him."

"Hold up," Skye said, putting her cup on the table. "Covert employees? You in the spy business?"

"No James Bond stuff here," Gagnon said. "But I am in the information business. Staying at the leading edge of next generation technology is how I maintain my advantage over my competitors."

"Industrial espionage is as vicious as the nation-to-nation stuff," Ike added. "The corporations with the latest tech first wins."

"Okay I get that," Skye said. "But I ain't no spy."

"My man in Atlantic City is," Gagnon said, crossing his legs. "He has acquired some very valuable information for me. But another group wants it badly and I'm afraid they'll take it and, sadly, dispose of my employee. Unless you two can keep him alive."

Skye shook her head. "I think you on the wrong track. I don't do bodyguard stuff."

"Of course not," Gagnon said. "That's Ike's job. You deal in death. I understand that. But I have word that another particularly talented killer may move against my man. If the killer surfaces and is moving toward my man, I expect you to make said killer disappear."

Skye turned a skeptical eye toward Ike.

He leaned forward, elbows on knees. "Skye, I'm pretty sure you know this fellow I need to protect. He's a professional stage magician with the rather bland name of Alan Brown."

"Uncle Al?" Skye breathed softly. A rush of memories pushed her back into her chair. Soon after she graduated high school her adoptive father had started grooming her for some fate she never really knew. But in the process, he introduced her to a number of people with special skills. Alan Brown was a stage magician and escape artist who also specialized in close up sleight of hand illusions. In three weeks of intensive training, he had taught her a good deal about the most common locks and how to thwart many of them.

She turned to Gagnon. "You're saying Uncle Al is a spy."

"He travels extensively," Gagnon said, "touring for his stage act. It doesn't pay very well. I supplement his income. He has a gift for taking things from people without them knowing it, and for hiding things where they can't be found. That makes him valuable to me."

"And a killer's coming after him," Skye said.

Gagnon set his coffee down and drew a cigar from his inside jacket pocket. "Not yet," he said, clipping the cigar's tip and pulling out a gold Zippo style lighter. "My information is that a competitor is trying to co-opt him. They want the information he's carrying and are offering him a good deal of money for it. I expect Mr. Brown will remain loyal to me. However, my competitors know he has a ticket to Washington. As soon as he moves to leave Atlantic City, they'll know they've failed to persuade him. At that point I expect their hired killer to move on him. My countermove is to send Ike to pick him up and bring him in safely."

Was the lighter gold colored, gold plated, or actually solid gold? "You figure he's safe until he makes contact with Ike here. Then the opposition's killer will move on them. You want me to spot that individual and take him out of the game."

"Precisely," Gagnon said, lighting his cigar.

Skye turned toward Ike. "He said Atlantic City. I take it Al is performing at one of the casinos. When are you supposed to pick him up?"

Gagnon said, "He will meet with Ike tomorrow night, after the show."

Staring at Ike, Skye's expression shifted. "Seriously? You couldn't find me no sooner?"

Chapter 7

Skye waited until she and Ike were in the elevator before she spoke again. "I'm not real sure about this, man. It's just not my kind of job and besides that…"

"You want time," Ike said. "You're used to doing research on the target, scoping out locations, prepping the right weapons and tools. I get it. But this is kind of emergent."

"Yeah, I get that," she said. "I still need to think it through. Where you staying?"

"Got a room in The Fairmont."

"Damn. Personal security must be a nice gig," Skye said. "And I get why you don't want to make this run by yourself."

"I won't," Ike said, stepping out of the elevator and leading the way to his SUV. "I could get another operator or two to back me up. That's not the point. I want you."

"Flattering. But I need to think it through. How about you meet me in the hotel lobby in a couple of hours? I'll give you a definite answer then."

"Guess I can live with that," Ike said, reaching for his vehicle's passenger side door. "Where can I drop you?"

"Thanks, but I'll walk a bit," Skye said. "It'll help me clear my head."

Skye watched Ike's Bronco until he was out of sight, then she pulled out her phone, dialing while walking.

"This is Jayla."

"Hey, Jayla, it's Skye. Got a couple minutes?"

After a beat of silence Jayla said, "Skye, are you in crisis? Patients don't call my personal number except in emergencies. What's happened?"

Skye chuckled. "I wanted to see if you were free. If you were with one of your crazy people you wouldn't have answered. Where you at?"

Jayla breathed ice through the phone. "I'm at lunch."

"Perfect," Skye said. "Where?"

"That's not how this works. Make an appointment."

As Skye started across the street a car wheeled around the corner. The driver tooted his horn. Skye stopped in the middle of the street, gave him a hard look, then proceeded. "You know what, no problem," she told her phone. "I'll just go to your office and tell your next appointment to get out and take his place."

She listened to Jayla chew for a few seconds, then the psychotherapist's tight voice said, "Ocean Prime."

"Cool," Skye said. "Colorado Building, right? Sit tight. I'm only five or six blocks away."

Jayla had snagged a table by the front window so she could watch the traffic pass her by. She watched Skye bouncing toward her, walking as if nothing in the world was wrong. But Skye smiling didn't necessarily mean good times. She considered again that she hadn't known all she was getting into when she made this deal with the devil. Maybe the professional and legal risks she accepted for keeping this fearsome sociopath's secrets were too great. She was walking on a moral razor's edge every time they met. Did she need to let this patient go?

She remembered that first phone call from Skye. She stated right off that she was not crazy, She described herself as a professional assassin and that her profession sometimes called on her to deal with some confusing ethical issues. She was prone to self-examination and didn't always love what she saw. She didn't need therapy, Lord knows, but she wanted someone to talk things out with.

Before Jayla could hang up, Skye offered her an odd incentive for accepting her as a patient. She knew she was a unique case and doubted any psychologist has ever gotten inside the head of a freelance high-end killer. Understanding her motivations could be the path to the Award for Research in Psychiatry, the prize they used to call the Hofheimer Prize. When Jayla pointed out that the prize was for a contribution that has a major impact on the field, Skye had laughed. She was certain that the inner workings of the mind of an independent professional killer would qualify. It was the right bait and despite her own moral and ethical reservations, Jayla had swallowed the hook.

Months later that incentive still hung at the back of her mind, but her focus soon shifted. She came to care about Skye, as she did every person she saw in her office and turned to finding a way to help this unique patient. Part of her still felt that helping Skye define a moral compass might save lives, but more, she hoped to save this soul.

Introspection stopped when Skye reached the door. She didn't exactly fit in with the sophisticated décor of this upscale restaurant, but she walked in as if she were the owner come to inspect the service. She dropped into the chair opposite Jayla and said, "What's up?" as if they were any two black girls meeting for lunch. "That looks good. What the hell is that on your lettuce wedge?"

"It's crab." Jayla did not return her smile. "What can I do for you, Skye?"

"It's about an upcoming job," Skye said. "I have to make a decision fast and I kind of wanted to talk it out with somebody."

She interrupted herself when the waiter approached offering a menu which she ignored. "Dude, is it possible I could get a cheeseburger in this classy place?"

"Of course. And welcome to Ocean Prime. Would you like to start with a beverage?"

"Since you asked, a Moscow mule. And make that burger as rare as they let you make it, okay?"

As the waiter walked away Jayla leaned in. "You know we don't discuss things you are about to do. I'd be under a professional obligation to…"

"Will you relax?" Skye gripped one of Jayla's hands, looked down at her nails and back up. "Hey, I like that color on you. Red but almost purple. And the job I'm looking at isn't my usual kind of gig. That's why I wanted to talk to you."

Jayla raised an eyebrow. "You're thinking of doing something less… sanguine?"

"I know what that means," Skye snapped, "and yes."

Jayla quickly backpedaled. "Hey, I wasn't trying to…"

"Sure you were." Skye leaned back and lowered her head but maintained eye contact. "You're always trying to sound superior to me. But it's okay. Part of the game between you and me. But I put up with your shit cause you put up with mine."

Jayla wasn't sure where to go with that and was grateful when Skye's drink arrived. While her patient wrapped her lips around the copper straw, Jayla forced herself into therapist mode.

"Of course, I'm curious about your new endeavor, and why you're considering a change."

"First of all, it's a one-off," Skye said. "I was asked to help out with a personal protection gig, out of town. It's for that Gagnon dude I told you about. I'd kind of be running interference against one of my competitors. Get it?"

"My sense is that you're not wholly comfortable with that role."

Skye's expression of uncertainty dissolved into a smile when the waiter placed her plate in front of her. Skye nodded thanks and quickly sank her teeth into the cheeseburger. Caramelized onions and mayo oozed out the other end. Skye cleared her mouth but didn't put down her meaty prize.

"Damn! Now that's a cheeseburger. You eat in the best places, Jayla."

"Glad you like your lunch," Jayla said. "It sounds as if you don't like this new job you've been offered. Want to tell me why?"

"It's just not my thing," Skye said. "And I don't know anything about the opposition. For all I know this other fellow might be a right guy. Besides, I like being the hunter. You control the action and anyway, it's just more fun. And to be honest, it's always safer playing offense."

"Considering all that, what's tempting you to take this job?"

Skye shoved a couple of fries into her mouth. "The guy who recruited me for this used to work for my dad. The man that adopted me, not that asshole that split when I was little. Anyway, this guy, I bet he's got some great stories to tell. And the guy we're protecting turns out to be one of the guys who helped me learn my profession, even if he didn't know what he was training me for. You know I only had Papa for three years before I lost him, fighting for some other country's freedom. This could be a chance to plug into… I don't know. Something. The past, I guess. Papa Maddox's past."

Jayla waited until Skye had taken another big bite and chewed a few times before she steepled her fingers and tipped them forward to point at Skye.

"And how do you feel about that?"

Skye sucked more drink to clear her mouth. "Why you always got to go there? How am I supposed to feel? Could be great to hear more about who Papa really was. But what if this isn't what he had in mind when he took this orphan in? What if he'd be disappointed in me? I don't know, it could be so cool to hear more about Papa's early days. But scary too. I can still say no, but am I going to look back on this as a missed opportunity?"

Jayla sat back, nodding slowly. Skye's adoptive father's approval would be important to her. And despite her apparent fear, Jayla knew Skye wanted to know if she would have gotten it. It seemed she was there to ask Jayla's permission. For her part, Jayla was eager to prompt Skye down any path that led away from the life of the hired killer. As counselor, she was more than Skye's therapist. She was Jiminy Cricket. But she had to speak Skye's language, had to work within Skye's pre-existing moral construct.

"You said you knew the person in danger. He helped to train you?"

Skye chewed a big mouthful and pointed at Jayla's plate. Hint taken, Jayda sliced a bit of her lettuce wedge, scooped a lump of crabmeat onto the fork, and eased it into her mouth. She savored the blue cheese and louis dressing, but part of her envied her patient who clearly didn't worry about her figure.

Skye wiped her mouth with the napkin and smiled at some memory. "Alan Brown, Uncle Al, showed me a whole lot about locks and how to open them. Thanks to him I can get into just about any place. And it was a nice break from the fighting, weapons, and demolition training. He was a magician, not a criminal, and he presented his lessons kind of like a game. He'd even throw word games and puzzles at me while I was working on a lock, getting my brain to do two things at once."

Jayla saw her opening and seized it. "The question you haven't asked yourself is this: how will you feel if Alan Brown dies because you weren't there and didn't have his back?"

Jayla watched the expressions chase each other across Skye's face. Surprise at the question. Anger, perhaps at herself for not thinking of it. Open mouthed confusion, wondering and deciding how she would feel. Lips clenched and head nodding at the decision. Then eyes on Jayla in recognition.

"Yeah, I'd feel like shit if that happened. Guess I go play defense for a couple days. See, this is why I pay you. You see shit I don't, even shit inside me." Skye pulled out her phone to check the time, then dropped two twenties on the table. "Okay, I got to jet." Skye stood and for a moment stared at her boots. There was more. Something hard.

Skye looked up, muttered "Ummm… thanks," and hustled out of the room.

Jayla grinned. Progress. Skye could be challenging, but Jayla knew she certainly couldn't abandon her patient, not this close to a real breakthrough.

Chapter 8

Walking north on Fourteenth Street, Skye felt more relaxed. Uncertainty didn't sit well with her, but having made a decision her brain fell into its familiar planning mode. It was maybe a mile and a half walk to Ike's hotel. On a warm Fall day with low hanging clouds and a nice breeze, the walk would provide thinking time.

She had mentally made her packing list for the trip by the time she made the left turn on K Street. She had no idea how many blocks it was to Washington Circle Park, although she could tell you it was an easy fifteen-minute walk. The traffic circles dotting the city were laid over a grid pattern, so the streets emanating from the circles cut the blocks into odd shapes. In terms of walking, some were much shorter than others. It was one of the quirks Skye liked about her city.

The Fairmont was just north of the circle. Skye stared up at the beige stone edifice before marching up to the door. This hotel was one of the most pretentious buildings in the city, and in Washington DC that is really saying something. Ten steps in she spotted Ike, who stood when he saw her.

"Nice to see you," he said. "Even nicer if you've come with the answer I need."

"You kidding? How could I say no to working with an old pro like you? I mean, you're so charming. And inconspicuous."

Ike glanced around at the hotel's décor, its marble floor and modern art, then at Skye's denim and combat boots. "Yeah, you blend right in. Now, can we sit for a minute?"

Ike led her to the narrow hall that held a long row of meeting setups, each composed of four comfortable chairs clustered around a small glass table. They passed five empty sets before sitting. A brick wall stood on her left. The wall to her right was glass, facing into the hotel. She had a long clear view past Ike, as he had of the space behind her. She would have to remember this for a meeting space.

"The basics here are pretty simple," Ike said. "We fly up to Atlantic City in the morning and kind of get the lay of the land. Tomorrow night we go watch Brown's magic show. He'll recognize me in the audience, and we've got a standard signal if he wants to wave us off. Otherwise, we meet him at his dressing room afterward and escort him to the airport."

"I take it the other side have been watching for a chance to grab him," Skye said. "What they waiting for?"

"Brown got hold of some tech they want," Ike said. "Actually, it's just a computer program. Some big innovation in telecommunications that will give this other company a huge leg up in the industry. They've been trying to buy it back from him."

Skye held up both index fingers, looking down for a second while she put it all together. "So, our boy stole this program from another company. They been trying to get it back from him. First, legally. Growing offers of cash. Then they probably tried to scare him out of it."

"Sounds right. I don't know how he got it in the first place."

Skye chuckled. "He's a magician. But this means they got people on him, raising the pressure. When they see him with you… us… they'll figure he's picked his side and he's on his way in. At that point…"

"At that point I figure they'll throw the switch. If they kill him, he can't hand off to anyone."

"Right. Once we make contact, they'll figure he might already have handed it off." Skye's eyes drilled into Ike's. "They'll want to kill all three of us. But you knew that."

Ike didn't even blink. "Sure. Problem is, when they come at us, they won't come in like a military attack. I might not see it coming. That's why you."

"That's why you need someone in my business. But why me, specifically?"

Ike took a deep breath. "Look, I had a lot of respect for Master Chief Maddox. He talked about you at the end, on that last mission, and I wanted the chance to get to know you."

"Wait. You was on that last mission with him?"

Ike nodded and sat back. "Now it's my turn. Before I told you I knew your daddy, you knew I was a SEAL. How?"

"Look at you," Skye said, raising both hands, palms up. "The military bearing just oozes off you. And Spec Ops guys move a certain way. But Rangers are thinner, built for long walks. Recon guys too, they tend to hike in. SEALs are built for swimming. You get that broad back, but your legs are a normal size. You all look a little top heavy."

"Fair enough," Ike said. "Now, you got questions for me?"

"Lots. Most of them can wait. Right now, I want contact info." She handed Ike that week's burner phone. "I don't deal with middlemen. After you put your number in there, give me a direct number to Gagnon. One he'll answer."

"No problem," Ike said, taking her phone and pushing buttons.

"By the way, you already got plane tickets?"

"Of course," Ike said.

"Good. If they know you, they'll be watching the airport. But we ain't going that way. We'll drive in tonight. That way I can bring all my favorite tools along. And, when we get in a car after the show, they'll think we're headed to the airport, but we'll really just be getting on the road back to here."

"I don't know," Ike said with a grimace. "Don't like having my hands on the wheel when I'm watching somebody."

"Oh, don't worry," Skye said, planting an elbow on the table and waving the objection away. "I got a guy."

Skye made the phone call as she and Ike parted company. She was leaning against the front of the building when Morris Gardner pulled up in his black Honda Accord. She opened the back door and dropped inside, instantly feeling less exposed. Mo's car was a safe space for her.

"How's it going today, Mo?"

"A day like any other, Skye," he said, pulling out into traffic. "Heading home, right?"

"Yeah, but take your time. We need to talk."

Morris glanced at her in his rearview mirror. "Uh oh. That don't sound good. It ain't about whatever your business is, is it? I mean, I don't know what exactly you do, but I'm happy you keep me at a distance from your work."

"I do everything I can to keep you from getting wrapped up in my business, That's why I don't tell you nothing except where to pick me up and where to drop me off. And why all the money goes through Uber. So far."

Early on, Skye had decided to use Uber to get around the city for several reasons. First, owning a car made her too easy to track down and left an unavoidable paper trail. Calling an Uber made her movements harder to trace. So she paid Mo a monthly retainer to always respond when she called. He was both reliable and very good at not asking questions. Over time they had settled into a comfortable relationship. She didn't trust easily, but he had become a trusted agent.

After a moment of silence, Mo repeated, "So far?"

Skye watched the city roll past her window as commercial property slowly gave way to the more residential look of Georgetown, her own neighborhood. "What if I wanted to deposit some money for you outside of Uber?"

"I appreciate the thought," Morris said, "but I don't want no trouble with the IRS. And why would you be doing that anyway?"

"Need some help outside of the normal routine."

Mo started shaking his head. "I don't want no more dead bodies in my car. That thing a couple of months ago, the shooting, talking to the police for you, and them dead men? I don't want no more of that."

"Nothing like that, man," Skye said, sliding to the right so she could see his face better. "Just a longer drive than usual."

Mo stopped at a corner on M Street and swiveled to look at her. "You don't usually pussyfoot around, girl. How much longer? You mean like to Baltimore?"

"I mean like to Atlantic City."

"You kidding?" Mo took a right, easing down one of the narrow streets that always has cars parked on both sides. "That's three or four hours, easy. And then I got to drive all the way back. That's a day."

"Well, sort of," Skye said. "You'd be staying in town for a few hours while I took care of some business, then bringing me back. While I'm working you could spend some time in the casinos. We'd probably leave town around ten."

"Oh yeah," Mo said. "Yolanda would love that. 'Hey, babe, I'm going to spend the day and half the night in Atlantic City with this sister I drive around. Be home around two in the morning.' I know how that'll go over."

"It's really me and a friend," Skye said. "And we'd be bringing another guy back with us.

And I get that your wife might not be down with this. But," she leaned forward between the front seats, "would five grand make it easier to sell?"

"Five large?"

"That's right. But we need to leave tomorrow morning."

Morris pulled into a parking space two blocks from Skye's apartment. He took a deep breath and let it out slowly. Still looking out the windshield he said, "you know, half the time I think you're a government agent, then I think maybe you're some kind of criminal. And I honest to God don't want to know what you do between when I drop you off somewhere and when I pick you up. But now you bringing in a partner and I need to know. Is he in the same business?"

"A related field." Skye smiled at her own description. "Ike's not involved in anything crooked, if that's what you're asking. And I promise we're not going up to Jersey to do anything illegal, but we need someone we can trust behind the wheel. I need you on this, Mo." She could see he was on the fence about accepting her offer. She didn't know what else she could say to persuade him, so she stayed quiet. She watched his internal monologue expressed through nods and head shakes until he finally pressed his forehead into his palm.

"Are you going to be in danger up there?"

"Mo, I swear to you I will not ask you to be anywhere near anything risky. I wouldn't do that to you."

Mo unhooked his seat belt and turned to face her. "That is not what I asked you, girl. Are *you* going to be in danger up there?"

The question honestly startled her, and she took a moment to decide how best to answer. Finally, she said, "I'll feel a hell of a lot safer if you're there to get me out of that place when I call."

Mo turned back around and buckled himself in. "Okay. Let me go tell Yolanda I got a long haul to do."

Skye popped her door open. "Thank you. Seriously, I wouldn't trust anybody else to…"

"Don't you have to make arrangements with this Ike guy or something?"

She rested a hand on his shoulder. "You right. Can you pick me up at like eleven tomorrow? Then we'll collect Ike at the Fairmont and head north. And trust me, this gone be fun."

Chapter 9

Some people drift up out of sleep in slow waves, clinging to the warms and comfort of that near-dream state. For others there is a thick black line between asleep and awake. To Skye, sleep was not anticipated relaxation but a necessary function to stay fit. In her ideal world it was simply a blank space with no perceived passage of time. She woke up all at once, ready to start another day.

This time she awoke to an unfamiliar sensation. This was not the usual sharpness of being on a job, nor the relaxed feeling she generally had after finishing a job. It was something in between and she found it unsettling. She thrived in fight or flight mode, but "wait and see" didn't suit her.

Stepping into the shower, Skye went over her last conversation with Ike the night before. It all sounded so simple. Cruise up to Atlantic City, check out the environment, have dinner and watch Alan Brown's magic show. After his performance, make contact in his dressing room, get him into Mo's car and head home. Easy peasy. And two long drives during which she could get some background on the man who adopted her after her parents disappeared and her brother died of an overdose.

She scrubbed in water as hot as she could stand it while she mentally assembled her packing list. She shouldn't need much for the few hours she'd be out of town. Then she scrubbed her teeth and combed out her short hair. Her skin tended toward dry, so she moisturized her face and entire body. All her self-care products were cheap store brands.

She knew the stuff chain drug stores sold under their own label came from the big-name companies that made the expensive stuff they sold on the next shelf.

In her white terrycloth robe, she turned on her television as she walked through her small living room on the way to her galley kitchen. There she popped two slices of bread into the toaster and started browning some ground sausage while she listened to the local news. She heard her most recent job reported with no more or less attention than the other two shootings that took place on the same day. Two teenagers facing off at a party, a drive by while the victim sat in his car, and Skye's work, with no mention of the dead man's crimes. Just another murder. Just the way she liked it.

She poured out the excess grease and added diced onions, mushrooms and green peppers to the pan. The aroma soothed her. This was what the start of a good day smelled like. Papa Maddox used to make omelets on weekends. She added two beaten eggs to the pan, covered it all with shredded cheese, and left it on a low heat while she buttered her toast. Then she folded her omelet, slid it onto a plate and sat it on the island where she took all her meals. Hot black coffee completed her breakfast. She slid up on the high stool and ate with her bare feet swinging free.

As usual during meals she stared out the window of her Georgetown rental. The brick house across the leafy, narrow street looked pretty much like the one she lived in, but it was all the view she needed. Familiar and boring so often equated to safe.

As soon as she finished breakfast Skye washed and put away her dishes. Then she returned to her bedroom and pulled on another pair of black jeans and an earth tone Henley. To soften her often severe look she added a pair of suede side-zip Timberlands. The three straps with buckles were just for show.

Her second bedroom served as her workshop and storage area. There she scanned the pegboard wall that displayed a variety of weapons. It bothered her that she couldn't be sure what she would encounter in Atlantic City, but she knew she wanted to carry something small and light. She selected the Sig P365. At around six inches long and under five inches tall it was 18 ounces of bad news for anyone who crossed her. At one of the benches, she pulled out a drawer and fished out a box of ammunition. Then she wore out her thumb pressing 9-millimeter rounds into the half-staggered magazine. With 10 there and one more in the chamber, the Sig was fully loaded and fit snugly into her waistband holster.

Next, she pulled out an overnight bag. She would need a change for the evening show. After all, she didn't want to embarrass her escort. She opened the closet, revealing a broad spectrum of clothing. Her real wardrobe was in the closet and dresser in her bedroom. The outfits in this room were just costumes, tools of her trade allowing her to be whoever she needed to be to go wherever she needed to go to fit in. In this case, the long black dress would do nicely, and the thigh-high slit would allow her freedom of movement if things went sideways and they ended up in a fight. The matching black pumps and custom-made black handbag would complete her outfit, and her defenses.

She kept her new Coach purse in her bedroom. She'd never risk carrying it on a job, but she needed to visit it on her way out. Then she stepped out of her place, set both the key bolt and the cypher lock, activated her alarms, and jogged down the stairs to the shaded sidewalk. Her street was narrow and that, plus the trees, made for perpetual shade except for the hour on either side of noon.

Two blocks later she tossed her suitcase into Mo's trunk, slid into the front seat of his car and dropped a thin white envelope in his lap. His mouth dropped open.

"What the hell?"

"Cash," Skye said. "Fifty bills"

Mo stared at the thin white envelope for a moment, as if someone had dropped a grenade in his lap. Then he gripped the wheel and staring straight ahead, said, "Would you put that in the glove compartment please. Jesus, girl, you couldn't just write a check like a normal person?"

"I don't write checks. Anyway, this way it's invisible to the IRS."

Mo nodded, put his car into gear and moved off through the familiar streets. A few minutes later they pulled up in front of the Fairmont and Ike walked up to the car. Jeans and a sport coat seemed to be his comfort zone, and he also had an overnight bag. As soon as he squeezed into the back seat, he offered his hand between the seats.

"I'm Ike. Pleased to meet you. Morris, right?"

"Call me Mo," was the response. After a firm handshake Ike sat back, stretching is arms across the back of the seat, nearly touching both sides of the car.

"Big son of a bitch," Mo said under his breath, pulling away from the curb. He cranked his stereo with his usual mix of seventies and eighties soul and R&B. Skye had had enough by the time they reached the Baltimore-Washington Parkway and was just about to ask for some more contemporary sounds when Love Rollercoaster came on. Ike leaned forward pushing his head into the front seat space.

"Ohio Players? I love that band."

"Really?" Morris asked. "Didn't see that coming."

"What, the white boy can't dig funk?"

Morris glanced quickly at Skye who was shaking her head in frustration. "You saying you like James Brown? Sly?"

"Hey, everybody like James, but Sly and the Family Stone was funk unit number one," Ike said, grinning. "Her pop turned me on to that stuff."

"Her pop?" Morris repeated.

"Tell you later. You got any Isley Brothers in there?"

"Guys," Skye spoke through clenched teeth. "I'm glad you boys are bonding and all, but can't we hear nothing from this century?"

Morris shook his head, "Sorry girl, nobody's making great music like this no more."

"Not true sir," Ike slapped Morris' shoulder like they had been friends for years. "Need to find you some of Trombone Shorty's stuff. That boy is dead funky."

At that point Skye decided to tilt her seat back and sleep all the way to Atlantic City.

When they rolled into town Morris followed the GPS to the Borgata, one of the hotels well off the crowded strip but down the street from the Golden Nugget. It looked to Skye like a giant flat mirror with a vertical tube at one end.

"This where your other friend's staying?" Morris asked.

"Don't know where he's staying," Ike said. "He kept that secret for security reasons. But he's doing a show here after dinner."

Skye took Morris' arm and leaned close. "Listen, you don't want to be too near us until we're getting ready to leave. Why don't you park the car and go hang out in the casino? I'll need you to be back here by like eight-thirty tonight. I'll text you when we're on our way out. Then we'll just head home, okay?"

"I get it," Morris said. "Be invisible until I'm needed."

"That's right, bro," Ike said. "You're our secret weapon."

Ike trailed Skye into the cavernous lobby where she signed in as Skye King, one of her many aliases. She looked around for a minute, orienting herself to the hotel layout.

The round wooden table at the center of the space served as a landmark if you got lost. From the check-in desk, the opening to the casino was in plain sight. The other way, just steps away from the check-in experience, the luxurious Lobby Bar beckoned.

"Upstairs to change?" Ike asked.

"No, first I want to see the venue. Where in this giant complex is Uncle Al performing?"

"He'll be in the B Bar at seven," Ike said. "Looks like it's right on the casino floor."

Skye headed toward the casino with Ike trailing. She ignored gambling opportunities and went to the center of the bar area, positioned in the middle of the action. Even before five it was buzzing with energy and pumping upbeat music. The round bar dominated the space. For those who couldn't stay even this far away from the casino, there were poker machines at each bar seat. Bench seating lined the walls. Small round tables lined up in front of those seats, with comfortable chairs arrayed facing the wall. The setup made good use of the big room, without crowding people in. It would be easy to move around without disturbing others. The small stage stood in front of a floor-to-ceiling curtain but there was no backstage area and only one way to approach the stage without crashing through a room full of patrons. It would be easy to follow Brown out of the room. As public spaces go, it was a good one to work in.

"Nothing tricky here," Ike said. "The danger point will be leaving the hotel."

"Agreed." Skye said. "I'm starting to feel a little better about this job. The great thing about casinos is, they don't want to present any obstacles to people coming in so, no metal detectors or any of that crap. They depend on cameras and guys that look like you for security. Let's drop our bags upstairs and come back down and grab some dinner. Plenty of time after that to change for the show."

Stepping out of the elevator, Skye steered them to the buffet. It was another big, open white space with a domed ceiling that appeared to be supported by a ring of pillars. Skye stood for a moment, paralyzed by the array of decadent choices. She scanned several pasta selections, all sorts of comfort foods and seafood and even Asian options. She saw Ike head for the lobster bar, but she decided to start at the beef carving station. Now this part of the James Bond stuff she could handle. As the chef loaded her up with Kobe beef she wondered if she could forego sides. She'd be fine with just beef and desserts for dinner.

She selected a table that gave her a good view of the entrances. On her way, one couple stood out on the other side of the room. The man was tall, blonde and mildly handsome with pretty blue eyes. He looked away as soon as she looked at him. The woman held her eyes for a couple of seconds. She was Asian with long, straight, black hair. She wore a yellow floral blouse and wrap skirt that revealed trim, strong legs, not as thick as Skye's. An athletic build. Her hands were still on the table, not fidgety at all, and she looked at Skye as if appraising her. Skye offered half a smile and nodded. Then she dropped into her chair at her chosen table. Ike soon followed but she stopped him before he sat.

"Want to get us drinks?" Skye asked. "There's iced tea over there, and you should check that couple opposite us. Pretty sure they're the opposition. The girl in yellow? She's got the look and I think she just tried to stare me down."

"Roger. Be right back."

As Ike left the table Skye took a sample bite of her food. At her usual steak places, she'd use salt, pepper, steak sauce and sometimes hot sauce. She wouldn't insult this steak that way. It was perfect as is. That first bite was still melting in her mouth when Ike returned. He opened his mouth to speak, but she cut him off.

"This is the reason you stay in a luxury hotel, right?" Skye asked with a grin. "And you know your boss is picking up the tab for all of this, under the heading of expenses. What do you think?"

Ike smoothed the napkin on his lap. "I think you're right about that other couple. And I think you're not used to working as part of a team." When Skye raised an eyebrow, he added, "You're used to making all the decisions and don't really want anybody else's opinion."

Skye chewed the succulent meat while she considered, and rejected, the idea of apologizing. "I ain't a soldier and I ain't a bodyguard, dude, I am what I am. It's assassin's rule number ten: never give up tactical control."

"I see," Ike said with a wry grin. "You learn that from the Master Chief?"

"Him and this ex-CIA guy I trained with. But never mind that. We got some time. Tell me more about Daddy."

"No," Ike said, popping a crab leg open. "You first. I want to know how you came to be with him. He called you his stepdaughter, but I know he never married, and he never talked about how or why he decided to adopt."

Skye was glad she had decided not to waste space on her plate with anything green. "Okay. My junior year high school. I'm fifteen. I was damn good in school, headed for scholarships and a way out of the hood. But it was a tough year. My brother OD'd. We was real close. Then a couple months later I come home from school and Mama's gone. Just gone. Like, all the closets was empty."

"Your dad?"

Skye gave one sharp laugh. "Never knew my dad. So then I was alone but I was still chasing the dream. I was handling it, but they don't let fifteen-year-olds live alone. As soon as the school found out, they moved to put me in the system. But before they got me into some random family, in walks this big nigga. He said he saw something in me. I always thought he might have found out about the dealer."

Ike chewed through a silent ten seconds before asking, "The dealer?"

"My brother's dealer." Skye stared down at the bloody au jus spreading on her plate. "He was my first." She said it before she knew why she was opening up like this to a man she just met. She had never told anybody about her first kill except Jayla.

Ike chewed on that, and his food, for nearly a minute. Skye focused on cleaning her plate. Then she stared at him, waiting for him to break the silence, not sure what response she was expecting.

Ike finally nodded. "I think he knew. Master Chief always did his research. Changes my picture."

"Of me?" Skye asked. "Or him?"

"I think maybe he didn't turn a young girl into a killer. I think maybe he saw something in you. Something he could work with. But what do you think?"

"What do I think?" Skye turned to the side, her mind wrenching loose from the table for two and out to the wide world. Then she turned back. "I think I'll have that chocolate espresso cake *and* the bourbon creme brulee."

Chapter 10

They returned to the luxury hotel room that for them was nothing more than a changing room. Unasked, Ike grabbed his bag and stepped into the bathroom to change. Ten minutes later he tapped on the door as if he was on the outside.

"Are you decent?"

"No," Skye replied. "But I'm dressed."

He stepped out, in the kind of simple navy-blue suit that people see but don't notice. A look of surprise preceded his smile, and that made her grin. She was sure his reaction came mostly from the shoulder length auburn wig, gold hoop earrings, and lightly applied makeup. The long black sleeveless dress was slit high enough to show her left leg to mid-thigh and cut low enough to display more cleavage than he probably thought she had to offer.

"That's a bit of a different look for you, isn't it?"

"Got to fit in, to get in, right?" Skye said. "It's a classy joint, so I wear my classy broad disguise."

"I wouldn't say disguise, and I think you look very nice." Ike looked her up and down, then stepped a little closer. "Good fit too. If you're packing, I can't see it"

"In here," Skye said, raising the little black purse hanging from her shoulder. "If I have time to pull this end zipper down, I don't have to ruin the bag to shoot."

"Nice," Ike said. "Got a blade in there?"

"Too obvious," Skye said. "But if I get in a fight, I got a surprise or two on me." She put her left foot up on the bed and reached down to her shoe. She grasped the heel which appeared solid but was in fact covered by a sheet of heavy black cloth. She slid it up to reveal the shiny steel spike it covered.

"Anybody grabs me I can nail them to the floor," Skye said with a smile. "Now, want to go down and see a show?"

"Yeah, but I don't think I'll go dancing with you. Don't want you accidentally stepping on my feet."

The late afternoon crowd they met when they arrived at the Borgata had swelled to a tightly packed mob when they got back downstairs. The noise level had doubled, largely from people trying to converse over the constant clanging and ringing of slot machines, each one trying to draw attention to themself. Casinos are loud, busy places, and the B Bar sat in the center of the casino floor, across from the main cashier. Skye felt the slight air conditioner breeze, trying hard to draw the odor of human bodies out of the room. Crowds were nice when she was on the hunt. You could slip up next to someone, stab them four times in the kidney and abdomen, and vanish into the milling throng before anyone knew what happened. Good conditions when she had a target.

When she might be a target, not so much.

She and Ike edged their way through the happy mob and found two facing seats. Skye hesitated for just a moment before taking the chair. Ike slid into the bench facing her with his back to the wall. Both maintained their smiles while the waves of people flowed past them.

"You look uncomfortable," Ike said. "I'd guess you hate sitting with your back to the room. You want to switch? I've got a good panoramic view of the whole bar."

She leaned over the small table. "Yeah, but you're kind of pinned. I got more mobility out here. It was a tough call, but I'll stay here."

A waitress swung by and got their drink orders, then hustled off. Skye wondered how she could remember five tables of orders without writing anything down but would trust her until there was a screw-up. She had too much that mattered on her mind.

"So how long did you know Papa?"

"Oh, hell, worked with him off and on for the better part of a decade," Ike said. "Hey, you know that couple you spotted earlier. They're here."

"Yeah, I saw them over to my right. You think they'll be trouble?"

"Later," Ike said, then leaned back as the waitress returned with her Moscow mule and his Jack on the rocks. He gave her a credit card and she faded again. "My intel is that Brown has kept the other company away by negotiating a return of the info he has for a price. As long as they think they can get what they want with money they aren't likely to get frisky."

"I get it," Skye said. "When they see him make contact with you, they'll figure that option is gone."

"Right. And by the time they're ready to make their move, we should be halfway to Washington."

"Cool," she said, sipping her drink. A little too much ginger beer, but still good. "So Papa didn't tell you how he adopted me. What did he tell you about me?"

"Well, it was clear he loved you like a daughter," Ike said. "He wanted you to…"

He stopped talking when another couple settled into the seating on his left, Skye's right. The black guy was model-handsome in an Armani suit and high-end Nikes. He shuffled his chair a little closer to Skye. His partner, blonde over blue with porcelain skin, wore a short, sequined, navy-blue dress and a bit too much Chanel. She worked for eye contact with Ike while the man spoke to them both.

"Hey, these seats aren't taken, are they?" He sounded New Jersey, but like he had practiced it. "I hope not. You look like the fun couple here."

Ike began his brushoff with, "Look, we're in the middle of..."

Skye cut him off. "No, those seats are free. And as it happens, so are we."

"I knew you were a party couple," the man said. "I'm Ricky. This here is Chantelle."

Now the woman slid a little closer to Ike. Skye took his hand to forestall any reaction.

"Come on, honey, don't be like that." When he finally turned to her, she gave him a wink. "I'm sure it's not what it looks like. They probably spotted us earlier and let's face it, we're surely just what they're looking for. Can't we just get to know them a little and see what happens?"

The new couple had to be a pair of amateurs given a challenging task. The opposition company, Oneida, must have sent them. That meant they knew who Ike was, and knew he was supposed to make contact with Brown after his magic act. These two must have been told to get close and monitor him. They probably expected him to be traveling alone. Her presence made their orders a bit more challenging. It's not easy to attach yourself to a pair of strangers in public. All they could think of was to play a hot couple wanting to hook up with them for some swinger fun. It was weak, but Skye thought it would be better to let them stay where she and Ike could watch them. If they rejected Ricky and Chantelle, they would move away but it wouldn't stop them from monitoring Skye and Ike. It would just make them harder to keep track of.

Skye didn't expect Ike to see all this or come to the same conclusions. But she held his eyes with her own, silently screaming at him to trust her. When he leaned in closer, she knew by his returned smile that he did.

"I don't know, Kitten. You think you can handle this? She's cute, I'll admit but this guy… what if he likes it rough?"

Skye glanced at their new friends, then back at Ike. "You never know, dear. We might want to switch partners."

Now it was Ike's turn to look the new couple over. "Okay, Kitten. I'll follow your lead."

For their parts, Ricky and Chantelle stuck to their original script. Chantelle slid closer to Ike, rested a hand on his thigh and said, "It might be fun for us all to play together."

There followed a few minutes of reflexive small talk. Where are you from? Where are you staying? What do you do? How long have you been together? Ricky and Chantelle were well rehearsed. Ike and Skye alternated responses, each careful not to contradict the other.

Then the lights went down, a white spotlight highlighted the stage, and Skye swiveled around to face it. A swarthy guy with dental veneers and Peter Lorre's stringy black hair came out and introduced mystifying illusionist Alan Brown. The magician rolled a small table onto the stage and greeted the room with a big smile. He was as she remembered him: slender, deep brown hair with white on the sides and a pointed nose. Old enough to be her father, he still showed the impish grin of the practical joker he must have been in school.

In that small space he leaped into his act with a flourish. He did the three cups with balls vanishing one by one, to be found under the cups, then the balls that penetrate the cups. He pulled out a series of rings and linked and unlinked them quickly and smoothly. These were his warmup tricks. Then he called for a volunteer in the audience to hold up a casino chip. People waved their hands in the air and Brown scanned the room.

Recognition flashed in his eyes when they landed on Ike, followed by a second reaction when he recognized her. His smile seemed to lift a tiny bit, and he gave a subtle wink.

For a moment she flashed back to those two weeks she and her adoptive father spent in Las Vegas. It was a dry, sunny afternoon when Papa introduced her to Al Brown in a small but expensive hotel room. He had given her a silver dollar and showed her how to roll it between her fingers It looked hard, but she focused and managed to do it pretty smoothly in less than an hour. All the while he had engaged her with riddles, verbal puzzles and other word games. Watching her move the coin Brown had raised his eyebrows to her papa and said, "This one's got promise." The same day he handcuffed her behind her back and showed her how to get out of them. When they left that room, she had smiled up at the man who had already introduced her to marksmen, martial artists and demolition experts that summer.

"Papa, you know the most interesting people," she had told him.

Now, one of those interesting people had selected a volunteer two tables from Skye. He got a strong reaction from the audience when he accepted the black hundred-dollar chip and bit it in half. Of course, after a moment of the volunteer's distress, he popped the half chip into his mouth and spit a whole one into his hand.

In the midst of the wave of applause, Ike said, "Keep your head on a swivel."

Papa used to say that, Skye thought. But already her eyes were always in motion. It was much like driving, watching Brown (the windshield) but regularly checking the couple they thought might be trouble - the tall blonde man with the Asian girl (the rearview mirror) and checking Ricky and Chantelle (side mirrors.) As long as no one made any unexpected moves, she could enjoy the show. She sipped her drink while Brown returned to the stage and began to introduce the next trick from behind his table. It would be nice to catch up with him. She wondered if she would tell him what she did for a living. It could be that he already knew. What *did* he think he was training her for that summer?

Brown grinned as he fanned a stack of playing cards in his hand. Then his eyes bulged, his mouth dropped open, and his shirt jumped away from his chest.

That was not part of the act.

Chapter 11

Shock threw Skye's world into slow motion. She saw Brown falling forward like a felled tree. No huge exit wound, so a small caliber bullet had pulled his shirt forward away from his chest. Half of the bar patrons were lurching to their feet. Skye was the first person standing, with Ike and the tall man she thought of as Blondie only a fraction of a second behind her.

"Time to change partners," Skye said, gathering a handful of Chantelle's hair and slamming her face down into the table. Ike swung over Skye's head, smashing a right cross into Ricky's face. Ricky flew backward over his chair to crash onto the floor. Skye had snatched up and slung her purse and was already moving toward the stage, but Blondie was ahead of her.

Screams, chairs shoved back, and glasses knocked over filled the room with white noise. Fighting her way through the chaos of frantic drinkers, Skye focused on the man already kneeling over her uncle Al. She had expected a kidnapping attempt after Brown's act was over, not a murder before she had a chance to speak to him. Either the opposition's plan had changed, or Gagnon had misjudged their intent. Now, a few feet away, Brown lay on his back and Blondie held his hand. It almost looked like they were talking. Was he there to finish Brown quickly, or try to save him? Not wanting to take a chance, Skye body-checked him away from Brown, then turned back to the magician.

"Uncle Al," were the only words she could muster. His white shirt was turning deep red in all directions out from the center of his chest. She glanced up at the curtain behind him. A wisp of smoke drifted out from a chest-high hole in it. The shooter would be long gone. Brown was already gone.

"Leave him alone! God, don't hurt him." This came from the tall stranger who was struggling to his feet.

"He's past that," Skye said.

Then Ike landed on Blondie, flattening him to the floor, an instant before a knife flew over them both. Skye caught the anger in the woman's face. It was the Asian girl who had been sitting with Blondie. She had thrown the knife and now she charged toward them. Ike lifted Blondie by the back of his jacket and shoved him toward Skye.

"Get him out of here," Ike shouted over the crowd screams. "I've got your back." He was faced off against the Asian woman, blocking her path. Why had Blondie's date tried to kill him? It didn't matter. Ike wanted him kept safe. And as much as she wanted a moment to process her loss, to just to say a proper goodbye to the man she called Uncle Al, there was no time. They had failed him. She wouldn't fail again.

"Come on," she growled, grabbing Blondie by his arm. He looked confused, stumbling after being slammed down and yanked back up. Skye practically dragged him through the room. With her other hand she pulled out her phone, shouting over the screams of stampeding gamblers.

"Mo! Where you at?"

"I'm in the garage," he replied. "I'm seeing a lot of people running out of the hotel. What's going on? Are you…?"

"Fine," Skye said. "I need you out front right now."

"What the hell?" Blondie said. "I need to get back to him."

"They want you dead," Skye said. "Ike don't. So, you come with me, and we sort this all out later."

"Why would anybody…" Blondie started to ask, but an elbow hit him from behind and he stumbled forward. A muscular arm wrapped around Skye's neck, pulling her back. The crowd was still packed too closely for her to manage a throw. Her attacker was too strong for her to fight free. He lifted her off the floor, so she couldn't stomp his feet. He squeezed hard around her neck. She would black out in seconds. She would lose sight of the man she was supposed to protect. She would fail, twice in just minutes.

No!

"You done fucked up now," she said between clenched teeth. She raised her left foot, snatched her shoe off with her right hand, and swung her spiked heel around into her assailant's neck. As he gurgled and fell away, she pulled off her other shoe and raced forward, shouldering people out of her way. Nothing smells quite like a panicked crowd. Fear sweat is somehow different. She maintained her view of the big man wrestling Blondie through the mob. The fool was wearing a blue Hawaiian shirt. Maybe when he got dressed that day, he didn't know he'd want to get lost in a crowd. Too bad.

Skye was behind the big man before he knew she was there. She slammed the heel of one shoe into his right kidney and as he half turned, the other heel slid into his stomach. As the thug crumbled to his knees Blondie turned, staring at her with widened eyes.

"Go!" she screamed. "Get out the door, or you're next." He glanced at her bloody shoes and turned to run. She stayed on his heels until they burst out of the air conditioned cool into the warm, muggy night. When he stopped, she grabbed the back of his jacket and kept moving until she was yanking the back door of a familiar car open.

"Get in," she shouted. Blondie complied. She slammed that door shut and yanked the front door open.

"What's going on?" Mo asked. "And where's Ike?"

"Circle the hotel," Skye said, climbing into the car and putting her shoes back on. "Had a surprise. Things got hectic. We got separated." Blondie gasped when she pulled her pistol from her bag, but she didn't have time to deal with him. She hoped that after putting down the knife throwing girl Ike would manage to get out of the building through one of the alternate exits.

Mo drifted forward out of the drop off area, his bumper nudging people out of his way. He negotiated his way around the Borgata, which was more challenging than expected. The complex was huge. Mo fought his way through a tangle of access roads and finally got around to the back of the building. They rode along beside a broad body of water that Skye couldn't name. She scanned the complex on her right and a waterfront walkway on her left. At the other end of the complex, they turned right, past the wine bar and yet another restaurant. The sound of sirens was getting louder. They were seconds away from drowning in a tidal wave of blue uniforms. Faced with this kind of chaos the police knee-jerk reaction would be to close off as much of the area as possible, then try to question everyone they could.

"Get us out of here, Mo."

"And Ike?" he asked.

"He's probably tucked into a hidey hole somewhere," she said, stowing her weapon. "He's not going to risk getting caught up in the net all these cops are going to throw down. He'll hide and find his own way home when the heat dies down."

After seven or eight turns Mo got them onto the Atlantic City Expressway before speaking again. "Where now? Your place?"

"Yeah. No, wait. Take us to The Fairmont. That's where Ike will head when he can."

Mo nodded, then jerked his head toward the back seat. "And this is the fellow you came up here looking for?"

"No," Skye said, twisting around to stare hard at their passenger. "That guy's gone. Murdered. But Blondie here was with him at the end. Ike wanted me to bring this guy with us and I think I figured out why. That man we were here to pick up, I think he gave something valuable to Blondie here."

"It's Carter," the backseat passenger said. "Carter Brown. I just watched my father die."

Chapter 12

Skye reached an empty hand over the seat. "If that's true, I'm real sorry you had to see that." If he was lying he could be one of the opposition, ready to give away their location. Either way, if his date had his number she might be able to track him. "Right now, give me your phone."

"What?" Carter said. "Why on earth should I…"

"You've seen what happens to people who piss me off," she said. "Phone. Now."

Mo muttered, "I'd do what this lady asks, man."

Carter pulled his phone out of a pocket and slapped it into her hand. "There. Now. Who are you?"

"Call me Skye."

"Just Skye?" Carter muttered. "Like Cher, or Madonna? Whatever. Where are you taking me? Why were you looking for my dad? And what the hell makes you think I'd give you anything I got from him? I mean, even if he gave me something."

Skye clenched her fists and took a deep breath to avoid screaming when she did speak. Instead, her voice came out in a deep, low tone filled with both frustration and menace. "Look, asshole, you don't mean shit to me, but Ike does and Al… did. Now I'm going to try to finish what Ike came up here to do but if you don't seriously shut the hell up, I will put you out of this car and I won't ask the driver to slow down. Do you understand?"

Carter shrank back into a corner. Skye pulled out her phone. She called Ike. His recorded voice asked her to leave a message. Not knowing if he still had the phone, she decided not to. She was glad she had insisted on getting a direct line to Gagnon and called that one next.

"Yes?"

"Listen, things went sideways in Atlantic City," Skye said. "Headed back to The District now."

"Alan Brown is with you?"

"Al Brown is dead."

A short pause. "I see. Ike?"

"Unknown," Skye said. "Gone to ground I think, after we got separated. But he told me to grab this other guy, who might have what Al was supposed to give you."

A longer pause. "All right. What do you need?"

"Need a place to land," Skye said, "I ain't taking this dude to my place. Get me a room in the Fairmont, as close to Ike's as possible. I'll want to see him as soon as he gets back."

"Done," Gagnon said. "Let me know when you've arrived safely."

"Yeah, okay. Later." Then Skye looked at the back seat passenger. His eyes darted around in terror. She felt a little bad for him. He looked like he had no idea what was going on. She wasn't able to produce a smile but she managed a less menacing glare.

"Look, dude, I don't know who killed Al but it's pretty clear they killed him for something he had, something Ike and I were supposed to get from him after the show. I think you got it. Whoever did him thinks the same thing, so they want to kill you too. But you're safe as long as you're with me. So just relax for a couple of hours and we'll straighten all this out in the District. Okay?"

Carter nodded. That was all she was going to get for now. Fine. She turned to Mo who sat yardstick straight with both hands on the wheel.

"You okay for this drive? I know sometimes after you get a burst of Adrenalin…"

"I'm good," Mo said. "In fact, I've never been more awake in my life. If I need you, I'll holler."

Skye nodded and leaned her seat back. She spent the rest of the long ride back to The District in silence except for Mo's classic R&B filling the car. A nap would have been nice, but her brain refused to settle.

This was what happened when you got mixed up in somebody else's job. She felt safe in Mo's car but had no idea what came next, and she didn't know the opposition at all. Was this how corporations truly acted? What she did know was, they had killed a man for information he was carrying. She knew people who killed for power. Some who killed for money. Most of Skye's work had been for someone who wanted revenge or to take a loose cannon out of a criminal organization, or occasionally to preempt the plans of somebody who was a threat to somebody else. To murder somebody for info they were carrying seemed to cheapen her profession. Uncle Al may have been involved in a dirty business, but he was a sweet old guy. He didn't deserve to die.

Just shy of eleven o'clock Mo pulled to the curb in front of the Fairmont. He looked at Skye as he had so many times before, with a mixture of confusion and fear.

"I don't know much, but I know your trip didn't go as planned. How can I help?"

Skye smiled and shook her head. "Brother you already saved my ass today, just by being where you needed to be, and staying under the radar. Thank you. But the best thing for you to do now is get your ass home so your family knows you're okay. I'll probably give you a call tomorrow. Got to get back to my place. I can't go around dressed like this all the time." Then to Carter she said, "Let's go in. After we get settled, we can exchange stories. I'll tell you what I know, which ain't much, but if you decide you don't want to trust me, you can split. Okay?" Carter's lips were a straight line, but he shook his head. He did have nice eyes, Skye decided.

Inside, Skye didn't approach the desk with her usual level of confidence. The Fairmont wasn't the kind of place people usually checked into without any luggage. At least she was dressed for the place, and she doubted anybody there would recognize her, even if they were there when she went in the day before. When the clerk greeted her, she handed over her ID du jour and said she had a reservation. The clerk perked up when she saw the name.

"Oh yes, Miss King," she said tapping buttons. "you're part of Mr. Gagnon's group. I hope you traveled well. I have instructions to add you to Isaac Thomas' room. Here are your room keys, the elevator is right over there, and please let me know if you need anything."

And like that they were on their way to the room, which wasn't very different from the one she had for a few minutes in Atlantic City except it was bigger, maybe twenty by twenty feet. She waved Carter into the bathroom and when he emerged, she took her turn. Then she tossed her purse on the one king bed and pulled the little refrigerator open. There she found a tiny bottle of scotch, a brand she didn't recognize. With a shrug she emptied it into a glass and gulped half of it. It burned on the way down, but a couple of swallows of good scotch was just what she needed. Carter dropped into one of the chairs at the multi-functional table looking worn out, like he had walked down from New Jersey.

"I know I had a lot of questions before," Carter said, "but after sitting and thinking for the last three and a half hours I know what I want to know most. Everything else will follow from there. So here it is. Why is my father dead?"

Skye sipped her drink, wondering how much she should share with this white boy. He was maybe six two. He'd have towered over her Uncle Al, but he was slim like Al, the hair was right, and he had that pointed nose. He might be who he said he was.

"Let me see some ID."

"Why should I?" he asked, leaning forward.

He was trying to look tough, but Skye had a genuine hard look that cut right through him. "Let's not do this. I got pulled into this game and I don't know who all the players are yet. You want answers. I got to know you're for real."

"Hey, you know more than I do," Carter said, but he pulled his wallet out of his hip pocket, slid a card out of it and flipped it like a frisbee at Skye. He looked surprised when she snatched it out of the air.

She stared at the Nevada driver's license photo, then up at the man. Brown, Carter Blaine. Six feet, two inches, 180 pounds. Birth date made him 22 years old.

"Blaine?" Skye asked, flipping the license back to its owner.

He let it land on the table, then picked it up. "A magician Dad was working with at the time. He got a lot bigger than Dad. You satisfied?"

Skye dropped onto the chaise lounge, kicked off her shoes and crossed her ankles. "Did Al tell you he had branched out from stage magic to industrial espionage?"

"What? I…no. We don't… didn't talk much," Carter said. "We had some great times when I was a kid. But the last few years he's been on the road all the time. How come you talk about him like you knew him."

"My dad knew your dad," Skye said. "We spent a couple weeks with him in Vegas. He taught me a bit about locks and such. And I was there tonight to meet him, to get some information from him. I think he's dead because somebody didn't want him to share that info."

"Sounds like a bad spy movie," Carter said.

"I know, right? But I don't have the whole story. When my partner gets here, he can fill us both in. He knew your dad too."

Carter stared down at the table, shaking his head back and forth slowly. Skye knew it was a lot to take in and figured he just needed a moment to process it. She decided on another drink while he did. She opened the mini fridge and selected a random tiny bottle.

"Hey, you want a drink, dude?"

"Is there an iced tea in there?" Carter asked.

To Skye's surprise there was. "It's called Gold Peak."

"Hey, that's the best."

Skye shook her head, pulled out a bottle, walked down to Carter and dropped it on the table. "Can't handle the hard stuff, huh?"

"That's what Harmony used to say," Carter said, twisting the top off his drink.

"That the girl you were with in the bar? Pretty. She your girlfriend?"

"Sort of," Carter said, taking a long drink.

"Sort of. So you don't know her all that well."

"Met her about a month ago," he said. "She knew dad too, but I think it was like a business relationship. Anyway, we met, and she was way into me."

"Of course she was," Skye said. "I'll bet she suggested staying close to your dad, too."

Carter rolled his eyes. "She thought it would be cool to see Dad's show tonight. Nothing weird about that. Dad and I haven't been close in a long time so I thought we could talk after. But now, I guess…"

Carter's words trailed off and he seemed to be choking. Skye felt an unexpected rush of emotion and they shared a moment of pained silence. She had counted on chatting with the magician about how he and her own father had connected. Until that moment she was so fixed on her lost opportunity that she he wasn't really mourning Al Brown's death. Now she remembered her sense of desperation when she learned of Papa Maddox's death. The news hit her hard and suddenly she had no direction, no purpose. With Papa gone she was alone in the world again, with an odd set of skills, but emotionally unsuited for military service or even law enforcement.

When she snapped back to the present, she steadied herself by grasping what she had: the mission. Not her usual kind of work but she had agreed to it and knew her only course was to see it through. She walked over to Carter and extended her right hand, palm up.

"Sorry about your loss. My father's gone too. You'll get through it, just like I did. Now let me see what your dad gave you."

Carter looked up and for the first time she noticed the tears. "Can't I just be sad for a minute?"

"Plenty of time for that later," Skye said.

"Fuck you," Carter said. "I told you he didn't give me anything."

Skye shook her head. "Nope. Ike must have seen it. He wouldn't have told me to get you out of there if you didn't have what we was sent for. Hand it over."

Carter's face flushed red as if anger and grief were tripping over each other inside him. "I'm supposed to trust you? You abandoned your partner when things got crazy. I should have stuck with Harmony."

"You mean the bitch that threw a knife at you?"

Carter was almost panting now. "Like you're any better? You weren't there to help my dad, and you don't give a damn about me. You just want whatever Dad had."

"Look, it's late and I'm tired. Just give it up. I don't want to have to strip search you."

Carter rose to his full height, fists clenched. "I'd like to see you try."

Now barefoot, Skye stared up into his eyes, a good eight inches above her own. He probably didn't see her as a serious threat. She didn't want to hurt him, but she was short of patience right then. She drove the fingertips of her left hand deep into his solar plexus. She was fast enough that he probably never saw the strike. But his mouth dropped open, his eyes bulged, and weakness shot out to his limbs. His legs gave way and he dropped to his knees.

Skye stepped behind him, grabbed his collar, and yanked his suit coat down and off him. She carried the jacket to the bed. She checked all the pockets and ran her hand over every seam searching for a note or a key or anything the magician may have palmed. Nothing. She turned back to Carter, now on hands and knees trying to catch his breath.

"Okay, shoes next," she said. When he didn't move, she asked, "You think I'm playing? Did you not see me kill that man with the heels of my shoes? Come on."

She took two steps toward him before he said, "Wait." He rolled to the side, pulled off his right shoe and held it with the toe pointed to the ceiling. He thumped the heel on the floor and a small object fell out. Skye scooped it up. It looked like a flash drive, only a lot shorter than any she'd seen. She pulled the cap off to be sure. Yep, a flash drive but, the USB plug was half of its length.

"See how simple life can be?" Skye said. "What my client wants is probably right on here. And check it, if you don't have it, nobody got any reason to want to kill you. So, you safe, and this gets to where Al wanted it to go."

"I'm not so sure of that," Carter said, pulling his shoe back on.

Skye hated dresses. No pockets. She picked up her purse to drop the flash drive into it. "Now why would you say that? If he was going to give it to the other company, they wouldn't have shot him, right?"

"How do we know there's only two groups that wanted that drive?" Carter asked. "I don't know who he…" Carter stopped mid-sentence and Skye nodded, considering that the situation could be more complex than she assumed.

"Okay, did Al say something before he… did he give you instructions maybe? What to do with the flash drive? Look I got a client, but this thing wasn't the job I was hired for so I'm down with whatever Al wanted."

"That's just it," Carter said. "I'm not sure what he said. Something about, a lineal manhole, I think. Then Wallops Island. That part I'm sure of. But at the end, not sure if he said help them or stop them."

"Well that's clear as mud," Skye said. "How can a manhole be lineal? I don't think they have ancestors. So, a place where manholes are in a line? Or maybe things that just look like manholes. And what the hell's a wallop island? Might make more sense after some sleep. Why don't we…"

Carter jumped and Skye froze in response to a loud knock at the door.

Chapter 13

In less than a second Skye opened the hidden compartment in her purse, dropped the flash drive and drew the slim Sig P365 from its hiding place. Could someone have followed them down from Atlantic City? She sprang to the bathroom door, standing almost concealed behind it except for the automatic she aimed at the room door. The knock was repeated.

"Yes?" she called.

"Skye? It's Eric."

Gagnon? At this hour? She lowered her gun a few inches. "You alone?"

"Of course not," Gagnon said. "Two security personnel. Now, may I come in?"

Skye waved Carter back into his seat and opened the door. Gagnon was dressed formally, as were the towering hulks to his left and right. Paid muscle, but not on Ike's level. She saw Gagnon's eyes go to her pistol, held close to her side, pointed at his navel.

"That hardly goes with the outfit," Gagnon said. She swung the door wide, turned back into the room and tossed the gun on the bed beside her purse. When she turned back, bodyguard number one, the black guy, signed for her to raise her arms and started toward her. Skye glared at him.

"You don't want to do that." She glared at Gagnon until he waved a dismissive hand at the bodyguard. "You already seen my gun. And besides," Skye said, turning a slow full circle, "What the hell could I hide in this?"

"I trust Skye," Gagnon said to the room. "And we need her on our side." Then he turned to the room's other occupant. "Who is this young man, and why is he here?"

"This is Al Brown's son, Carter," Skye said, moving to stand between him and the newcomers. "He was on the scene when Al was killed. Thought he might know something."

Gagnon reached past Skye to offer a hand. "How do you do? Eric Gagnon. I am so sorry for your loss."

"You're *the* Eric Gagnon?" Carter said, rising and shaking the offered hand. "Did you know my dad?"

"Your father was a loyal and valued employee," Gagnon said. "Independent contractor really. While on tour, he often brought me valuable information about my competitors."

"I had no idea my dad was doing anything other than magic shows when he was away." Carter pulled his hand back. "It sounds like whatever he was doing for you might have gotten him killed. What kind of information gets you shot in the back? Government stuff?"

"Communications stuff," Gagnon said. "Did he say anything to you before he passed away? Maybe he gave you a key to fetch a package of information. Or it might have been loaded on a flash drive or scribbled in a notebook."

After a glance at Skye, Carter said, "If it was, he didn't share it with me. And look, your business problems don't really concern me. I want to know what was so important they killed my dad for it."

"I'd kind of like to know that bit myself," Skye said, sitting on the bed. "Maybe if we knew, whatever Al said to Carter here might make some sense."

Gagnon lowered himself onto the chaise. His two guards remained standing and moved with him, so they always flanked him.

"I suppose you deserve to know," Gagnon finally said. "As I'm sure you know, most of the world's information exchanges take place through satellite transmissions. One of my rivals has developed software that would allow a person to selectively tap into those transmissions and corrupt them. Imagine if you will, technology that would be able to turn off one of our television news programs. Or stop one radio station from reaching anyone. You see how this could disrupt the industry."

"Yeah I see how it might mess with your cash flow, Skye said.

Carter said, "Sounds like we're talking about a computer program. You're worried about somebody being able to knock one of *your* programs off the air. I'm not so sure Dad would have given such a thing to you so you could do it to somebody else. Knowing him, maybe he was just going to sell it back to the original owner."

"That would have left them no reason to hurt him," Gagnon said. "Now, you mentioned something your father may have said to you?"

Carter stared at Skye. She figured he had finally decided on who he would trust. He took the woman who saved his life over the billionaire who wanted more control over what was on the air. She gave him a wink no one else could see and said, "Tell him what your dad said. Maybe it will make sense to him. It sure didn't tell me shit."

Carter nodded. "I've been going over this in my mind, over and over. Best I understood he said something like, 'stop the lineal manhole of wallops island.' Or maybe get to the lineal manhole of wallop island."

Skye didn't feel like she had a dog in that fight, but figured it was smart for Carter not to mention the flash drive. It was his only bargaining chip and if Gagnon was right, it might have a lot of value on the open market. She stared at Gagnon. His face was frozen, but she could almost see the gears spinning behind his eyes. After most of a minute of silence he abruptly snapped to his feet and pulled a credit card out of his pocket.

"Mr. Brown, I don't imagine you want to share a room with a woman you just met. Why don't we get you your own room elsewhere in the hotel?" When Carter reached toward him, Gagnon handed the card to the black bodyguard. "Fellows, would you please escort young Mr. Brown to the registration desk downstairs? Get him into a room and stick with him to make sure he's secure. I need to talk a little business with Skye here."

Carter looked at Skye as if he were trying to choose the lesser of two evils. She smiled and patted his arm. "Relax, you're safe with these guys. I'll catch up with you when we're done here."

Carter sighed and followed the larger men out. The second the door closed Skye's smile dropped.

"Seems to me our business is done, so this better be good."

Chapter 14

Gagnon stood and went to the little refrigerator. He read the label on every bottle before selecting one. While he was checking bottles he said, "The North Koreans. That's who else wants this new software." As he reached for a glass Skye sensed that energy she felt the first time they met. "I don't want to meddle in international affairs, but I can't have a foreign power interfering with my transmissions."

"Hang on," she said. "You think some Korean spy took out Al Brown?"

"No, I'm quite sure it was a professional killer being paid by the North Koreans. And this would be the third man this murderer has taken from me."

Skye pulled her legs up under her on the bed, knees apart and ankles crossed. "Seriously? You think the North Korean government is after you in some big conspiracy or something?"

"You think me paranoid," Gagnon said. "Or perhaps I'm just an old man with delusions of grandeur. Let me tell you a story."

Sipping his drink, he probably didn't see her roll her eyes but she knew he must have heard the sigh. It didn't stop him.

"Quincy Page was a reporter on one of my papers for several years," Gagnon said. "I got to know him well. He wrote a lot of great crime stories. He learned about people at the Oneida Communications conglomerate working on a way to disrupt a rival company's signals coming off any satellite. I was both excited and horrified. His story would have damaged that organization once he had all the facts."

"Would have?" Skye asked.

"Quincy Page was murdered three months ago." Gagnon took a deep breath, as if he himself was hearing the news for the first time. "Him, his wife, his two children, in their vacation home in Nevada. Then the house burned to the ground. Took the police two days to collect all the bullets. Bodies were… well, identification was difficult."

"Uh-huh. Overkill," Skye said. "The kind of work you get from drug cartels or something. Can't never do it clean. Always got to make a fucking statement."

"My people were able to determine that the North Korean government had also learned of this software development. Naturally they wanted it and didn't want any American company to know anything about it. I believe they are responsible for the slaughter."

"So what? You want to go to war with North Korea?"

Gagnon shook his head. "Not the nation. One person. I sent Ike Thomas to investigate the scene. He said all the bullets came out of two guns. A lot of nine millimeters. Groups looked like a submachine gun in the hands of a pro. I think he said something like an MP-5 or the like."

Skye stopped him. "They let Ike on the scene that fast?"

Gagnon nodded. "Cops out there, they didn't really know what they were looking at. I contacted my good friend the governor. I offered some assistance."

"And he couldn't say no." Skye didn't even try to hide her skepticism.

"All politicians keep one eye on their campaign funding," Gagnon said. "Under the circumstances, he welcomed an expert consultant."

Skye bit back a chuckle. "Yeah, the local cops needed help gathering up all them nine millimeter slugs."

"It seems there were also quite a few forty-five slugs."

"Right," Skye said. "Bastard went inside to make sure, up close and personal."

"This… bastard is the issue," Gagnon said. "Quincy was supposed to be digging into Oneida, but it appears he had also gathered a lot of information about the North Koreans spying here in the U.S., and also about one particular killer they used here, to maintain a bit of separation from the violence. Like yourself she guards her identity well. She is known only as Abraxas. You know this name?"

Skye's snarky smirk evaporated. "Abraxas? She's a legend. She's with the Yakuza. Maybe the most sophisticated crime syndicate. Probably the wealthiest. Big time crime. Transnational, as they say. I heard about some work she did in Central America recently. Rumor has it she took out some big boys in Afghanistan who tried to push the Yakuza out of the drug trade. Can't see her working for Koreans though. The Japanese and the Koreans hate each other. Either way, she's not a freelance."

"A professional killer," Gagnon said.

"Well, yeah," Skye said, "But bound to a particular house, loyal to her master. Sort of like a..a…"

"A samurai."

"Yeah," Skye said. "Like a samurai."

"Yes," Gagnon said. "A samurai loyal to a transnational criminal organization instead of a shogun. A samurai who needs to die."

"Hold up." Skye stared hard at Gagnon, but the stare faded into a smile. "You sneaky mother fucker. This bitch slaughtered somebody you cared about before Ike tracked me down. Abraxas was going to be the job all along, wasn't she?"

Gagnon nodded. "I planned to hire you for this mission after we got Al Brown back safely. It would give Ike a chance to see you in the field. You had a strong reputation, but I had to be sure. Ike's endorsement would cement my plan, but before he could report back, she killed Al Brown. I'm sure of it. As I said, she needs to die."

"Okay, I'm down with that," Skye said, "but I think the Departments of Defense, Justice, Treasury, Homeland Security, and maybe State probably agree. And you've got the juice to put them on the scent. Lots of folks been after this bitch for a long time, but she still out there killing. So, why me?"

Gagnon smiled. "Those federal agencies are effective, they know how to capture drug dealers and hunt down terrorists. Perhaps even typical murderers for hire. But how does one defeat a samurai? With an army? Investigators? No. One sends a ninja." He then raised his hand and pointed at the spot between her eyes. "You are the one who can get this done."

"Uh-huh," Skye said with a grin. Pouring herself a third drink she considered what he said about her. She had not thought of herself in such terms. She was a soldier, a warrior who had turned her talents to one specialty. But then, what about her methods, her approach, her code, the rules Papa had drilled into her. A ninja? Maybe. But then another jarring thought pulled her out of the self-evaluation.

"Hold on, old man," she said, rising to her feet. "You talk like we old friends or some shit. How you think you know me so well?"

Gagnon raised a palm. "I know you by reputation. Ike had good connections. Through him I was able to interview a few international operators. A couple of them made reference to a woman known only as Skye. One I talked to had helped train this girl. A couple mentioned that in the past she traveled with a retired Navy Master Chief named Maddox who, as it turns out, Ike trained with at one time. And the others, who all turned down this particular contract, said that you were the right person to take this on. Were they wrong?"

Skye stared at the floor, thinking through how different such a job would be from anything she had done before. She would be hunting a hunter, and this predator was big game. "Well, there ain't nobody can't be got. But look, this girl, she's more than a rep. She's the real fucking deal. And she's a ghost. Comes out of nowhere and disappears after. No home base. No family. No friends. Nobody even knows for sure what she looks like. This ain't a woman you find. This a woman that finds you."

Gagnon waved her objections away. "I found you, didn't I? I'm sure I can position you to get the job done."

"What, you got X-ray vision or some shit?"

"We all have our powers," Gagnon said with a disarming smile. "Your superpower is turning creeps into corpses. And me? Money is my superpower."

"You gone need more than cash to flush this rat out."

"Oh, I have more," Gagnon said. "I have the last text Ike sent me. I have the perfect bait. And the vital clue that bait gave us."

Skye wondered about the content of that text, but another thought replaced that curiosity. "Wait a minute! Before you said Ike *had* good connections. Why past tense?"

Gagnon sat back on the chaise and emptied his glass. Skye figured him for a sociopath, like most rich, successful men, but he had a well-practiced bad news face. Just by his expression, she knew before he dropped the words.

"I'm sorry to tell you that just before I got here, I received word that Ike's body was identified floating in the little canal near the waterfront walk behind the Borgata Hotel. My third loss to this murderer, I'm sure."

"What?" Skye leaped to her feet and rushed in on Gagnon before he could react. Her face inches from his, she breathed, "That should have been the first thing out of your mouth when you walked in that door."

For the first time Gagnon looked unsure. They locked eyes for a tense moment, then the moment passed, and Skye turned away. Fists clenched, then relaxed. Breathing slowed. Voice calmed.

"Drowned?" Skye asked. "Shot? Stabbed?" She didn't really care how he died. She wanted to know if he went down fighting or if someone sneaked up on him.

"Shot," Gagnon said. "One in the leg, two in the chest, and…"

"One in the head," Skye said, turning to face him. "They had to make sure he'd stay down." She paced to the far corner of the room, fists again clenched, but she was composed when she turned. "How big a mess did he make?"

"Mess?" Gagnon looked confused.

"Damage?" Skye asked. "Total body count?"

"Ike was one of five dead men found."

Skye said, "Yeah," in a soft tone.

"I don't understand," Gagnon said.

"They sent an army," Skye said, slapping her hands down on the bed. "They knew Ike was going to be there, so they sent an army to take out one magician. I know they expected Ike cause they had people watching us. Me and Ike, we knocked them out but sounds like there was lots more. Don't know how many men they sent, but Ike took down four of them before they got him. He went out good. Since you got spies everywhere, any word on a girl?"

"No but one was mentioned in Ike's last text to me. He said you two had spotted a couple who looked dangerous. The woman was Asian. I believe this was Abraxas."

"No way," Skye said. "I sized her up. She was a lightweight, not a top-notch assassin. Besides, that guy you just sent out of the room was the other half of that couple. I don't think he hangs out with killers."

"She was there to kill Alan Brown," Gagnon said, looking over the rim of his empty glass. "Or maybe Al was there to meet her and give her the information. A threat to his son might have swayed him. Either way she's a threat. Will you kill her for me?"

Skye stared out the window into the darkness. This Harmony did not kill Al Brown. Skye had eyes on her when Brown was shot. But she could have been there to get the program everybody wanted. She could have been a Korean agent negotiating with Brown. Staying close to his son would be a good way to subtly threaten Brown. Give me what I want, or something might happen to your boy. And she was a killer, or at least wanted to be. She had tried to kill Al's son, evidently to keep him from sharing what he learned from his dying father. She wasn't who Gagnon thought she was. Abraxas wouldn't miss with a knife throw. Still, she fit rule number one – she deserved to die.

"If you want her taken out, whether or not she's Abraxas, I might be down with that. Problem is, she could be anywhere."

"Not quite," Gagnon said. "The boy had a clue, even if he didn't know it."

"You kidding?" Skye asked. "A lineal manhole on a wallop island?"

Gagnon chuckled. "You have no reason to know, but Wallops Island is a real place. It's a small island in Virginia, just south of Chincoteague Island. There's a Flight Facility there that supports NASA with, among other things, special orbital programs."

"Orbital? Oh, you mean satellites," Skye said.

"Indeed," Gagnon said, "and I'm certain the North Koreans keep an eye on this place, so it makes sense they'd have an intelligence cell in the area."

Skye nodded. "Could be. But even if we have the right town, it would be a bitch to flush her out. I could wander around down there for weeks. She's got no reason to introduce herself to me."

"I'm not so sure," Gagnon said. "Am I right that Brown's son was the first to reach his father after the shooting?"

"That's right." *How in hell did he know that?*

"Did the woman he was with see him?"

"Oh yeah," Skye said, "and it pissed her off. She threw a knife at him. But Ike shoved him out of the way."

"Well then, she must think, as I did, that the boy got something from his father. If he goes with you to Wallops Island, she won't want to miss a second chance at him."

Skye got to her feet. "You a crazy old man if you think I'm going to use this kid as live bait. And he'd be crazy to go along with it anyway."

"Oh, you let me worry about that," Gagnon said, rising. "I'll explain the realities to him in the morning. Why don't you get some rest, and we'll deal with the details tomorrow."

Chapter 15

The sun had been up for almost an hour when Skye trotted down the stairs of her Georgetown rental. Her pre-dawn walk from the hotel to home had helped clear her mind, but it was being in her own space that energized her. She changed into her comfort clothes, denim, a Henley and boots. She gathered weapons and tools into her shoulder bag, made one difficult but important phone call, and texted Mo. Thirty minutes later she was out the door, still not really knowing her next move.

On the street, she wondered if her neighbors noticed her at all. It was a predominantly white neighborhood but not exclusive by any means. Did she attract attention because of her generally casual mode of dress. Her neighbors tended to wear business clothes, especially on a bright, clear morning like this when they were all rushing to work or the university. Did anyone register her wavy auburn hair. Nothing odd about a black woman wearing different wigs from day to day, but if they didn't know that it might make her stand out. In her profession, standing out was not a good thing. She needed to blend in.

Maybe she *was* a ninja.

One block to the left, another to the right, and she was opening the back door of Mo's Honda. As she pulled the door shut, he turned down the radio a click or two. *He must have it blasting when he's in here alone*, she thought. It was his usual mix of eighties R & B, well stocked with people she thought were mostly forgotten: Dazz Band, Al B. Sure, Freddie Jackson. Right then it was Gregory Abbott. *"You read my mind. Girl I want to shake you down."* Not her tastes, but it comforted her a bit. It was the stuff Papa used to listen to when he was in his Hennessy and telling his war stories. Except he never talked about times of actual combat.

"Well, this is different," Mo said, never taking his eyes off the road.

"What you mean?" Skye asked, shifting to the right so she could see his profile.

"This is that stop you make every couple of weeks up on Connecticut. You always call it a meeting, but I was thinking maybe you had a man up there."

"You trying to get all up in my business old man?"

"Oh, hell no," Mo said. "I like my head right where it is, on my shoulders. Just saying you pretty regular with this one. Most of the time at night, sometimes late in the afternoon. Ain't never took you there in the morning. Just saying it's different is all."

Mo was generally good at minding his own, but he wasn't stupid. She never told him her profession, but he had seen enough to know she was in some covert, dangerous business. It was sometimes hard to keep him in the dark about other things. Maybe she didn't need to.

"Not a man," she said, turning to stare out the window. "Actually, a woman. A counselor of sorts."

"Oh, like a shrink?"

"No," Skye snapped. "Just, you know, somebody to talk to. About my stuff."

"Somebody to talk to."

"Yeah."

"About your stuff."

"Yes."

"You pay her," Mo asked, "to talk to her about your stuff?"

Long sigh. "Yes."

"Yeah. That's a shrink."

Jayla pulled the blinds on the office windows. She knew Skye didn't like it too bright in there, and she always wanted patients to be comfortable. She wasn't sure what to expect. When a patient calls for an appointment ahead of schedule it often means they are in crisis. Two such calls in the same week might mean a total breakdown. In Skye's case the possible definition of crisis was broader than usual. And Jayla was keenly aware that their relationship had evolved over time to a place where her advice or even a casual suggestion to Skye could literally mean life or death for someone. As often as she regretted the position she had let herself get pulled into, she admitted to herself that Skye's psyche was just too fascinating for her to let it go. She took a deep, calming breath and settled back into her office chair before telling her receptionist to send Skye in.

Skye wore her emotions close to the surface and her agitation was clear. She paced into the room and glanced at the chaise where she usually sat but stayed on her feet and nailed Jayla with her eyes. "Need your help with something."

"Good morning," Jayla said with a smile. "And how are you today?"

"Look I ain't got time for…"

"Not the way this works," Jayla said, keeping her tone soft. "This is my house, and we work by my rules. Now sit down. Please."

Jayla understood the risks of pushing Skye, but she needed to maintain control in the office. Skye's lip curled into a snarl, but she stepped back and perched on the edge of the chaise.

"Now, what seems to be bothering you today?"

Skye blew out of puff of frustration. "Well to start with, that last job I took didn't turn out too well. Them two people who knew Papa? The ones I wanted a chance to talk to? They both dead now. I should always work solo."

Jayla managed to keep her mouth from dropping open, but it was a challenge. In the time she had known Skye she had never heard about a failure. She saw no sorrow or pain in Skye's eyes, but there was plenty of anger and frustration. And something else she rarely saw. Confusion.

"I'm very sorry to hear that. How are you handling this?"

"Never mind that," Skye said, waving the issue away. "Thing is, when I got back last night, the same client offered me another job. A real job. My kind of job. A great job. Dream job. But again, it ain't what I usually do, and I don't know if I ought to take it or pass."

Jayla raised her palms. "All right let's take this one thought at a time. First of all, what makes a job a dream job for you?"

"You sure you want to know?" Skye asked. "You don't usually want to know about a job until after it's over."

"Well, you aren't saying you'll do it yet, right? This is all hypothetical." Jayla maintained her calm smile, although inside she was wrestling with her professional ethics, knowing her ethics were losing the fight.

"I've got an opportunity here to go head-to-head with a … a person in the same line of work as me, only they working for the Yakuza. A pro like me, and a woman. The girl's rep is huge, and I can face off against her."

Jayla saw Skye's eyes flashing, excitement and doubt twisting her features, and it took her a second to guess why. "Is this about proving that you're better?"

"Duh! I'm the best there is, girl, and yeah, this is how I prove it."

"I see. You can test yourself against the competition," Jayla said.

"Yeah, and to your way of thinking, either way it would work out for the best," Skye said with a smirk. "No matter how it came out there would be one less killer on the loose."

Because she could see the embedded hook Jayla chose not to rise to the bait. She also didn't want to reveal that she saw this as an ego issue. Instead, she probed further.

"I think I understand the attraction, but I don't see the conflict. Why would you not want to take the job?"

"I see only one way to catch this bitch with her guard down. I know who she would want her next target to be. He's probably safe if he stays hidden. But to draw her out, I'd have to use him as bait. No matter how good this woman is at being invisible, when she makes her move to take out her target, she'll reveal herself."

As realization dawned Jayla tried hard to suppress her smile. "What I'm hearing is, you don't want this competitor's target to die. Is this someone you know?"

"Just met him yesterday."

Now Jayla let her smile show. "You're concerned for this stranger's life."

"Hey, don't get it twisted. I'm not about getting in another professional's business. I think I just don't want some dude to get smoked cause of *me*. Don't know how I feel about using somebody like that."

Jayla scribbled in her notebook. She wasn't really writing but she wanted to look like she was. Her patient should think she's recording her reactions, but in truth she needed a moment to think about what was happening. Skye was never unsure of her feelings, at least not in this office. She would never reveal such a thing. She would wait until she was sure before she would share anything with Jayla. Then it occurred to Jayla that Skye had brought this to her when she usually had to drag Skye's feelings out of her. Skye was staring at her expectantly. Did she expect Jayla to have answers? To advise her?

"Well, does that sound like a good thing?" Skye asked. "Worth it to take a killer off the board? A woman who might be responsible for dozens of murders?"

Jayla's eyebrows rose and she covered her mouth. Skye was looking to her for absolution. She wanted to be absolved of the guilt she'd feel if she let someone die to get her job done. Skye's mother had abandoned her in her teens. Was she now casting her therapist in that role? If Jayla was right, it was an awesome responsibility she was ill-prepared for. But if she handled it right, she might save lives in the future. And in this case, Skye might not even see that she faced more than two options. Jayla laid down her pen and leaned forward on one elbow.

"Well, I guess you'll just have to stop this other killer before she reaches her target."

Skye shook her head. "But that's not what I do, Doc. I already said I'm no bodyguard. Like I said, this last bit didn't work out too good."

Jayla paused to consider her next words. Just yesterday Skye went to help protect someone and had somehow failed. Now she was weighing putting another person at risk. Clearly there was more to this story, but she thought she might have enough of it to speak.

"If you refuse the job, will this other woman give up? Or will she eventually, given time, still kill the target?"

"Sure as shit," Skye said.

"You know who this other woman's target is. You said you met him."

Skye closed her eyes and nodded.

"Does he deserve to be murdered?" Jayla asked. "Does he meet rule number one?"

"Not so far as I know."

"Well then," Jayla said, holding both palms up. "There you have it. This other person would be violating the first rule that you say would qualify her to be what she is. It appears to me that you can accept this assignment, but you have to keep that next target alive. It's the only option available that fits your code."

Skye carried that thought back to the Fairmont. She chose to walk this time because the crisp autumn air cleared her head. She pictured Ike, who dies with honor, and Al Brown, who never had a chance, and put them in their appropriate boxes in her head, out of the way of today's thinking. Today it was about the boy with the pretty blue eyes.

Jayla's reasoning made sense. Skye was prepared to prevent her Japanese opposite number from violating what should be a universal assassin's code. But Carter Brown had to be in total agreement with the plan before she would move forward. So, she went straight to his room.

"Carter? You there?"

"I'm here. Hang on a sec."

He sounded tense and she couldn't be sure he was alone. Just to be safe she unzipped the front of her purse and pushed her hand into the hidden opening at the back, wrapping her fingers around the slim gun butt. The door swung open but instead of Carter she saw Gagnon waving her in. Still not sure, she stepped inside. The two bodyguards were on station flanking Gagnon. Carter stood alone on the other side of the room, hands deep in his pockets. His eyes were red. He looked upset but not afraid. She relaxed and withdrew her hand.

"Hey dude, you okay?" she asked.

"I'm fine," Carter said. "Not happy, but fine. Give Mr. Gagnon the flash drive."

Her eyes went to Gagnon, but his face revealed nothing, so she turned back to Carter. "You told him?"

"Yes, after he told me some things. Give it to him."

Skye walked over to Carter, stared up into his eyes and spoke softly. "Are you sure this is the guy who ought to have this stuff?"

"He says the flash drive proves my dad was a traitor," Carter said. "Says he was there to meet Harmony, to give her the program. That he gave it to me figuring I'd give it to her since we were dating. Well, I don't believe all of that. My dad was loyal to our country, and so am I, so give it to him."

Carter's heartache was so clear even Skye could feel it. She turned to Gagnon, standing between the two muscle men, holding a tablet. Yeah, she could take them all out but she stood between them and Carter. She probably couldn't finish the two guards before Carter got killed by their return fire. Besides, without Gagnon's support she was unlikely to manage her face off with Abraxas. Muttering a coarse obscenity under her breath, Skye dumped the contents of her purse on the bed, fished through the variety of tools and makeup, and pulled up the tiny flash drive she had dropped in there when Gagnon had come to the door the night before. She flipped it like a coin at Gagnon. He caught the tiny prize with a smile and plugged it into his tablet.

While he poked at electronic buttons, Skye asked, "It's just a computer program, right? Why the hell didn't he just email it to you or something?"

"Oh, this file is far too large for that," Gagnon said without looking up. "And much too precious to risk putting it up in the cloud where someone else might hack their way into it."

Carter moved closer to her. "He's wrong about Harmony, you know. He has to be."

He sounded like a petulant child. Skye held her hands wide and shrugged. "Dude. She threw a knife at you."

"She killed Ike," Gagnon said through clenched teeth. "He was the best security specialist I ever had."

"Look I'm sorry your friend got killed," Carter said, "But it wasn't some plot like you think. Harmony was only there because she was with me, and I wanted to see my dad perform."

Without looking up, Gagnon said, "You are easily manipulated, young man. I'm afraid your father was working for a competitor, even while he was working for me. It makes sense that he was also negotiating with the North Koreans. He would have given this to the highest… Oh. What? Damn it!"

"What's up?" Skye asked.

"This program can't possibly do what it's supposed to. There isn't enough… Wait. I see. Brown was smarter than I gave him credit for. This is, in fact only part of the program."

"Well ain't that a shame," Skye said with a tight smile. But Gagnon wasn't laughing. Nor was he acting angry. When he closed his eyes, Skye imagined him mentally shuffling the facts looking for the best plan. Best for him in any case. When his eyes opened his focus was on Carter, not her.

"What do you do, young man? What is your profession?"

"Engineering," Carter said. "Well, it will be. Working on my Masters now."

Gagnon seemed to be considering Carter, getting his measure. "You are an intelligent young man," he said. "Educated. Your chosen field tells me you are a man of logic and reasoning. You will understand. I will need your help."

"Screw you," Carter said with more heat than Skye expected. "You're trying to make it sound like I'm the reason my dad is dead but looks to me like you're to blame. Why the hell should I help you?"

Gagnon's voice was an icy calm. "Well, I can't say where this computer program came from, but no one would believe you wrote it. Yet I found it in your possession. I could have you arrested for theft of intellectual property."

"What? I didn't…" Carter looked to Skye, who plopped down on the bed.

"Don't look at me, college boy. I like to keep a low profile around law enforcement types." Gagnon had come up with his play pretty fast and she thought it was kind of interesting. It was BS of course, but Carter was naïve. Gagnon had showed him a stick, and now she wondered what the carrot would be.

Carter's expression moved from anger to desperation. He accepted defeat way too fast. She knew it when he dropped his head, looked up at Gagnon and asked, "What do you want?"

Just as quickly Gagnon turned on the charm, throwing the full energy of his personality at Carter. "You have the opportunity to redeem your father's mistake and make both him and yourself into national heroes, my boy. This woman you were with is somehow connected to whomever killed your father. And we know she wants this little flash drive. Just as I assumed you had it, she probably does too. If I understand the events of last night, she may have even seen you receive it. And we know that your father intended for you to get it to someone on Wallops Island."

"Or keep it from somebody there," Carter said.

"All right. Either way someone down there wants it. All you have to do is travel there and locate them. Skye here will protect you. If you find this Harmony, I believe she can lead us to the Korean agents who want to control our communications. Then we can bring in the federal forces to shut them down. You see, you have the power to stop this plot, this threat to national security. You're the only one who can."

Carter's hands curled into fists. His eyes sparkled and he gave a small slow nod of agreement.

By God, he's got him, Skye thought. Gagnon had somehow injected Carter with patriotic fervor with those few words. None of this had dulled her own sarcastic skepticism.

"And naturally you're hoping the rest of that computer program's going to surface and find its way to you," she said.

"It would certainly be the right thing for someone who is working for me to have in mind. There could be a generous cash bonus involved."

Skye looked him in the eye. "And that's why you want me chasing this bitch instead of the feds, ain't it? If they got hold of it, no way they'd give it to you. Well, that's bullshit. You know damned well that's not what I do."

Gagnon switched to his grim face; teeth bared. "I know exactly what you do, Miss. And your mission hasn't changed. I want the person who killed Ike dead. That is what you get paid to do. And I'm certain that in the process you will eliminate the person who killed Alan Brown. I think his son would want that. Yes?"

Gagnon turned his hard stare on Carter, who nodded.

"Then we are agreed," Gagnon said. "I will deposit your funds before the day is out. You will be provided with a credit card for expenses, and I will supply a car for you to take to Wallops Island. I have a new Audi A6 available, or a Jaguar XF if you prefer."

Skye laughed, shaking her head. "Yeah, I don't think so. Going to need something a lot less flashy. An older muscle car. I ain't trying to get nobody's attention. What we going to need is a getaway car. So here's what's going to happen. You going to give me back that flash drive so I can flash it at somebody for leverage if I have to. Then you and me, we going shopping for a good ride. You'll put one of your other car's plates on it. While we out doing that your boys will get Carter a couple days' clothes and a suitcase. I'll pick up a couple changes at my place. Then him and me, we take ourselves on a road trip down to Virginia and see if we can find his killer girlfriend."

Chapter 16

Sunset was still a half hour away when Skye and Carter rolled onto US-50 pointed east toward Annapolis, but a cloud bank sliding overhead made it darker than it should have been. They had grabbed dinner at a fast-food drive thru. Skye had tuned to WPGC and was savoring French fries one at a time from the container stuffed into the map pocket of the driver's door. She had Carter using the GPS feature of Google Maps in his phone to play navigator. She was relaxed, sitting back, holding the wheel at arm's length, jamming to the urban sounds as she became part of the steady flow of traffic. Aside from giving directions, Carter had ridden quietly to this point, and she was good with that. But of course, that couldn't last.

"So, you rejected the offered Audi A6 which is, as I understand it, a pretty sweet ride," Carter said. "Instead, you put us in a plain blue… what is this exactly?"

"It's a 2006 Pontiac GTO. A nice blue car that hardly anybody is going to look at twice, and a lot of people would mistake for a Honda Accord."

"Yeah, kind of drab," Carter said.

"That's kind of the point, college boy," she said after a sip of the soda jammed into the center console cup holder. "And I like a six speed. It don't look like nothing special, but she'll pump 400 horses to those rear wheels. It's what I told Gagnon we needed. A muscle car. A getaway car."

"That guy who drove us out of Atlantic City," Carter said. "He's one of your partners?"

"Mo? Nah, he's just a driver I use."

"You know your cars," Carter said. "And clearly you enjoy being behind the wheel. Why would you employ a driver?"

How much should she tell him? After a moment's hesitation Skye decided that once somebody has seen her kill, a little openness was a small risk. She finished up her fries and checked the vehicles around her for suspicious activity.

"I don't pay a driver because I hate to drive," she said. "I use Mo because I want to stay off the grid as much as possible. Once a car's registered in your name the government sees you. If you only use Uber, you're a lot less visible, especially if you change the name on the account frequently. Most of the time I call Mo before I go into the app, so he's always the closest car when the call goes out. But this is small talk. Why don't you ask me what you really want to know?"

Carter stared out his window at the uncluttered roadside area. Gas stations and restaurants few past, but it looked like the commercial area was only one building deep. The dark skies began to release their tears, spattering the window.

"Okay," he said. "Do you think Harmony is this big bad villain Mr. Gagnon says she is?"

Now we getting to it, Skye thought. She put the wipers on at their lowest setting, hating the squeak of rubber on glass. "Do I think your date is a master assassin? No, she don't read like that. But she is a nasty bitch. I figure she got close to you so your dad could see she could hurt you if he didn't cooperate with her team. I think he knew she was a threat, but didn't want to scare you so he never said anything. I do think she had a hand in Ike's death. And in your dad's death too. What else?"

After a few seconds of silence, she glanced over at Carter. He looked frozen, his breathing getting deeper as he stared out the window. It took Skye a moment to realize why he was close to hyperventilating.

"First time over the Chesapeake Bay Bridge?"

"What the hell," Carter said, fingertips digging into the bucket seat.

"Don't feel bad," Skye said. "There's people that think it's the scariest bridge in the country. A couple hundred feet high and around four and a half miles long. It don't bother me, but then, I ain't most people. Now come on. What do you want to know?"

Carter stared at his hands in his lap. Just before they left the bridge he asked, "You really think we'll find Harmony?"

"If you heard Al right we will. Somebody down here wants this flash drive. They know who you are, and by now probably know who I am. We got the flash drive for bait. If we stay visible, they'll surface for sure. When they do, trust and believe they'll give up your girlfriend."

He didn't look up, and the rain on the roof became a white noise background.

"And what happens when you find Harmony?"

"Oh. She dies," Skye said, speeding up to escape the cluster of cars coming off the bridge.

"Is that really necessary?"

"Are you serious?" Skye asked. Carter gripped the door handle hard when Skye made a sudden lane shift. "Do you not get that this bitch thinks you betrayed her by running off with that flash drive? She'll off you first chance she gets. And besides all the other good reasons, seeing her off is the only reason I'm here. That's the job."

Of course, that was only if Gagnon was right, that Harmony was Abraxas. If not, Skye was sure she could make Harmony lead her to Abraxas. *Then* she'd kill her.

Carter sat back and returned to silence. Skye had to admit she was starting to like the boy, or maybe she envied his innocence a little. She didn't spend much time with guys like him.

Embedded in a pack of cars, Skye merged onto what looked like a new road on the right. Routes 50 and 301 had shared the road up to this point but this was where they parted company. While 301 continued north, Skye followed Route 50. The two turn lanes became the highway, cutting through what looked like farmland on both sides. Actually, it looked like tall grass with the occasional house stuck in it, but Skye assumed it was farmland. The rain was trying to become a thunderstorm, but the terrain was flat and the road straight, so none of the drivers around her reacted to the weather. Slowing down was just not part of the Maryland driving style. *The real danger*, she thought, *was those drivers who try to be too careful.*

When she started this drive, she hoped to ride in silence. But Carter had talked for a while and now, to her surprise, she wanted the conversation to continue.

"So, what did you do last night?"

"What?" Carter asked.

"DC is a big tourist town. What did you do?"

Carter released a ragged sigh. "I cried a lot."

"You... you cried?"

"Yeah," Carter said the way people talk when somebody touches a nerve. "I cried. You know. Grief? That thing people do when they lose a loved one? Actually, I think I'm all cried out."

Skye lapsed back into stillness. She thought about the day she found her brother lying there in their tiny apartment. She remembered kneeling on the linoleum and how soft his hand was between hers. She could feel the life draining out of him, chased out by the heroin in his veins like the drugs owned the space and refused to share his body with his soul. Daddy was gone. Mama was never quite sober. Skye was only 12 and she was sad, but she didn't think about grief.

She had to do something, to take action. She decided to find that rusty gun Tyrone carried. It made him feel like a man. Then she would find the bastard who sold Tyrone that poison. She hurt, but she had needed to strike out, not cry about it. When things went wrong you did something about it.

Just like now. She was motoring due south but at a light she made a left onto Rte 404.

"Hey, I didn't say turn," Carter said. "The GPS says it's south on that same road for another couple of hours."

"We're taking a little detour," Skye said. "We've picked up a tail."

Carter turned to stare out the back window. Skye had left the bulk of the traffic behind and wondered if the follower knew yet that he had been spotted. The strengthening storm was forcing him to stay closer than any good tail would want to be, just to keep her in sight.

"Which car?" Carter asked, raising his voice to compete with the rain pelting their vehicle.

"Take a guess," Skye said. "I told you why I picked this car. I'm thinking the tail is a pro too."

Skye sped up just a bit, momentarily pulling away from her followers. She did like the feel of the GTO, its engine snarling almost as loud as the rain. She searched for the next intersection, her headlights slicing through the blackness almost far enough for comfort.

"Not the pickup truck," Carter said. "That black car looks like a BMW. So must be the old sportscar."

"Yep. You strapped in?"

"Of course. Why…?"

Skye spotted the small side road just in time to brake on her approach. Then she popped the clutch and pressed the accelerator. She cranked the wheel and yanked the handbrake. That broke the rear tires loose. She drifted farther than planned, hydroplaning a bit, and Carter's shoulder hit hers, but when she released the brake, the GTO shot down the side road. Now she raced down a two-lane blacktop with narrow shoulders and no overhead lights.

She thought she heard Carter shout, "What the hell" under a base drum rumble of thunder. Ten seconds later her pursuer came back into view, gaining on her at a dangerous pace. As that vehicle grew in her rearview mirror, she recognized it and couldn't fight a grim smile. It was a Mustang.

"Respect," she whispered to herself. It wasn't just a Mustang but, judging by the fat tires, it was the Bullitt model, which actually blends in better than a standard Mustang. And it was the original dull green, just like the one Steve McQueen drove in the old movie.

As they were the only two vehicles on that road her tail had clearly given up on stealth or subtlety. He was closing on her. Was he going to try to bump her? In a storm, in the dark, she was not about to try to outrun him. But with fields on either side instead of buildings or trees she could probably run off the road without much trouble.

"Push your seat back and get on the floor," Skye snapped. "This asshole might ram me." Peripheral vision told her Carter was even whiter than when she met him.

"I think I'm safer in the safety belt."

"Boy you better get your ass down there in front of that seat," Skye said. "If I have to do some evasive shit, I don't want you banging into my arm while I'm trying to control this beast."

Lightning flashed off to her left and Skye could smell the ozone. The two vehicles were all alone on that narrow country road. Neither the darkness nor the weather seemed to bother the other driver. In her mirror Skye saw him push the Mustang into the other lane, risking a head on crash with anybody unlucky enough to be driving in the other direction. Was he going to try to push her off the road? She gripped the wheel tighter. She was prepared to swap paint with the Mustang.

As the other car pulled up beside her Skye muttered "Bring it, bitch" through clenched teeth. From her right she heard Carter moan. At least he was where she told him to be, knees in his chest, back against the door. But then, her view of the other driver became much clearer. His passenger side window was down.

Fear gripped her heart and her breath locked in her lungs. Through her rain spattered window she saw his stringy black hair and a pistol pointed at her face.

Chapter 17

Skye clenched her teeth, stiff-armed the steering wheel and locked the brakes. The roar of a heavy caliber round cut through the night. The car shook Despite her GTO skidding forward the Mustang shot past her. Carter screamed. The Mustang's tail lights receded ahead of her. He was leaving her behind.

"Like hell," Skye said, slamming the stick down into first and popping the clutch. Her car jumped forward like a scalded cat, pulling the Mustang's tail lights closer. The shooter was racing away, trying to escape her, but he was still handling the road at a safe pace. Skye had no interest in safe. She needed to catch the man who had the arrogance to shoot at her.

"What the hell's going on?" Carter asked. Skye ignored him. Most of her focus was on the vehicle ahead, still the only other one on the road. The rest of her mind was on the driver. She examined her mental snapshot of him, certain that she had seen him someplace recently. It might not matter though since she had no intention of seeing him again.

The storm was easing into a gentle but steady rain. She drove to within three or four car lengths of her quarry. She remembered her training for the "Precision Immobilization Technique." more commonly known as the PIT maneuver.

An inquisitive moon peeked down through two parting clouds. Skye took that as a positive sign. They started down a gentle hill, offering a better view of the road ahead. Now it was Skye's turn to move into the oncoming lane and speed up, but she wouldn't pass the other car. Just before her front bumper was even with the Mustang's rear wheel, she jerked the steering wheel to the right.

The thump of metal on metal combined with the squeal of tires and another open-mouthed scream from Carter. Skye pulled halfway onto the right-side shoulder, her right rear tire spitting gravel behind them before she got back into her lane. She watched the Mustang turn fully sideways and move to the left. One of its front tires went off the asphalt and must have dug in. Both left tires rose up and it spun like a pinwheel, rolling in the air before falling into the field off the left side of the road. It landed on the roof but rolled at least once before Skye had driven past it and couldn't find it in her rearview mirror. Near her feet, Carter was panting like a thirsty great Dane.

Skye slowed down, the car and her breathing. She relaxed back into her bucket seat, grinning at Carter's efforts to right himself. After a couple minutes she pulled onto the shoulder, stopped and reached over to pop the passenger side door open.

"You can climb out now," she said. Carter's head fell back, eyes closed against falling drops. He got his hands on the ground and slowly stretched out in what, to Skye, was a comical movement. He stood up in the rain for a few seconds then dropped back into his seat.

"Want to tell me what happened back there?" he asked as Skye pulled back onto the road. "I don't see anybody else out there. What happened to the other car? Did you lose our tail?"

"Yeah, he's gone. I think he went off the side of the road and got stuck."

Carter matched her smile. "Oh, wow. Bad luck for him, I guess. Bet he's back there pissed off to the max."

"Oh, yeah, I'm sure he really flipped out when we got away," Skye said, grinning to herself and wondering how

Carter would have reacted if he knew what really happened to that other car. "Now get your phone out and get us back on track. I'm about ready for dinner."

Soon they were rolling through the middle of what looked to Skye like every small town in that part of Virginia. The locals called it the Delmarva. The peninsula held the state of Delaware, but Maryland and Virginia each also owned a slice, hence the name which combined the first letters of the three states. Skye felt out of place, urban woman out in the country surrounded by country people. Chincoteague Road appeared to be the main drag, and she could see that if she didn't slow down, she'd run out of town pretty quickly. The closest she'd ever been to this place was Ocean City, but at least there they were trying to look like civilization. Of course, in the dark she might be getting a bad impression.

"Looks peaceful," Carter said, tapping his phone. "Want me to find a hotel. There's a surprising selection here."

"How about a camp site?" Skye asked. "Or an RV camp?"

Carter looked around. It seemed to be what he did when he was confused. "It's a big car, but it's hardly an RV. Like I said, there are some nice inns here. After all that excitement aren't you ready to lie down in a nice warm bed?"

"What I want," Skye said, stopping at a light, "is to wake up in the morning. The guy in the chase car might have called ahead with our location and direction before we got away from him. It might not be hard to guess our destination. And this ain't no RV but it's real easy to spot if you know what you're looking for. If anybody is looking for us, hotel parking lots are the first place they'll check."

Carter grumbled. "Okay. Let me see what's out there."

Town appeared to end with a view of what must be the Atlantic, and the road curved around to the north. There was no development for a while. Then Skye saw what looked like a runway on her left. A small-town airport?

"Hey, you said RV parks?" Carter said. "That's easy. Just stay on this road. We can stay at Jellystone Park."

"Seriously?"

Two bridges and ten minutes later they rolled onto Chincoteague Island. The storm passed and the rain stopped as they pulled into a strip mall where pickup trucks outnumbered cars in the parking lot. After sandwiches and sodas at Subway, Carter pointed them to Jellystone Park. Carter explained it was part of a national chain tied into the cartoon bear from the 1960's. Skye had never seen a Yogi Bear cartoon, but she recognized the image on the campground signage that directed her to the office. While she navigated the idyllic setting, Carter watched her eyes.

"Sounds like we'll be spending a little time together," Carter said with a lopsided smile.

"That a problem?"

"Oh, no," Carter said. "I know I was in no condition for company last night with all that happened, but I'm more together now. And with all we've had to deal with I didn't really have a chance to actually look at you."

"So?"

"So, you're nothing like any woman I've ever known. And, well, you're kind of cute. Fate has thrown us together, and I was thinking maybe, you know, you and me…"

Skye raised the pointer of her right hand. "Don't even think about it, college boy."

His smile weakened. "Oh, I'm sorry. I didn't think. Maybe you don't you like men. Are you a lesbian?"

"Hell no," she said. "I loves me some dick. I'm just picky about which ones."

Carter's smile thinned further. "I get it. You only date Black men."

"Black, brown, white, yellow, tried them all," Skye said. "But I got standards and, college boy, you don't meet them."

Carter nodded, watching her face closely. "So, what do you look for in a man?"

In truth, Skye never over-thought it. Some guys gave off the right vibe. It was a matter of feel, not something she could explain, and it was almost always somebody she picked, not somebody who stepped to her. Aloud she simply said, "Not you."

Carter's face fell while he clicked around on his phone. She knew her words stung, but it seemed he was trying not to show it. "Okay, whatever. It's just that they've got some nice little cabins here. AC, full kitchen, a shower would be nice."

"And a parking space where anybody can spot my whip," Skye said. "You missing the point here. I ain't looking to get cornered in some cabin because you want a shower. Now chill while I lie to this guy about what we're driving and hook us up with a space."

She parked, climbed out of the car and crunched across the gravel to the rental office. In ten minutes, she was back in the car. Carter was staring out his side window. She sat for a minute, pulling her thoughts together.

"Look, you must think I'm a real bitch," she said, "but I wasn't trying to diss just now. I mean, I meant what I said but even if you were my type, this ain't the time or place for that stuff."

Carter nodded and managed a small smile. "I get it. Thanks for saying that." After a short pause he added, "I don't want you to think I'm just a horn dog. Really I'm just kind of lonely right now and sometimes when you want to connect with somebody… anyway…"

His words trailed off, and Skye let them. She drove through the grounds in slow motion. It was too late for so many children to be running around but there they were, loud and fast and not watching out for cars. She crept down a narrow lane between a row of cottages and a line of deluxe RVs. At the end of the lane, she turned up the next path, eventually driving into a vacant space between two smaller RVs. She killed the engine, looked around and smiled. It was a pull-through site surrounded by mature trees that gave a feeling of privacy.

"What now?" Carter asked.

"Well I don't know about you, but now I'm getting some sleep," Skye said, laying her seat back as far as it would go. "Grab those blankets out of the trunk."

"Wait a sec. Are you talking about sleeping in the car?"

"Safest option," Skye said. "Nobody would look for you here. Except maybe me." She popped the trunk and closed her eyes. Ten long seconds later she heard his huff of frustration and his door opening. He returned, and the folded blanket landed on her chest. She slipped the gun out of the waistband holster at her back and held it at her waist. Then she opened the thick gray blanket and pulled it over herself.

"This was your plan all along," Carter said.

"Not really. I just like to be prepared."

"I guess," he said. "Everybody keeps a roadside emergency kit and first aid kit. But blankets, towels, emergency rations?"

"Got to be flexible."

Was he mad or just surprised? After a pause, Carter said, "Well, you may well have saved my life before, so I guess I'll follow your lead. But I think I'll take the back seat."

"Suit yourself."

Again Skye heard the passenger door open. Heard the seat tilted forward. Heard the strained, "What the hell," and Carter dropping back into the front seat.

"Whoever heard of bucket seats in the back seat too?"

"You are observant," Skye said. Then came the sound of his seat being tilted back and the shuffling of a tall man trying to get comfortable. She relaxed into her seat, breathing in the darkness, clearing her mind for the next day's target search.

"Who do you think is coming for us?"

Well, damn. He wanted to talk. Probably too scared to relax. "Don't really know. Maybe this Yakuza assassin, but more likely this Oneida group Gagnon told us about, the people who wrote the program he wants. I recognized the driver who was tailing us. He was at the Borgata."

"What? He was there?"

"He was the MC, the guy that introduced your dad on stage," Skye said. "And he sure as hell wasn't Korean or Japanese. Looked a little Middle Eastern to me."

Quiet returned, except for the insect chorus outside the car. Two spaces down someone was creating more smoke than anything else in their fire pit. Their laughter carried on the clear night air. With her eyes closed, Skye thought she could see the sandman approaching.

"Do you think my father was a traitor?"

Skye's sigh fogged the windshield momentarily. "Does it really matter?"

"It does to me," Carter said.

Skye hadn't given it any thought. It didn't impact her feelings about her Uncle Al, or her mission to eliminate his killer. "Don't know, don't really give a shit. I could see why he might switch sides. If I understand what this program they all want can do, I'm not too sure it's a good idea for Gagnon to have it. If all the players are dirty, maybe your father decided to give it to the highest bidder. Or, hell, maybe he was going to give it to the feds? That would make Gagnon think your dad was betraying *him*. And I don't think there's any way to find out for sure, so why waste time thinking about it?"

"You really are a cold-hearted bitch."

"Right now, I'm really a tired bitch," Skye said, pulling her blanket aside and thumping Carter's thigh with her pistol. "Don't make me slap you across the face with this piece. Tomorrow's going to be more dangerous than the last two and if you want me to keep you alive, you going to have to shut your mouth so I can get some rest."

Chapter 18

She was a teenager again. She stood before a door she knew was unlocked. She walked right in. She would never lose the smell of the place, a mix of sandalwood incense and vomit. The man was alone, squatting on a torn brown leather chair just to the left of one of the windows that faced the street. He looked at her like she had just landed from mars. She held her brother's rusty revolver in both hands.

She faced a very dark hard-looking man with short nappy hair and one gold tooth. When he stood up, he waved a corroded knife at her. The lamp on the table by the chair spread a circle of light around small plastic envelopes full of white powder. The deadly weapons that killed her brother, Tyrone, in plain sight. This was the man who sold that poison to her big brother and got him to commit slow suicide. Death by injection.

Her heart pounded in her chest and in her ears as he walked toward her, grinning his contempt.

"You that boy's little sister, ain't you?" he said. "Come up in here, all brave and shit, with that stupid piece of shit the boy used to carry around. It don't work, you know. But you got potential, shorty. I think I'll turn you out so you can make me some money. After I teach you how to act."

She squeezed the trigger. The gun gave off a loud click, but nothing more. She pulled the trigger again. The cylinder turned, the hammer rose and fell. Again, nothing.

He towered over her, looking down, reaching for her, maybe two arms' lengths away when she pulled the trigger again. This time the gun jumped as if it was trying to leave her hands and a roar bounced off the walls and crashed into her ears. She never thought it would be so loud. And the smoke! It burned her nose and made her eyes water.

But now there was a hole in the middle of the man's body. It seemed so small, but she could see a red mess behind him on the wall beside the window. He staggered back, eyes bulging with surprise.

Then he said, "You little bitch," He took another step forward, so she fired again. This time the hole appeared in his chest, a couple of inches higher than the first. She expected blood to spurt out of the holes, but it didn't happen. And how come he was still standing up? He did back up a few steps, but then leaned forward, reaching for her.

She pulled the trigger again but the gun seemed to have given up trying to fire. Terrified, she threw it. It hit him in the face, and he staggered back a few more steps.

"I'm gonna kill you, you little…" He had backed into the open window.

That's when it all changed. Skye's terror turned to anger. Anger became resolve, a determination to do what she had gone there to do. She rushed forward.

Her small palms crashed into the bigger man's chest. The glass behind him shattered. That sound stopped her, but he kept moving. The next sound was a thump from four stories below her on the street. It must be over. It had to be. But she had to be sure. She forced herself forward to lean out the window.

"Hey! Hey! You okay? Wake up!"

Skye's eyes snapped open. Someone was shaking her right arm. When she turned her head to the right, she was looking into Carter Brown's face, so close to her own in the dim moonlight. His expression showed only concern. It was his hand on her forearm. She realized that inches from his hand she held her pistol, pointed up under his chin. With a sharp gasp she opened her hand to drop the weapon.

'Sorry," she said, breathing deeply, trying to pull her mind back into the here and now. Terror hung in Carter's wide eyes for a moment after the gun hit the seat. He swallowed hard, but his next words surprised her.

"Seriously, are you okay? That must have been one hell of a nightmare. You shouted and thrashed like you were wrestling with the devil himself. What the hell?"

"I'm fine. Just a bad memory that comes back once in a while."

"I was worried," Carter said.

"Yeah, sorry. The gun thing was sort of a reflex, but I wouldn't…"

"I wasn't worried about *me*," Carter said.

Skye didn't know what to say to that, so she put her business face back on and lowered her voice. "Look, it was nothing. Go back to sleep."

The sun and the screaming kids seemed to get up at the same time. Skye quietly flipped the blanket off. Carter's hand was still on her arm. Taking liberties or trying to comfort her? Either way, it was unwanted, but she removed his hand gently. She shoved her blanket into the back seat. Beside her, Carter snored softly, covered completely by his blanket, even his head. They were about the same age but for some reason he seemed so much younger. She laughed at his naivete but had to admit she appreciated his concern when the dream shook her. She had given him no reason to care about her. Maybe he was one of those people who cared about everybody.

She watched Carter as she turned the key to bring the engine to life. He slept through her starting the car, easing it out of the space and driving to the bathhouse near the tent area. His head snapped up when she opened her door.

"Welcome back to the living," she said. "I pulled over to the bathrooms so we can pee. Then we'll find a place to check in and get a shower. After that we can scout the area for anything that looks or sounds like what your dad was trying to tell you."

Just before she closed the car door, she heard him say, "Yeah. Good morning."

The inside of the ladies' room was clean and nicely appointed but for all that it was still just a fancy outhouse. Skye took care of her needs quickly. When Carter returned to the car, Skye was waiting for him, ready to go. She retraced their path toward the mainland. It was a perfect day: clear blue skies, warm but not hot with a soft sea breeze, and a calm ocean that appeared to be sprinkled with sparkling diamonds as they approached the first long bridge. The only downside was her inability to find a decent radio station, so she turned it off and rolled down her window. She loved the smell of the ocean, the call of the gulls. Despite carrying live bait into the arena with her, Skye was in that positive energetic mood she always felt when she was on the hunt.

"Hey college boy! Find us a small hotel or motel in town. Then we can go see what Wallops Island is all about."

Carter worked his phone. "You do realize that the town we went through last night isn't Wallops Island, right? That was Wattsville."

"What?" Skye's mood was dented. "Then where the hell is Wallops Island? And why'd you bring us to the wrong damn place?"

"I didn't," Carter shot back. "You just jumped to the wrong conclusion. What made you think it was a town anyway? Truth is, it's an actual island, the next big one south of the one we're driving off now. Mostly that's a national Wildlife refuge."

"Well, hell," Skye said. "I hate the woods. Why would your dad send us there?"

related to outer space, Colonial Virginia and Hawaii. An odd mix of model rockets, oil lanterns and conch shells.

"Checking in for the night," Skye said, slapping the Gagnon credit card down on the counter. "In fact, better make it two nights. And I prefer the second floor."

Leilani nodded with an over-enthusiastic smile. Her accent and tan skin confirmed a Hawaiian or Samoan background. The extra girth around her middle was squeezed into a long, white, ruffled muumuu-style dress with puffy sleeves that reached halfway down her forearms. Straight black hair topped her round, jovial face and hung to the middle of her back. But her black eyes looked somehow wrong to Skye, like they didn't belong in that face.

"You're going to love it here," Leilani said while working her registration on a computer console. "Indoor pool, whirlpool, sauna, exercise room, and the wild ponies sometimes graze in our pasture."

"That's cool," Carter said. "You'll have to tell me more about that."

"Maybe later," Skye said, tugging on his sleeve. She hustled him up the stairs. Room 202 was nothing special: bathroom to the left as she walked in, then opening up past there. A king bed with its headboard against the wall to the left. Dresser on the right with just enough space between it and the foot of the bed for easy passage. A chair in front of a pole lamp in the far left corner. The far wall covered by drapes.

Skye directed Carter to shower first and went through to pull the drapes open. Standing at the sliding glass doors that opened onto the balcony she scanned from left to right, pleased with the view of the approach to the inn. That was why she preferred the second floor, That and the fact that it made it just a little harder for an uninvited guest to visit through the sliding door.

She pulled the curtains closed again and turned to unpack. She tossed her shoulder bag on the bed. She opened it, then pulled her holster out of the back of her waistband and dropped it, gun and all, inside with everything else. Then she covered her bag with her denim jacket, marking her territory. She sat to pull off her boots. She put her travel bag next to her shoulder bag and opened it. By the time she had fresh clothes in her hand, Carter stepped out of the bathroom, and she filed past him.

Not much water pressure, but what did she expect at a small, low rent motel? At least the water got really hot, just the way she liked it. She liked the smell of the hotel shampoo, so she used it and the little bar of soap provided. Refreshed and energized, she dried briskly with a towel so thin she feared ripping it apart. A layer of baby oil warmed her dry skin. She wriggled into her jeans and bra (both of which are always good for more than one day) and a clean light blue Henley top. She chose not to replace the light make up she had worn yesterday. No harm in the boy seeing what she looked like in her natural state. Smirking at that thought she scooped up her dirty clothes and auburn wig.

But at the door her smirk turned to a flash of anger. Carter was sitting on the bed in khakis and a polo shirt, going thru her things. She hadn't imagined that he would touch her tools or her weapons. He had partially unspooled her piano wire garrote, and now was waving her one-handed folding knife around. And in his other hand, the fixed blade.

"Put that down," she snapped.

Carter looked up, wearing what she thought was his default expression: confusion. "Why do you have all this stuff? And, hey, what happened to your hair?"

"Put it down NOW!"

"Hey, I didn't touch the gun," Carter said, as if he didn't even register her anger. "But this looks like a pretty mean knife." He held it like a cinema swordsman and when he thrust it forward the blade burst from the handle, flew past Skye's face and thudded into the wall beside the door. Skye reached him in two long strides and slammed a fist into his midsection. He dropped to his knees on the floor, gasping for breath.

"Asshole!" she said, in a sharp tone but trying to keep the volume low enough for her words not to escape their room.. "That what they teach you in college? To fuck with other people's shit?" She walked back to the wall where the first two inches of the blade were solidly embedded. The three slots in the blade allowed her to grip it well enough to wiggle it free. Then she returned to the bed to reload the long shank of the blade into its handle.

Carter was still struggling to catch his breath. "What… what the hell…"

"It's a ballistic knife, dumbass. Good thing you didn't pick up the flashlight. You'd have probably blinded yourself. I've burned through plastic with that halogen light."

While Carter struggled to his feet Skye pulled her denim jacket back on, slid her gun back into place at her back and started stowing other things in various pockets. Then she plopped on the bed and started reading through the brochures. She could feel Carter's eyes on her but couldn't be bothered with him right then.

"Sorry if I violated your privacy or something," Carter said. Was he being sincere or sarcastic? It didn't matter. She nodded.

"I am a little curious. Why two knives?"

Without looking up, Skye said, "Assassin's rule number five: always have a backup. For everything."

Carter blinked twice and leaned back against the dresser. "Assassin?"

Skye sighed heavily. "Assassin. That's me. That's what I do. Are you really that slow?"

"I figured you were some kind of corporate fixer or troubleshooter or something. Maybe a spy."

"Wake the hell up," Skye said. "In real life, spies deal in information. Killing is kind of a specialized skill. Now, when you were digging through the internet about this place did you see anything that made sense with your father's last words?"

Carter's eyes wandered for a moment. "No, I guess not."

"Did you look at street names?" Skye asked. "I could imagine a Lineal Street. Or how about business names? No bar called The Manhole or something? I just remember he loved to play with words."

"No. nothing I've seen seems connected to a lineal manhole, if that's what he said."

Skye nodded. "Yeah, I figured you either heard wrong or made that shit up. I just went along to see what your plan was. Now I'm guessing you don't have one. Well, assuming you got the location right, we move to plan B. We'll just wave you around like a fat nightcrawler until some fish rises to the bait. I see here that the Wallops Island Flight Facility isn't one site but three separate spots. There's the main base, that fenced in compound we drove past, there's this place they call the Mainland, and the launch sight that's really on the island. So I think we visit them all, and see what happens."

"You mean see if anybody tries to kill me," Carter said.

"Yeah, I guess," Skye said, getting to her feet. "Never know where the attack might come from. You got to admit, it's kind of exciting, right?"

"No. No it's not."

A few minutes later Skye led a pouty Carter Brown back into the visitor's center. Actually, the granite sign said it was the NASA Visitor Center - Wallops Flight Facility, Goddard Space Flight Center. The towering flagpole was as tall as most of the missiles scattered about the grounds and like most of them it was mounted on a cement platform. Skye wondered if the missiles were just models or if some were operational, part of some stealth defense system.

The rockets on display inside were definitely scale models, some in display cases, some out where you could touch them if you were that enamored with space vehicles. She had no interest in any of it so she moved straight to the counter. The puffy matron behind it wore a blond shock of big hair, at least blond down to the last half inch of dark brown roots. Skye matched the attendant's pleasant smile.

"Good morning. How do we sign up for a tour of the Main Base? I want to see what really goes on out here."

"Oh, so sorry honey," she said in a voice most people reserve for children under ten years old. "Tours of the facility are only provided to non-profit school and civic groups, and our security procedures require a minimum of four weeks advance notice."

"I see," Skye said, holding her frozen smile. "In that case, do you suppose anyone would shoot me if I just stood at the front gate and looked inside?"

The attendant actually chuckled. "Oh heavens no. Just don't take any pictures. They frown on that."

Skye had hoped to walk Carter around all three Wallops locations but since that was not meant to be, she pulled out of the visitor center lot and drove back up the two-lane road to the small spur that led to what appeared to be the Flight Facility main entrance. She pulled into a small parking area to the side. She imagined this was a waiting area where people sat while the security guards checked their clearance or maybe where wives sat to pick up their husbands after work. She climbed out and waved to her passenger to follow.

The guard house at the gate made it clear that this was no tourist attraction. The installation had the feel of a military compound. It was the same feeling she got from a prison. The man standing outside the guard hut was the only person in uniform she saw, but inside vehicles moved and people even walked with the kind of precision you might see at a military site. Or the way prisoners were moved around in the yard. The aircraft she could see all looked military too.

Beside her, Carter asked, "Why are we here?"

"Just to give anybody walking by a chance to see you," she said. "Never know who might know who, you know?"

She made eye contact with the security guard. She thought he really saw her for what she was. He offered a sliver of a smile and his right hand rested on his holster, just for a second. Then he folded his arms. His body language spoke volumes to her. Calm, relaxed, yet very alert. This was no rent-a-cop. He was a pro. She nodded acknowledgement and turned back toward the car just as a vehicle rolled through the gate on the exit side. She was a few steps from her car when she heard the other vehicle stop behind her.

"Jonesy? Schuyler Jones is that you?"

Chapter 19

Years stood between Skye and the last time she had heard her birth name. That name was printed on her high school diploma, but no one had called her that since graduation day. She forced herself to turn slowly and fought the impulse to reach for a weapon. The man stepping out of the silver Range Rover coupe stirred memories from that other life.

"Get in the car," she told Carter. He frowned but obeyed.

"It is you," the newcomer said. "I can't believe it. What in the world bring you here?"

"And it's you," Skye said. Omar Parker was a material ghost reaching out from that universe on the other side of the line that separated her childhood from her whirlwind life with Papa Maddox. Here he stood, much as she remembered him, tall and fit with his Denzel looks in an Armani suit and Ferragamo shoes. And there she was in jeans. She could count the people she was close to in high school on the fingers of one hand and Omar was at the top of that list. He had also been her first.

"How in the world have you been?" Omar asked, wrapping her in a warm hug. "Seems like you vanished the second you stepped off the stage after high school graduation."

"Yeah, well, my stepdad, he wanted me to see the world," she said. "You were headed for MIT."

"Yep," he said. "Followed the plan just like we talked about. Engineering degree and straight into a job with NASA. You were aiming at the military if I remember, or something in law enforcement. Which way did you go? FBI?"

"Well actually, I am an investigator, but I went private industry," she told him, because that's what the ID she was carrying that day said. The truth would probably have ended their conversation on a bad note.

Omar watched a black Mercedes roll through the gate toward them. "Investigator? You're not here about the test they were planning for today, are you? I can't talk about the payload, that's top secret and besides, they're talking about canceling it."

"Really?" Skye couldn't resist asking. "Is this the satellite signal control thing?"

Omar shushed her. "What the hell? Unless you've got a top-secret clearance with SCI access you shouldn't know about that."

"But since I do…" she said, stepping closer.

Omar sighed and rolled his eyes. "They decided it's too dangerous to do here. They're afraid it might interfere with signals it's not meant to mess with. I think the real issue is the signal from the ground intended to control it after it's in orbit. Talking about moving it."

"To?" She stepped closer. Omar was watching the Mercedes that had parked just past his own car. Two white guys got out.

"Trust me, you'd never find it. They'd be far from civilization."

"Oh, out with the wildlife on the real Wallops Island," Skye said.

"No, over on Saxis…" Omar cut himself off, as if realizing he was going too far.

The wider of the men from the Mercedes approached. Cheap suit, cheap shoes, cheap haircut, bulge under the right side of his jacket. Ferret face. Security.

"Hey, Omar," Ferret face said. "Who's your friend?"

Omar held his smile and slapped a palm on Skye's shoulder. "This is Schuyler, an old friend from high school, if you can believe it. Quite the coincidence I'd see her here, eh?"

"Coincidence," Ferret face said, turning searchlight eyes on her.

"Yeah, I don't believe in them either," Skye said.

"Schuyler, this is Walt Valentine," Omar said. "He runs security for the project I'm working on."

"No shit." She looked him up and down, as if they had just stepped into the ring together. While she considered the best way to take Valentine down the second man approached. This one was more a white version of Omar. Young George Clooney instead of Denzel, but the shoes and suit were probably from the same shops, and he looked like he spent a bit more time in the gym than her old schoolmate. He seemed familiar, and she tried to picture him in more casual clothes. He was one of those single focus guys. Right then he focused on Valentine, ignoring the others.

"What's going on, Walt? Do we have a problem here?"

Omar said, "No, Quinn, there is no problem. This is an old friend of mine. She's just here as a tourist, looking the facility over. Maybe she got a little too curious coming to the gate like this but she's not trouble. Trust me."

"Quinn?" Skye looked more closely. "Have we met?"

Quinn's eyes rested on Skye. "I'm sure not. I doubt we travel in the same circles." Then he turned to scan the parking area, "That's got to be your car, an older, inconspicuous sports car. And it looks like you brought back up." Then he refocused on Valentine. "Just for safety's sake I think we better impound the vehicle." His attention returned to Skye, and he wrapped a hand around her left upper arm. "I believe we should hold you for questioning until this is all sorted out."

"What the hell, Quinn?" Omar said.

"That would be a serious error in judgment on your part," Skye said. Her left hand reached out, not to grip Quinn's upper arm just the bicep. Her fingers dug in, as if she were trying to tear that muscle out of his arm. Their eyes locked, but neither moved until another voice broke in.

"What's going on here?" It was Carter, who had come back from the car. "Skye, do you want to introduce me to your friends?"

Quinn tore his attention away from Skye to focus on Carter for just a moment. Then back to Valentine. Then he released her arm. A second later Skye let go of him. Quinn smiled at Omar, rubbing his arm.

"Sorry," Quinn said, turning on a charm Skye had not so far suspected he had. "I suppose I over-reacted a bit. This project is making me jumpy." Then to Skye, "Forgive my over-zealousness, won't you?"

"Not a problem," Skye said. "Just glad you didn't try to frisk me or something. I'd have had to teach you some manners." While all the men laughed nervously, she reached for Omar's hand. He surprised her with another hug.

"Sorry this all happened," Omar said.

"No worries," she said. "But I think we should be on our way now. At least now I know where to find you. But next time, I'll call first."

Skye stalked back to her car with Carter trailing and occasionally looking back. She started the car but sat, watching Omar and Quinn pull away. Then she pulled to the entrance to Occoquan Road and sat until both the Land Rover and Mercedes were out of sight.

"Want to tell me what that was all about?" Carter asked.

"I would if I knew," Skye said. "I'm wondering if this Quinn guy would have held me if you weren't there."

"I don't think I'm that intimidating," Carter said. When Skye sighed and shook her head another thought seemed to

occur to him. "You think he recognized me? Like he's one of Harmony's people?"

"Not sure," Skye said, turning onto the road. "But the good news is, I'm pretty sure he didn't recognize me."

"That sounds like you've seen him before."

"Yep," Skye said. "He was in the bar that night when your father was killed."

Chapter 20

For launches from the main installation, the visitor's center was the recommended viewing area. They had already been there so Skye headed down the road to the secondary viewing area known as The Mainland. This was the best place to see launches from the island. Again, it was more modest than Skye expected, the two-lane blacktop leading to a space on the coast holding a handful of small buildings and parking for maybe thirty cars.

The day was bright and with no launch scheduled the viewing area was not overrun with tourists. Skye walked Carter around, making sure anyone who cared to see him did. She didn't see anyone who looked like trouble, and it was an awfully open space for an attack anyway, but she remained on full alert. She might have already met the people who wanted Carter.

She walked down to the water's edge facing into the warm, salty breeze. She looked across the bay at the small, wooded islands lying between her and the actual Wallops Island a couple of miles away. It was a perfect place for a wildlife refuge, out of the way of any reasonable travel lanes but easy to get to if you wanted to. She pushed her hands into her jacket pockets and was surprised to find one not empty. She withdrew her hand to find a card in it. It was Omar Parker's business card, showing his name, phone number and the NASA insignia but no mention of his job or position with them. He must have stuck it in her pocket during that second hug. She had joked about the next time she called him. Now she had a number.

Staring out across the calm water she wondered if she wanted to go out to the island. If Alan Brown had wanted them to get his drive to someone there, or stop someone there from getting it, he'd have had said, "Refuge" not "Wallops Island." And all that was assuming Carter heard those last words correctly. As he walked up behind her, Skye reminded herself that he was the locus of the mystery.

"What now?" Carter asked.

"Now lunch," she said. "We passed a deli a few minutes back that should do fine."

Five minutes later they pulled into the parking lot of the oddly named Ocean Deli. Odd to Skye at least because there was not a pastrami sandwich or bagel in sight. Instead, it was actually a pizza place that also served Greek food and a selection of quesadillas. She had seen Italian and Greek foods in the same place before, but the Mexican bit was a surprise, as were the shelves stocked with a pretty strong variety of wines and liquors. Maybe there was some confusion as to the definition of the word delicatessen. She and Carter decided to split a pizza and Skye selected a table that gave her a good view of the door. They ate mostly in silence, which was fine with her. She figured Carter was still feeling salty about being told to leave her tools alone. But it was okay. She might be able to use that.

Chewing her last bite, she said, "I think we should just tour this little town this afternoon. Maybe there's a store or some street sign that will have something that's close to what we're looking for, something that relates to 'lineal manholes'? Or we might actually see some kind of holes in a line."

Carter shrugged. On their way out Skye picked up a bottle of Tanqueray. They spent the next half hour driving the streets of Wattsville, with Skye reading street and business signs out loud, as if that might make a connection. When they ran out of streets to explore, Skye pointed the

GTO back to their inn. She kept a keen eye on the rearview but still no one was following. She parked in the free space farthest from the building. Inside she saw only the owner in the lobby and one maid in the hall upstairs. In the room, she pulled off her jacket and poured herself a drink.

"Well that was a waste of time," she said, "When you going to do something?"

"Like what?"

Skye, sat, pulling off her boots. "I don't know. Maybe find something that relates to your father's bizarre last words. If he said what you said he said."

Carter leaned toward her, hands on hips. "And just what's that supposed to mean?"

"Watch your mouth with me, college boy," Skye said, gulping half a glass of gin. "What I'm saying is, I'm starting to think you made this whole thing up. Random words that are supposed to mean something. Alan Brown didn't never do nothing random. I got no reason to trust you anyway."

"And why should I trust you?" Carter said, a little louder. "I thought we might get to be like friends, but then you hit me. Hard."

Skye laughed, almost spitting out her drink. "That wasn't shit. I should have knocked your ass out. Look, I'm here for one reason, to find this girl that Gagnon thinks is Abraxas, and so far, I don't see you being any help. You trying to look important, but I think you don't know shit, and you can't do shit. So what good are you?"

"Really?" Carter was turning red. "Doesn't seem to me like you're doing any better. What's your plan, huh? What's the next step?"

Skye emptied her glass and plopped back on the bed. "My next step is to take a nap. Why don't you go watch the horses eat or something?"

Carter muttered, "Screw you" under his breath, stomped out and yanked the door shut, not quite slamming it but it closing it hard enough to make his point.

"Thank God," Skye said. She bounced off the bed and went into action.

Chapter 21

Getting rid of Carter had been harder than she expected, and she didn't know how much time she might have alone.

Step one was to get the flash drive well hidden. It represented Carter's actual value. If the opposition managed to scoop him up, not knowing where it was might keep him alive for a while. She pulled out one of the more innocuous items from her purse, a pack of chewing gum. While she chewed hard on the wad of sweetness, she carried the green gin bottle into the bathroom and dumped three quarters of the contents into the toilet. After flushing, she moved to the dresser and pulled out the second drawer. She saw that pulling it free of the dresser would be a lot of trouble. Good. She returned to her purse, opened the hidden compartment and pulled out her gum and the flash drive. She jammed the drive into the wad of gum and stuck it to the bottom of the drawer. She closed it and pulled it out again to make sure the gum stayed in place. Even an ambitious search of the room could miss it, and if someone did reach under the draw and their hand slid over the gum, they still might just assume some past visitor stuck the gum there. They'd have to pull it off to find the flash drive.

That done, she returned to the bed, crossed her legs and pulled out her phone. In just a few seconds she had Gagnon on the line.

"That was quick," Skye said. "I must be important."

"You have something for me?" Gagnon asked.

"Yeah, hello to you too. And no, no sign of the other killer. In fact, ain't seen an Asian face since we got here. But I think somebody recognized the college boy. I figure the opposition must have an APB out for him. So I need you to check this dude out."

"My people can research anyone," Gagnon said. "Of whom are we speaking?"

"Of whom?" Skye chuckled. "Okay, let's start with this dude named Quinn. Not sure if that's a first or last. But he works for NASA at the Wallops Island facility. And he was at the Borgata, in the bar, when Alan Brown got shot, so I'm sure he's involved with all this. Six-one, one ninety, Brown hair, brown eyes, snappy dresser. Hell of a grip for a lab rat, but you never know. Think you can…?"

"Hang on," Gagnon said.

"Look you can call me back…"

"Just hold on a moment."

Skye huffed, leaned back and stared out the sliding glass doors to the balcony. Not much to look at. A swing big enough for three, a couple Adirondack chairs and a lot of green, but a nicer view than she had from her apartment.

Thirty seconds later Gagnon said, "Got him."

"What? That fast? What the hell?"

"Quinn is an unusual first name," Gagnon said. "I thought I'd heard it before but wanted to be sure before I said anything to you."

Skye wished she had grabbed some chips at the deli. "You saying you know this guy?"

"Sending a photo."

Skye checked the file on her phone. "Yep, that's the right asshole. He in with the other company, the Oneida gang?"

"This is Quinn Robinson," Gagnon said. "He is a legitimate NASA technologist. Brilliant mathematician, computer genius, one of the fellows who figures out how to get satellites into geosynchronous orbits."

"Okay, he's smart, I get it." Skye got up and pulled the sliding door open, drinking in the mix of salt air and forest smell.

"He was on my radar because he is one of the few men in the country who might be able to fully understand the signal stealing program, and I believe he has ties to the right people at Oneida. It is possible that he could have gotten hold of the program and given the flash drive to Brown that day. Brown's dying wish may have been to return it to him to keep it out of whatever he considered the wrong hands."

Skye nodded as if he could see her. "Yeah, maybe. Then again, Uncle Alan was a top-notch pick pocket with all that sleight of hand shit. So maybe he stole the formula from this Quinn character, and his dying wish was not to let him get it back."

"If either of those scenarios is right it leads us to the same conclusion. Robinson will want the drive back. He may have seen Carter get the drive from his dying father."

"Maybe," Skye said, picking up her pistol, "but he didn't snatch Carter when he had the chance. And he knew not to mess with me. No reason for him to see me as a threat unless he has some inside info. That kind of sounds like a leak in your team."

"Possibly," Gagnon said. "But you have the drive in a safe place, right? You won't let Robinson get it."

Skye dropped the magazine from her little automatic. "Don't get it twisted, brother. I don't give two shits who ends up with this program. I got one job."

"Yes, kill your Asian mirror image. I take it the nonsense syllable clues have led nowhere."

"You got that right," Skye said, lifting off the slide and pulling a small cloth from her bag. "I'm starting to think the boy made all that shit up."

"Possible," Gagnon said, "but why?"

"That part's easy," Skye said, wiping down her weapon and pulling out a barrel brush. "He had the location, right? He might not have expected you to want to use him for bait, but he knew you'd send somebody down here. Don't take a genius to see I wouldn't have brought him with me unless we needed him for something. Like if he had a clue nobody else was likely to figure out."

"You think he knows more than he's saying?" Gagnon asked. "Think he has his own agenda?"

"Could be," Skye said, pushing a cotton cleaning patch down her gun's barrel. "Anyway, I got a plan to find out. And I think he might be back soon, so I'll let you know when I know something."

"I could send some help down…" Skye hung up before Gagnon could finish that sentence. He didn't get that she was no team player, and she didn't feel like explaining it to him again. After her pistol was clean, she emptied the magazine, pulled the spring out, and cleaned it too with a small brush. She reassembled her gun and shoved it under her pillow when she heard Carter outside the door. She took a mouthful of gin and swished it around in her mouth before swallowing. She spilled a couple drops on her shirt and left the bottle cap off.

Skye had learned to imitate a convincing light snore. She curled up under the coverlet and feigned sleep. She heard Carter enter the room, pause, and slowly close the door. He stepped at half speed to the sliding door, but if he was trying to be quiet, he had a lot to learn. She heard the curtain close. He turned, and after a deep breath he moved toward the bed. He would be staring right into her face, surely thinking she was asleep. He was creeping toward her, maybe screwing up his courage.

As soon as one hand touched the bed Skye's eyes snapped open and she thrust her pistol forward, almost touching Carter's nose. He froze, mouth open, eyes wide, breath trapped in his throat. She laughed inside, enjoying the fear in his eyes, but her expression stayed stern.

"Nigga you can't be sneaking up on a woman like that. The hell you think you doing anyway?"

"I… I thought… I…" Carter's stutter was almost enough to make her crack up, but she held onto her pretended anger.

"What? Huh? I know you wasn't thinking about getting in this bed with me."

He pulled back and wrinkled his nose. Good. He smelled the alcohol on her breath and based on the nearly empty bottle, he'd assume she was drunk.

"No, no, of course not," Carter said. "I was going to wake you, to tell you I think I remember spotting something. Something that maybe matched Dad's clue."

"For real? Well good for you." She put the gun on top of the covers and let her head drop onto the pillow. "I think I'll go see what you got later. Head's a little buzzed."

"That's okay," Carter said, backing off. "I kind of wanted to double check on my own before I called you in. But it's too far to walk."

"Well you ain't driving the GTO, college boy," Skye sat up just enough to point at the dresser. "Take the credit card over there and get yourself a taxi or something. If it pans out you can call me, right? I'm not really up to…" She let her voice trail off and closed her eyes. Silence. She returned to the light snore. More movement. A minute's hesitation. Then the door opened again and eased closed.

She sat up and looked around. Yep, he had lived up to her expectations. The credit card was gone. More to the point, he took the gun. Together, they were proof positive that he had his own agenda. He must have put something together from what his father told him, and he wanted to follow up without her. The fact that he grabbed her pistol implied he thought there was trouble at the end of the trail he was following. Which would be fine with Skye.

She pulled her boots on and considered what weapons to take with her. She'd slip downstairs and ease out the side door while Carter waited out front for his ride. She would follow him to whatever meeting he had in mind. With any luck it would be with his old girlfriend.

But as Skye stood up, she heard steps in front of the door again. Damn. What did he forget?

Before she could lie down again the door burst open, slamming against the wall. Two bulky forms dressed in black from head to toe rushed in.

Chapter 22

The two-man black wave rushed at her. She fell back on the bed and rolled off the other side to get a little space, her blood already racing. Skye didn't like being taken by surprise and she channeled her anger into her defense.

She stood facing them, the sliding glass doors behind her, the chair on her right. The space between the bed and the dresser allowed only one person at a time and the bigger man came through first. Despite the black mesh hood covering his entire head she thought she recognized him.

He came on as expected, sacrificing accuracy for speed. His huge fist whipped over her head as she dodged to her left, spun, and drove her elbow into his ribs. It was enough to throw him into the chair. Skye had time to land a stamp kick to his groin before the second man reached for her, but she captured his wrist with both hands and a sharp twist spun him into the glass door, or rather into the upright steel bar in the middle. His head thumped hard but nothing broke. She twisted his arm in the opposite direction and kicked his supporting leg out from under him. He slammed hard onto the floor.

The first attacker stood and charged, slamming his shoulder into Skye's body and carrying her forward to crash into the wall. Stiffened fingers into his eyes weakened his grip. He staggered back, tripping over his partner's legs but catching his balance before falling.

"I've had enough of you," Skye said through clenched teeth.

Contrary to popular belief, a heel of palm blow upward into the nose is not a death blow. It will not drive cartilage up into the brain. It is, however, blindingly painful if the blow is delivered correctly. Skye felt the man's nose break when she smashed her palm up into it and her target howled and collapsed.

Her second attacker got to his feet, and she spun to face him. He backed up two paces and sprayed something at her. The mist dampened her outstretched palm. That would have spared her the worst of mace or tear gas, but this was different. She took one step toward him, but her balance was off. She lost her equilibrium and placed one hand on the dresser to steady herself. A sudden wave of nausea and vertigo stopped her forward motion. A nasty taste rose in her mouth and she was swaying on her feet.

"What the hell? Gas?" she said, her words slurring. Her attacker dropped the aerosol canister and stepped closer with a raised fist. Skye raised an arm but was too slow to block the right cross that knocked her to the floor. On hands and knees, she shook her head, desperately trying to clear it. The fog was too thick. The first attacker was back up behind her. He gripped her throat with one hand and her waistband with his other and lifted her into the air.

"Arrogant bitch," he said, slamming her down hard. Skye felt that impact roll through her whole body. She stared up at the blank face above her, working to breathe as deeply as she could.

"Cowardly fuck," she breathed. "Gas a girl half your size."

He bent to grab her collar and lift her up. He cocked his big right hand. She figured he aimed to get revenge for his broken nose by breaking hers. Maybe she deserved it for forgetting assassin's rule number 14: never get caught with your pants down. Her stomach clenched in preparation for the next burst of pain.

"Let her go!"

The unexpected voice came from just inside the door. Carter stood with both arms stretched fully forward. His hands were shaking, but since they were gripping her automatic, he commanded everyone's attention.

Skye's mind was fuzzy, but her vision was clear enough to see the terror in Carter's eyes. Surely her two attackers did too but they froze, eyes on the newcomer, and that should be enough. Skye could smell the blood soaking into the big man's mesh mask. She gathered what little focus she had and with a grunt, swung a right into his nose. The punch wasn't much more than half the power she could normally muster but it was enough to make him howl, and stagger back off her. That gave her enough time to drag her jacket off the bed. She fumbled for the hidden pocket and pulled her backup piece out of its built-in holster. The little Beretta Pico, less than three-quarters of an inch thick, carried invisible but would do the job when needed. She charged the slide back.

"Sit your asses down!" Skye said, breathing deeply to clear her head. "On the floor or sure as shit I will shoot you." Her voice was steadier than Carter's and from their faces no one in the room doubted her resolve. With her free hand on the bed, she got to her feet. The two attackers moved to the space in front of the glass door, eyes moving from Skye to Carter and back.

"Come on, you know how to do this," Skye said, backing toward Carter. "On your knees. Cross your ankles. And toss those gas canisters on the bed. Now, hands on the floor."

Carter moved forward and in a stage whisper, said, "They probably have guns too."

Skye half smiled, a burst of pain from her jaw preventing more. "Yeah, but that can wait a minute."

"Who are these guys," Carter asked. "Why did they come after you?"

"Not sure about the one on the right," Skye said, yanking the man's mesh head covering off. His face was unfamiliar. "But we just met this asshole." She snatched the bigger man's hood off. He howled in pain as the mesh scraped his nose. It was Walt Valentine. When she was at the Wallops Island gate, Omar told her he ran security for the project he was on.

"Oh shut up you pussy," Skye said. "Now, you boys want to tell me who sent you? Or do we just send you to the professionals for interrogation?"

Valentine looked up from under his brow and snarled "Fuck you."

"I take that as a vote for option two." Skye dropped her gun on the bed and scooped up one of the little cylinders. She pressed the smaller man's mesh mask over her nose and mouth and stomped down hard on Valentine's hand. He screamed in pain and rose up on his knees when she moved her foot. Just as he began to inhale Skye sprayed the aerosol into his face. His eyes stretched wide, and he bared his teeth. Rage reddened his face. He managed to mumble "You bi…" before his eyes rolled up and he fell forward, crashing into the carpet so hard his head bounced up before settling again.

"That's going to hurt like hell when he wakes up," Skye said, spraying more on Valentine's face.

"What is that stuff?" Carter asked.

"Don't know," Skye said. "They used it on me just before you came in." She traded the hood for her pistol and turned to the second man, looking at him over her front sight. He was better looking than Valentine, blonde with a pointy nose that had never been broken. "What is this stuff?"

"Sorry, I don't know. Got it from the boss. Told me it would knock you out for a couple hours."

This one sounded like he was willing to be reasonable. "I guess you didn't figure the two of you would need it to take down one girl, huh?"

"Well yeah, until you dumped me on the floor."

"Who are you anyway? Who sent you?"

"Anderson," he said. "Zack Anderson. Look, we're just contractors doing security for NASA at Wallops Island. Valentine's the boss but I never done nothing like this before. He said you was dangerous and I gotta say, he was right. But we are the feds so maybe you better just…"

"What?" Skye asked. "Let you go? Please. Besides, you're not feds you're federal contractors. Nobody gives a shit about you. Right now, I think it's nap time for you. But you don't have to bang your head like your asshole boss."

Anderson tried a tentative smile and nodded his thanks. Then he stretched out on his stomach with his face turned toward her and closed his eyes. Skye covered her nose and mouth again and gave him a good long spray.

"I'm keeping these," Skye said. "Glad they came loaded with this stuff and not ricin or sarin. That means they were sent to take me in, not kill me."

"So, what now?" Carter asked. His arms were drooping from holding the pistol at arm's length for so long.

"Well first, give me that," Skye took her gun out of his hands. "Now is when I frisk those guys and take their guns and phones and anything else I want. As for you… you never fired, or even held a gun before, huh?"

"No, and I'm sure glad I didn't have to shoot anybody."

"Yeah." Skye dropped the magazine and handed it to him. "Well, you can do this part. Under that bed spread there's a handful of nine millimeter cartridges. Gather them up and reload this magazine. Just push them in here, point forward, okay?"

"Um, okay. How many?"

"All that's there," she said. "They'll all fit."

Carter looked at the magazine, the gun, Skye's face and back to the magazine. "It was empty?"

Skye nodded, put the gun on the dresser and went to the two captives. She had wanted to embolden him so he'd keep any meeting with the bad guys he might have arranged, but she sure didn't trust him enough to hand him a loaded weapon. At least, that was true before he jumped in and saved her.

Kneeling beside Valentine she said, "Oh. Um. Thank you," over her shoulder.

"Anytime," Carter replied, focused on pushing bullets down into the magazine. "But what happens to them? I mean, are you going to…" His silence was an obvious question.

"Relax, they ain't the job," Skye said. She found zip ties in Valentine's pocket and used them to strap the two men's hands behind them. Then she collected two pistols, a nice folding knife, their wallets, two phones and two car fobs. She was calculating all that time. It was easy to know what not to do, but the best next step was less obvious. She needed more information from them, but this was no place to be interrogating people. It was a wonder nobody responded to the noise they already made. She wasn't going to leave a trail of corpses, but if she just left them there, they'd be back after her as soon as they got free. She was too far from home for any of her usual subcontractors to help. She could only think of one good option.

Turning back to Carter, she watched him force the last bullet into the magazine.

"Man, that kills your thumb," he said.

"Yeah," Skye said. "Now go in the top drawer and get out the box of nine millimeters. Not the box marked 380. They look the same but they ain't."

She took the magazine from him, tapped it against the dresser to make sure the rounds were aligned against the back of it, and slid it into her Sig. After charging the slide she dropped the magazine and added an extra round from the box. With the magazine back in place she slid it into her waistband paddle holster behind her. She felt better already. Carter, on the other hand, still looked nervous. Skye wasn't sure what he was freaking out about, but it was clear he was waiting for her to do or say something. He was a normal, mainstream white boy way out of his world. Was he just now realizing that he was in danger, that there were people out there who would do him in? *Well, welcome to the big leagues*, she thought. *Too bad your dad never showed you the real world.*

Aloud she said, "Okay college boy, it looks like we working together now. We gone have to get moving pretty soon but I got to make a phone call first. You need to be real quiet while I'm talking. I'll answer any questions you got after I hang up. Cool?"

Carter nodded and stepped over Valentine's head to get to the chair. He perched on the edge of the chair cushion, elbows on knees, glaring at the two men on the floor as if they might pop up at any moment. He was cute, the way a beagle puppy is cute. She sat on the bed with her back to him and made the call.

"You have something for me?"

Skye wondered what kind of response Gagnon expected to that. But only for a second. "Got attacked. Couple of big-ass white boys crashed in my hotel room and tried to drag me away."

She heard rustling, as if Gagnon was grabbing a notepad. "What can you tell me about them?"

She took a deep breath and let it out slowly. She gathered the two wallets and glanced over her shoulder at Carter who was still staring at the unconscious men. Into the phone she said, "Yeah, we fine, thanks. And maybe you can track them down. We chatted a little before I knocked them out. We got Walt Valentine, brown hair, brown eyes, and Zack Anderson, blonde with brown eyes. They claim they contractors doing security for Wallops Island, and they got the ID to prove it."

That was a pencil scratching across paper. Gagnon was a pencil guy, instead of pens. Skye liked pencils too. They made better weapons.

When he stopped writing Gagnon said, "I figured you were all right or you wouldn't be calling me. It's easy to assume these two are working for Robinson, but I'll have someone check them out anyway. If they're just government contractors, they may or may not know what he's really up to. They might just be doing as they are told."

"Yeah, could be," Skye said. "Couldn't get too much out of them without making a mess and a whole lot of noise. So I got a bit of a situation here. They tied up and pretty much in one piece, but I can't just leave them here and I sure as hell ain't taking them with me."

"I see," Gagnon said. "A logistical problem."

"I guess," Skye said. "Before you offered to send some help down here. Well, I don't need the kind of help you was offering then, but how about sending a team down here to take these boys someplace where they can't report back to they boss for a while. He don't need to know they failed, or where they at."

She could hear the pencil tapping on the pad. After a moment, Gagnon said, "These men may have valuable information. They need to be interrogated under well controlled conditions."

"If you say so," Skye said. "I just don't want no cops to come looking for me for some bullshit assault or kidnapping beef. And I bet you got people to clean up behind us too. You know, fingerprints and shit."

"Yes, I can take care of that too. Just tell me where you are."

Skye gave him her room number at the Mahelona Inn on Chincoteague Island and after terse goodbyes, ended the call. When she turned, Carter looked up, expectantly. He was built to be more a sidekick than a partner, but despite herself she had to admit she was beginning to like this stray pup that landed on her doorstep.

"Gagnon's going to take care of these guys," she said. "His people will gather them up and keep them out of contact with anybody for a while. Pretty sure they'll also find out who they work for, and that might be the next step on the trail to your dad's killer. But that's likely to be a couple hours, so we need to secure these boys better."

"Okay," Carter said, standing. "What can I do?"

She tossed him a zip tie. "First, pull those drapes all the way closed. Then zip-tie that one's ankles together. I'll do this asshole." Carter watched her closely while she secured Valentine's legs. Was he afraid he'd do this simple thing wrong? "Now go get me a couple of washcloths from the bathroom."

Skye frisked the two captives again, this time pulling their belts off. When Carter returned, she took the washcloths. He stood back and watched, the way she used to watch his father when he was about to do a magic trick. The cloths were the cheap, thin kind only cut-rate motels use, but that made them perfect for her purposes. She shoved one into Valentine's mouth. She wrapped his belt around his head to hold the gag in place and tied it tightly at the back of his head. While she did the same with Anderson, Carter chuckled. She imagined he thought she had just invented a new way to keep a guy quiet.

She stepped away from them to survey her work. They lay face down, hands locked behind them, ankles strapped together, and gagged. It would do for a couple of hours. On an impulse she unplugged the room phone.

"That's that," Skye said, offering Carter a smile which he gratefully accepted. "Now we get scarce. We need to get off this island and stay low until Gagnon's boys get something out of these two clowns." She pulled her jacket on and reached for her little backup gun. She stared down at it and looked up at Carter. He was staring at it too.

"You know how to work one of these?"

"Sure," he said, shrugging. "You point it at somebody and pull the trigger, and they fall down."

Skye weighed the pistol in her hand while she weighed the pros and cons of her next action. Then she handed the Beretta to Carter. "Well if anybody comes after us, this will give you six chances to knock them down. I'm not sure how they knew where we were, but if they found us once they can find us again so slip this into your pocket. But be careful. It's got no safety catch so if you fall hard, you could blow off your own knee. Or your dick."

Carter winced but accepted the weapon with both hands, tried aiming it once, and pushed it into the right front pocket of his khakis. Skye had quickly packed up her bags.

"Now grab your shit," she said. "Not sure where we going, but we got to get the hell out of here."

Carter's smile grew. "As it turns out, it does matter where we go." He paused a second for dramatic effect. "I think I've cracked my father's code and found a place that matches his clues. I know where we need to go."

Chapter 23

This job had put Skye on the road more than any she could remember, and she kept driving to unfamiliar places. She didn't like the situation at all. She liked being in charge of the hunt, but if she was going to find her elusive target this time, she would have to follow the trail and just keep her head on a swivel.

Beside her, Carter navigated from his phone. She drove back to, and through Wattsville and continued west, watching the suburban landscape phase into rural. She was an urban woman in every way. She liked Northern Virginia, which felt like the outskirts of The District, but real Virginia was just too much out in the woods.

"So, what's out here that Uncle Alan was trying to point at?"

"It's a classy looking hotel called the Molehill Inn," Carter said. He sounded proud of himself.

"I don't get it," Skye said. "What does another hotel have to do with lineal manholes or whatever the hell he said?"

"It's how I knew the message was for me," Carter said. "See, when I was little dad used to try to work my brain with word puzzles, especially anagrams. It became a game for us."

"Anagrams?"

"You know," Carter said. "When you rearrange the letters of one word to make something else." When Skye shook her head he added, "Molehill Inn is a very near anagram for lineal manhole, with just a couple letters left over. Go left up here."

Chincoteague Road ended, and Skye turned onto Lankford Highway. At least that was what the signs said. It was divided, but still just two lanes each way with regular intersections at cross streets, not on or off ramps. *They'll call anything a highway out here*, she thought. And they were driving through generic small-town scenery. The stores, homes and gas stations made her feel like she was moving through someone's toy train set.

"How far?" she asked.

"Google Maps says about a half hour."

Skye nodded. "What made you look that far away? Your dad said Wallops Island, right?"

"Yep. But this is on Saxis Island."

"Okay," Skye said. "Your dad couldn't know they'd move the test, so I'm thinking this was planned all along. Somehow, he knew but maybe the opposition thinks it's a big secret."

"Is that good or bad?" Carter asked.

"When people think they fooled everybody, that's when they get careless. If they get careless, we might spot somebody there."

Skye wondered why intersections entering the highway didn't have traffic lights. She wondered why people would build their houses next to it, so their driveways entered directly onto the highway. And she wondered how long ago Carter had his anagram epiphany. Maybe he knew it was a code the first time he heard his father's words. Maybe he kept it to himself because he didn't want Gagnon to end up with the satellite messing program. Not that she cared. Whatever got her within striking distance of the bitch that killed Ike was good with her.

Skye was just settling into the drive through small town America when Carter told her to turn west down Horsey Road. She passed a ball field and the school it was attached to, then some sort of grain processing plant and suddenly they were chugging down a two-lane road cutting through a dense forest. The woods were periodically broken by farmland. She rolled her window down to take in the shift from the smell of damp woods to dry farming air. Miles separated houses and even more miles went by between vehicles they passed. With no radio programming available she could tolerate, the only soundtrack was the throaty growl of the GTO's engine.

"Did you attend college?" Carter asked. The silence must have been too much for him.

"Not me," Skye said. "Why?"

"I was kind of wondering what you study to be a, you know, your business."

That gave Skye a genuine hard laugh. "I don't think there's classes to be an assassin. It's pretty much OJT. You grab your bag of luck and jump out there."

"Bag of luck?" Carter asked. She guessed he had never heard that expression.

"Yeah, you start out with a bag full of luck and an empty bag of experience. The trick is to fill up the bag of experience before you run out of luck. Of course, you learn from other professionals, and if you're really lucky you have a mentor who knows what skills you need and gets you tutored by the right people. Like your dad. He's the reason I can get past most locks. But what about you? What you studying?"

"Engineering. Planning to be a civil engineer." Carter stared out the window. "Of course, that was all before I saw my father gunned down in a hotel bar. Mama passed when I was in high school. Now there's nobody to…"

His voice faded away, and Skye wondered. Nobody to push him? Nobody to tell him what to do? Nobody to pay for college?

The next turn put them on Jenkins Bridge Road, surely named for the fifty-or-so foot long bridge they crossed soon after the turn. More woods, more farms, and Jenkins connected to Saxis Road. which rolled through what Carter described as a wildlife management area. Skye shrugged. To her wildlife management was something done with a rifle.

A few minutes later they drove into an area with the trappings of a small town. Carter said, "We're here. Saxis Island."

"Really? Why they call it that? It sure as hell ain't an island."

"Guess not," Carter said, "but sure looks like there's a lot of nice beach. At least that's what they say in all the stuff I see online."

To Skye, it was a dying town filled with run down, decaying houses and businesses that could use a coat of paint. She did catch the smell of the ocean, but it was off to her right, to the west, which just didn't seem right. Again, the locals favored pickup trucks and basic SUV's. But one vehicle caught her attention. That silver Range Rover coupe stood out like a ruby in a black man's ear. She pulled over to park behind it.

"That's an old friend's car," she said. "You saw him at the Gallup Island gate. Sit tight. Be back."

She hopped out of her car, headed to the store they were parked in front of. At the door she realized it was closed. So where was he? A path between this building and the next led to the beach. Maybe he was down by the water. Had he taken up fishing?

Skye followed the path to the narrow band of sand, wondering what she would say when she reached him. He would naturally wonder what she was doing there. He certainly wouldn't tell her where the remote satellite control team was set up. Maybe it was a bad idea letting him know she was in town. She walked until she was a couple inches short of where the ocean reached up to lap at the shore.

Looking around she decided it might not matter. Omar was nowhere in sight. All she found was a couple of kids playing in the surf, and one old white guy in a lawn chair staring out at the horizon. Too bad. She wasn't sure what made her want to talk to him. He couldn't be far. She pulled out her phone and his card. She hit the buttons, listened to it ring three times before the message came on.

"You've reached Omar but I'm not available at this time. Please leave a message and I'll get back to you."

"Hey man, it's Skye. Are you screening? Pick up, brother." She stared around the beach, then at the nearest buildings facing it, checking each window. He had to be nearby. Maybe he could see her from wherever he was. Maybe he didn't want to talk to her again or had been told not to. More disappointed than she expected to be, Skye returned to the car, slamming the door just a little too hard behind her.

"Okay where's this hotel you're talking about?"

Carter was pushing more buttons on his phone. "Wow. Was looking for their web site and it looks like the place is closed, permanently. Like gone out of business. Still, it's got to be what Dad was talking about. We ought to at least check it out, right?"

Skye looked up at the ugly clouds rolling in from the horizon. "We're going to lose daylight soon," she said. "Not sure I want to go right up to the place with darkness coming on. Maybe drive past to get the feel for the place."

"I'm with you. Let's check it out tomorrow," Carter said. "I'm beat. How about we find a place to crash for the night, get some dinner, and chase the clues in the morning?"

Skye slowed to a crawl. They appeared to be on the main drag, but if there was a downtown, she didn't see it. She was sure they hadn't been followed. They hadn't heard anything from Gagnon. She was a little hungry. Why not? There was something to be said for having someone else to deal with petty details while she just did the driving and killing when the time came.

"I'll go along with that."

"Take this right," Carter said. "There's a cute little bed and breakfast over here."

The house was white with blue trim and close enough to the beach to have a beautiful ocean view. There were only two other cars in the parking lot. Skye parked and they gathered their bags from the trunk. As always, she led the way. As she reached for the doorknob with her free hand, the door swung open.

"Freeze and you may live."

It was Quinn Robinson. In the dim light of the hallway Skye could just make out the revolver he was pointing at her chest. Beside him, Leilani Mahelona, the Hawaiian manager of the hotel where she was attacked, aimed an automatic at her forehead.

Her mind hopped over the questions, cutting to possible responses. She could drop the bag, dive to the side, draw her pistol, take at least one of them out. Those thoughts evaporated when she felt the steel tube press between her shoulder blades.

"Please," Carter said behind her. "Don't make them do anything ugly."

Her mind reset. The men inside were relaxed and probably amateurs. The man behind her certainly was. Her right hand opened. While her bag was falling, she spun to her right, her elbow pushing Carter's gun aside. Her right hand captured Carter's sleeve. Her left palm slapped into his upper arm, swinging his body around so he was between her and the guns in the hallway. She pushed him forward and reached for her gun. She just might put all three of them down.

The blow to her temple short circuited those thoughts. A second to the side of her left knee dropped her to the ground.

Dazed, she looked up to see the woman, Carter's girl, Harmony Knight, raising a collapsible baton for a backhand blow. Skye lacked the focus to defend herself. She heard Mahelona say, "Your trade-craft sucks" just before Harmony swung the baton into the side of her head again and the world went away.

Chapter 24

In Skye's experience the biggest difference between sleep and unconsciousness was the nausea. There was the headache of course, but sometimes a normal day started with one of those, especially during allergy season. But when she awoke from a restful sleep her stomach felt fine. When she returned from being knocked out, she was fighting to keep from throwing up.

Also, when she was asleep, she was never awakened by a slap in the face. The second slap was unnecessary. Even with her eyes closed she was able to anticipate the third well enough to move her head at the right time to just feel the air blow by her face.

"Do it again and I'll break your wrist I swear to God."

Mahelona's chuckle came from across the room. "She's awake, Quinn. Back off before you get hurt. Let's give her a minute to get oriented and realize her situation."

Skye accepted the invitation and opened her eyes. Vertigo prevented her from sitting up all the way, but even without it she wasn't sure she could. Her wrists were secured together behind her. Her ankles were duct taped together. It was a small room but big enough that they were all out of reach even if her hands were free. She lay on her side on the threadbare carpet that smelled like someone had sprayed lilac scent on it. The bed was behind her. They were standing in a loose semi-circle against the opposite walls: Quinn, the tech; Carter, the traitor; and that bitch Harmony. Only Mahelona sat, forearms resting on the arms of her overstuffed chair. with a Glock aimed at Skye's face. Only she seemed to know who she had on the floor. She knew Skye was dangerous, and that made Mahelona dangerous.

"Okay," Skye said, looking only at her Hawaiian captor, "Want to tell me what's going on here?"

"That would take a lot of time," Mahelona said. "But the bottom line is that you have something I want. It's not in your duffle bag, and despite a number of interesting items I didn't find it in your purse. Where is the flash drive?"

"Do I look like a computer girl?" Skye wriggled enough to work her way into a seated position, knees up, back against the bed.

"My friends here don't like you much," Mahelona said. "Your immediate future will be quite unpleasant if you don't give it up."

"Hang on, Leilani," Carter said. "We had a deal. I did my part. You promised not to hurt her."

"Seriously?" Skye snapped, turning her eyes to Carter. "You set me up, you sold me out, and now you expect this bitch to play nice? Are you really that stupid?"

Mahelona's voice was hard, her words clipped. "I understand that you might not want this program to get into the wrong hands. What you don't know is that I don't really need that drive. I already have the entire program thanks to Quinn here being a traitor to his country."

"Hey!" Quinn said. "You're lucky I split the program so only half got stolen. And I had sense enough to make another set of flash drives."

Mahelona ignored him. "Harmony here was resourceful enough to find Quinn, get the flash drives, and get him out of the Borgata. Of course, now that we have it, I don't want anyone else to have it. The tech is brilliant but given the latter half of the program a smart enough team might reverse engineer the rest. My current client would like to maintain his exclusive on this for a while after he uses it tomorrow."

"If you had just let me give it to you to begin with, we wouldn't be here," Quinn said.

"Not the way this works," Mahelona said with a bit of an edge to her voice. "I was not going anywhere near Atlantic City. All you had to do was hand off to Miss Knight here. She would have gotten it to the right place."

Quinn stepped closer and pointed at Harmony. "She failed you. She kept me waiting, didn't make contact at the appointed time."

"No," Mahelona said. Unlike Quinn she didn't raise her voice. But she very smoothly moved her gun to her left hand. Her right hand moved like a striking snake. She gripped Quinn's outstretched finger and snapped her hand up in a quick, sharp movement. Everyone but Skye jumped at the loud crack of the finger breaking.

"You let the magician identify you," Mahelona said. "More importantly, you let him pick your pocket. You are the reason we are here."

Quinn tucked his injured hand under his armpit. His mouth opened wide but barely a squeak came out. After a couple of deep, ragged breaths he whined, "I risked my career to get that program out of the facility."

"You are fortunate that the magician's son felt this black killer disrespected him," Mahelona said. "Had he not betrayed her she would have put it all together, the mission would probably be lost, and you would be dead."

Skye's jaw dropped. "You made a deal with these assholes to get back at me just because I dissed you?"

"Did you think this boy's actions were about patriotism?" Mahelona asked. "Or some drive to protect the world from dangerous technology? He is a child."

Carter took two menacing steps toward Mahelona but one hard look from the seated woman backed him up.

"So, you running it, huh?" Skye said. "And I let this boy drop me right in your lap. Twice! Does college boy know them assholes that jumped me in your other hotel were your boys?"

Carter returned to his default confused look.

Mahelona smiled. "I suppose he does now. But, as you can guess, they were not following my orders. Quinn here, he sometimes thinks this is his operation. I think he understands the situation better now."

Mahelona turned her gaze to Quinn. He tried a defiant stare, failed, and turned away. She went back to talking to Skye. "It was a clumsy attempt. You and I, we are too sophisticated for such nonsense. Quinn didn't know that I had the Brown boy in hand and had a much easier way to pull you in. And as I haven't heard from his two hired hands, I presume you left them in some drainage ditch."

Carter started to speak but Skye cut him off. "She don't need to know where them losers are. Damn, you really are that stupid. And I guess I am too. You been leading me around by the nose this whole time, ain't you?" Skye closed her eyes and leaned her head back against the bed. She had gotten too relaxed, too trusting. The clues were everywhere and not paying attention was about to cost her her life. When she opened her eyes, she again focused on Mahelona who smiled, perhaps anticipating her next words.

"Should have known something was up as soon as I saw you. What the hell is a woman named Leilani Mahelona doing running hotels in Virginia? All the foreigners I know who got into business in the U.S. Americanized their names so people here could say them easier. You kept yours to stand out, to be memorable."

"Chose it, but yes, your reasoning is sound." Mahelona said.

"Alan Brown did know you. If he stole the flash drive, like you said, it was cause he didn't want you to have it. He was trying to tell this asshole that you were the woman to keep it away from." Mahelona nodded. Skye closed her eyes and tilted her head back while she fiddled with the name in her head. She gave up in a few seconds.

"I'll be disappointed if the puzzle is too hard for you," Mahelona said. "You are surely smarter than this child."

Skye glared at Carter. "So that anagram shit was real! You steered us to that Inn cause you saw her name online. I can't quite do this in my head, but Leilani Mahelona sounds like it might be an anagram for the clue, that 'Lineal Manhole' bullshit."

"Yes. Yes." Mahelona looked almost gleeful. "It is very close to that. For most, my cover name is innocuous, but it appears that the senior Mr. Brown had been playing with it. It was a clever way to warn his son about me without being obvious to anyone else. But I didn't know about this anagram business until the younger Brown told me about it."

"When he left the hotel room, he wasn't going anywhere," Skye said. "He just went downstairs to talk to you. He probably thought you'd tell him if you and his dad was tight. But you filled his head with a lot of bullshit."

"An alternate story," Mahelona said. "One in which I was his father's friend and the rightful recipient of the flash drive. Sadly, he didn't know where you kept it, so we formulated a low-key plan to capture you with limited violence. He just wanted to teach you a lesson, you see. You should be flattered that he insisted you not be harmed."

"Yeah," Skye said. "How long is that going to last?"

"Well, that depends," Mahelona said, "on how quickly you surrender my flash drive."

Skye let out a derisive puff of air. "You been talking like you know me."

"By reputation," Mahelona said.

"So you must know I ain't gone give you dick."

Mahelona shook her head. "Such an impractical attitude. I know you're a loner. You don't have any cavalry waiting to rush in and rescue you. Are you hoping your friend Omar Parker will come to your aid?"

"He works with Quinn here," Skye said. "Soon as I saw him, I figured Omar was part of your crew."

"Oh, no." Mahelona crossed her legs, which seemed too thin for her body. "Parker was never read in. In fact, I don't think Quinn has informed anyone on his team or anyone at Wallops Island what we're really working on. But when I learned Parker knew you, he became a risk too great to bear. I had to drown him in the surf."

Skye jerked forward, teeth bared. "You bitch! Yeah, I knew him but from years ago. He was innocent. Didn't know a thing about what I do or why I'm here. Now I really ain't gone tell you a damned thing."

Mahelona gave a knowing smile and jerked her head toward the other woman in the room. "Miss Knight here likes to hurt people, and she's quite sure she can make you talk." Harmony looked down at Skye, extended her baton and swished it through the air.

"No," Carter said. "That wasn't the deal." He reached into his pocket and pulled out Skye's gun. Mahelona didn't react. Harmony snapped her baton down on Carter's wrist. He howled. The gun skittered across the floor and stopped just past Mahelona's feet. Harmony snapped a crisp jab into Carter's jaw. His head hit the wall behind him, his eyes glazed over, and he slid slowly down the wall to land, seated, with his legs straight out in front of him. His eyes rolled shut.

"I will ask you one more time," Mahelona said. "Where is the flash drive?"

"Then I only have to tell you one time," Skye replied. "Kiss my black ass!"

Harmony swung the baton hard into Skye's right shoulder. Skye grunted in pain but maintained eye contact with the other woman. Harmony wound up again but switched to Skye's left thigh. Then she turned to the side and whipped the baton, backhand into Skye's solar plexus. That finally drew a pained moan.

"You talk or I start breaking bones," Harmony said.

Skye looked up at her, working to shut out the pain that just breathing caused. "You need a weapon to do that? You ain't nothing, bitch." Then Skye breathed deep and worked to retreat from the scene mentally. She knew her body was going to hate the next few minutes, but she didn't have to stay present for it.

Harmony snarled and dropped the baton. She bent to land a hard right cross on Skye's jaw followed by a left that rolled her onto her side. The stamp kick was a little off center and Skye wondered if she felt a rib crack. She tried to block the pain, but it was coming in from too many different locations. Luckily, Harmony seemed too impatient to give anyone a good beating. She gripped Skye's shirt with both hands and pulled her back to a seated position.

"You better talk, bitch!" Harmony screamed into her face. "I'll beat you to death if I have to. Do you know who I am?"

Skye swallowed the coppery taste of blood. "I know who you ain't. You a killer all right, but you ain't who people think you are."

"Oh no?" Holding Skye's shirt in her left fist, Harmony punched her once, twice, three times. Skye moved her face to control the impact points, sacrificing mouth and jaw to spare her nose and all-important orbital bone. She'd need her eyes later when it was time to kill this bitch.

When Harmony paused to assess the damage, Skye said, "You ain't her. You a pretty good decoy, but no way you're Abraxas. But hey, why don't you untie me and we start over and you can prove me wrong."

Harmony bellowed, "Fuck you," and released Skye's shirt to swing a hard backhand that snapped Skye's head around and laid her on her side again. Skye braced for another kick.

"Enough," Mahelona said. All eyes turned to her. Quinn was pale. Skye figured he'd never seen a beating like this before. And Carter was just waking up, his face again reflecting fear and confusion.

"We have places to be," Mahelona said, standing.

Skye looked up at Harmony and when she spoke her voice was dripping contempt. "You better kill me now. Otherwise, at some point, it's going to be you and me. Then, it'll just be me."

Harmony pulled her foot back for another kick, but Mahelona snapped "No. Our time is limited. The client is waiting for us. This phase of the operation is ended thank the gods, so this silly cover is no longer needed."

Skye's eyes widened. Mahelona's accent had suddenly disappeared. It was gone, not replaced by another. The woman now spoke in a flat, mid-western voice, accent free.

"I'm rather glad this part of the plan is completed," she continued. "Harmony, fetch my sweater and slacks from the next room. I'm going to change." She reached up and pulled the long black wig away. Her own straight, black hair was cropped short. She pulled the muumuu dress up, over her head and off, revealing foam padding around her torso and arms. She pulled a folding knife from under her chest padding and opened it with her thumb. She grinned at Skye while she began cutting the tape that held the padding in place.

"Totally worth it," she said. "The look on your face is priceless."

With padding gone the form revealed in leotard and tights was lean, athletic, muscular. A quick glance told Skye that only she and Carter were surprised. The woman they knew as Leilani Mahelona slid small pads out of her cheeks.

That made her face less round and now those eyes belonged in that face.

"Holy shit," Skye breathed. "You're her. You're Abraxas."

Chapter 25

Bucket seats are just not as comfortable when your hands are zip-tied behind you. Skye chafed as much at Harmony driving her GTO as at her uncomfortable seat behind the driver. Carter, seated beside her, kept his eyes cast down, frowning at the floor. Sadness? Fear? Guilt? Whatever he was feeling, he had earned it.

Another car trailed them, its headlights throwing jerky splashes of Halloween light around the inside of the GTO. Quinn, Skye guessed. She did get some small joy at the thought of what this bumpy dirt road was doing to his Mercedes.

In the front passenger seat, the woman Skye now knew as Abraxas was dressed for business. She had pulled a black sweater over her leotard. Over that, in plain sight, she wore a double shoulder holster rig with a knife scabbard between her shoulder blades. She could grip the knife by reaching up to the back of her neck. Skye decided she would take it from Abraxas if she got the chance. At that moment, Abraxas was staring at her as if she could read her mind.

"What?"

"I don't understand how you got involved in this business," Abraxas said. "Why do you care about the computer program that Alan Brown stole from Quinn?"

"Oh, we asking questions now?" Skye asked. "Well I got some. You say you know my rep. You know how dangerous I am. Why the hell am I still alive?"

Abraxas smiled. "I still want that flash drive. More to the point, I want you to tell me where it is."

Skye sensed there was more to it than that but held her thoughts. "Okay, why him then? He don't know shit."

"He's here because of you," Abraxas said, never glancing at Carter. "Despite his betrayal, you still care about him. You're more likely to behave while we have him, and when I have time, I will see how badly I have to hurt him to make you talk."

It looked and felt like they were driving through a dark tunnel just wide enough for the car. In fact, Skye knew they were rolling down a narrow dirt road, their headlights carving a path through the deep woods ahead. The engine snarled with anger at being held to third gear by a tentative driver. With unexpected turns and banked curves left and right, it could have been a scary, claustrophobic ride at Disney World, except that the most frightening bit would come after the ride ended.

"Torturing the college boy won't make no difference but hey, if you believe that, why'd I have get my lip split and my ribs cracked."

Abraxas grinned at Harmony, then returned her gaze to Skye. "I just wanted to be sure. I had to see if you were all I had heard. And you lived up to the hype. You are, as they say, the real deal. But this is the source of my confusion. You are a professional, but my research says that you are apolitical. You're not a government agent. You appear to be working for a corporation but clearly industrial espionage is not your field."

"Tried to tell you," Skye said. "I ain't here because of some computer program. I'm here for this bitch." She snapped her chin toward the driver.

Abraxas drew back, her brow knit in surprise. Inside the dark car her stern Asian features nearly disappeared. "They sent you for Harmony Knight? Understand my surprise. Harmony is heartless, and dangerous to a degree, but she's a just a vicious child, well below your stature."

"Hey," Harmony snapped. Everyone ignored her.

"That's what I said," Skye responded. "Although I might cut her throat for what she's doing to my transmission right now. But they sent me for her cause they thought she was you. My client thinks she's Abraxas."

After a beat of silence, Abraxas burst into a high squeal of a giggle. Her body, racked with laughter, rocked the car for a minute. When she regained her breath, she reached back to slap Skye's knee.

"I can hardly believe my little deception worked!" Abraxas' small, even teeth glinted in the darkness. "I pay Harmony to let the word out that she is the deadly assassin known only as Abraxas. She enjoys carrying the cachet of my reputation. In this way I can stay in the shadows where a true assassin belongs. It sounds as though it may have saved my life."

"Clever," Skye said after a moment. "Anybody that's hunting you follows the trail and goes after her. I get it. But what happens when somebody like me catches up to her and takes her out?"

"Her?" Abraxas jerked a thumb at the driver. "This one is easily replaced."

There was no audible response from Harmony. Skye wished she could see the girl's face, but the fact that she didn't say anything was itself a clear statement about the level of fear she had for the real Abraxas.

The car hit a bad bump and then jerked everyone to the right. All the passengers were alone with their own thoughts for a couple of minutes. Then Abraxas spoke again, in a softer voice.

"Days ago, in Washington D.C., a Haitian child abuser was killed in an appropriate fashion, struck down with no warning and leaving the police no clues. Your work?"

"Yep. That guy needed killing. And since we trading stories, what about this guy Page in Nevada three months ago. His whole family. Messy as hell. You?"

"Yes, I'm afraid so," Abraxas said. "The client requested that be a death that would instill fear in anyone who might pursue the same line of investigation Page was on. A lot of wasted ammunition, but I think it made the point. Now, the creator of this computer program the client wanted so much. That was more my natural style."

For the first time Carter spoke up. "Wait, I thought Dad stole the program from Quinn. Didn't he write it?"

Again, Abraxas chuckled. "That idiot? Oh, I suppose he's a genius of sorts, but not a creative one. A scientist at Oneida Communications named Dan Kim developed it. When the company realized what they had they weren't sure how to handle it. Quinn knew the man and became close to him. My client learned about it while the company was trying to decide what to do with their new discovery. He co-opted Quinn, and I was assigned to make sure the creator could not share his secret."

Now Abraxas pushed her face between the bucket seats. The following vehicle lagged behind after a sharp curve. With only the light from the dashboard and the harvest moon Abraxas made eye contact with Skye.

"Quinn was in his office, downloading the program during the lunch break. More than a hundred people work in that building. About half of them go out to lunch every day. The entrance is fourteen steps up from the nicely landscaped ground level. My target, the designer of the satellite interference program, was jogging up the stairs. I was walking down, in his path. Just before I passed him, I called his first name. Dan! I sounded surprised to see him, as if I were an old friend. He turned to me. I slid a one-inch blade into his throat. Three quick jabs, unnoticed by the mass of workers rushing back to their desks. I was lost in the crowd before anyone noticed him stumbling and falling to the stairs. I walked calmly to my car and drove away."

Skye nodded. "Like a bolt of lightning out of a clear blue sky."

"Yes. Exactly."

Skye felt Carter shiver beside her. This was how a true assassin strikes. Skye knew it as assassin's rule number 18.

And then the light increased as if the sun had suddenly risen. They drove into a broad clearing illuminated by flood lights mounted high on three stone and wooden structures sitting in a rough semicircle. The buildings on the left and right were low and long like old style military barracks, only with big satellite dishes on the roofs. Beside each dish stood a smaller structure that looked like a one-man guard post. Whoever sat in each rooftop post was tracking the car with a rifle. The building in the middle looked to Skye like the towers park rangers sit in, in the movies. The first floor had windows on either side of the door. An exposed outdoor staircase led to the second level. The second floor had windows all around and was surrounded by a deck like a wrap-around porch with a waist high railing. The car stopped in front of the center building.

"Time to get out," Abraxas said. "The client wants to meet you."

Chapter 26

Abraxas got out and tilted her seat forward. She gripped Skye's upper arm and guided her out of the back seat. Harmony had not moved.

"What about Carter?" Skye asked.

"The client has no need to see him," Abraxas said. "Only you are of interest. Now, after you." Abraxas waved her toward the door. Two men stood in the shadows on either side of that entrance. Both were big, both were armed with submachine guns, and both looked vaguely Middle Eastern under their brimmed caps. Skye shrugged and walked between them. Abraxas followed her up the long, open flight of stairs on the outside of the right side of the building. At the top she pushed a door open and ushered Skye into what looked like a NASA control room; all computer screens and blinking lights and one big monitor on a side wall. Theatrical and bright. The kind of setup a giant ego would demand. The guy rising out of an overstuffed chair at the other end of the room had to be the owner of that ego.

"So, this is the troublemaker," he said. "I had to see for myself."

Skye blinked in surprise. She had expected a Japanese boss but this guy was clearly an Arab. He was wide, with a cap of short hair, black eyes and a full beard. He wore a bright yellow shirt covered with huge black flowers and a huge gold Rolex on his left wrist. As he stepped closer Skye knew she was supposed to be scared but she wasn't getting the fanatic vibe. This was no crazed bomber. This was a guy who sent others to blow themselves up.

From two feet away, he locked eyes with her. "What do they call you?"

"I'm Skye. Who the hell are you? DJ Khalid?" Abraxas' short punch to her kidney was just hard enough to make her grunt.

The man facing her smirked. "You may call me Rajul al-Baghdadi. I am simply a man of Baghdad. But tomorrow I will be the face of what you call The Islamic State."

"Oh, more terrorists," Skye said. "Like the Taliban, right?"

Rajul's bushy eyebrows went down. She had touched a nerve. "We are far more dangerous than the Taliban. And the world will know that after tomorrow, thanks to the accidental discovery made by one stupid American."

The door opened. Only Skye turned her head to see Quinn Robinson enter. He paused, perhaps waiting to be acknowledged. His gaze went from one face to another, his body language the opposite of confidence. Finally he walked behind her to take a chair. It seemed he wanted to maintain a low profile, not speaking until he was spoken to. It occurred to her that he was afraid of everyone else in the room. She stepped to her left so Abraxas wasn't right behind her. She wanted to be able to see them all.

"You guys are so dangerous," she spoke to Rajul, then snapped her head toward Abraxas, "but you subcontracted a Japanese killer to get you this program you wanted so bad. And when she killed the reporter who might have been on your trail, you threw the blame on the North Koreans."

"Stupid zinji. Hiring a Japanese killer was a master stroke. If anything went wrong no one would suspect we were connected to this theft. Not until we told them."

Skye wasn't sure what Rajul had called her, but if felt like when a white boy called her nigger. She just met this clown, and she already hated him. "That sounds like bullshit to me," she said. "You hired a Yakuza girl cause you got nobody on her level. Your boys are clumsy and artless."

Rajul curled his massive fists. Skye relaxed her knees, primed to moved. Abraxas did not react. After five tense seconds Rajul's hands opened and he flashed a broad smile.

"You see, this is why you are here. I wanted an American to see my face and know who launched the greatest terrorist attack in history on your sad country. When we are finished here we will destroy the compound but we will take you with us and drop you someplace where you can tell the world the whole story."

"You don't need her," Quinn said. "I can be your witness."

Skye's brow wrinkled. "What, you going to stop NBC from broadcasting for a few hours? No Al Roker in the morning? Yeah, that'll destroy the country."

Rajul glanced at Abraxas.

Abraxas shook her head. "She wouldn't know. She had no reason to know."

"You mean you don't know what this program can do?" Quinn asked.

"Sure," Skye said. "You can cut off a signal from one of the satellites. Maybe pudgy here will replace a TV or radio show with his propaganda. I get it."

Rajul's body shook with a true belly laugh which, for some reason, chilled Skye. "Clearly someone has lied to you. With this program, and the equipment here, I can stop all transmissions from any satellite. From all satellites in a broad specified area. Like, for example, the entire American Mid-Atlantic region. As an amusing side effect, it will also send a singular transmission down from the satellites that will disrupt all cell towers in that area. When the creator of this program realized what he had discovered he didn't know what to do with it. He confided to the wrong friend, the traitor Quinn. He realized the value of such a capability and betrayed his country for the promise of riches."

Quinn's face dropped, like a child berated by his parents. "Hey, you could never have done this without me. Besides, people in your part of the world would consider this capability to be much too dangerous to let the U.S. government get its hands on it. And now with this threat, you can blackmail them for millions, maybe billions."

"This one is not a suitable witness," Abraxas said. "He will be totally discredited by both his government and the scientific community when his part in this comes out. But beyond that, he has let me down. First by letting his pocket get picked before the planned hand off of the flash drive. Then he compounded his error by sending his NASA security team after this woman. We can assume they've been dispatched and are lying in a drainage ditch someplace covered with quick lime."

Quinn was fidgeting. He was slow on the uptake, but even he had to see where this was going. He stood up, eyes roaming from Rajul to Abraxas and back. Skye stepped back out of the way. This could get messy. Abraxas held her hands up, palms forward, stretched away from her weapons.

"Settle down, Quinn." Abraxas' tone was distilled condescension. "Don't let your last act on earth be to embarrass yourself."

No, the idiot was desperate, beyond caring what anyone thought of him. His last act would be to reach under his suitcoat for a weapon hanging under his left arm. He moved with speed born of that desperation.

Quinn's gun was almost past the jacket's lapel before Abraxas reacted. Her right hand rose to pluck something from behind her neck. The throw was too fast for even Skye to see. Suddenly a knife handle appeared, growing out of the back of Quinn's hand. The blade pinned his hand to his chest, still clutching his gun. Abraxas was across the floor before Quinn's expression had time to change from shock to pain.

Abraxas' hands became blurs of motion, driving fingertips or fists into Quinn's torso half a dozen times. She took one step back and swung the edge of her right hand into Quinn's throat, cracking his larynx. Then she stepped aside to watch him crumple to the floor.

That was unnecessary. She had killed Quinn at least three times. She was showing off, but for who? Maybe both of them, but for different reasons.

Abraxas knelt and flipped Quinn to retrieve her throwing knife and wipe it on his sleeve.

"Last time," she said, without looking up, "Where is the flash drive?"

Skye was ready for that one. "I told you I ain't got it."

Now Abraxas looked up. "Carter Brown says differently."

"Sure. I told him that, so he'd tell whoever grabbed him. The flash drive was just a lure to draw Harmony out so I could finish her off. Truth is, I tossed it in the ocean."

Abraxas opened her mouth to speak but Rajul cut her off. "That no longer matters. If it is destroyed, all well and good. Even if someone does have that half of the program it is far too late for them to take any action. Tomorrow all Americans will learn to fear us. For six hours, beginning with the evening rush hour, I will cause a communications black out across your East Coast. With no warning, the death and confusion will bring your nation to its knees."

Skye had had enough of this arrogant bastard. She could kill him right then and for a moment considered if it would be worth her own death. Her eyes cut to Abraxas who shook her head just enough for Skye to see it. Skye had seen this woman move. She really was Skye's Japanese equivalent, maybe even a hair faster. Still, Skye figured she could take her, but not with her hands tied behind her back. That confrontation, and the Arab's death, would have to wait.

"Now take this one downstairs with the others," Rajul said with a dismissive wave of his hand. "She will see the destruction tomorrow. When the investigators find her, she will be able to tell all in her corrupt nation who is responsible."

Abraxas smiled and offered a cordial wave toward the door. Skye moved in that direction but paused as she passed Abraxas.

"You wrong, you know. This ain't what we do."

"This," Abraxas replied, "is exactly what we do."

Chapter 27

Abraxas unlocked the steel door with two keys, pulled it open and pushed Skye inside. The lower level of the tower was laid out as one big open office. The only light came through the windows facing the courtyard. There were two big desks to her left, and two more facing them on her right. Carter sat in the chair behind the first desk on her right. Beyond the second desk on that side stood three gray metal filing cabinets. Doors at the other end of the room were marked as men's and ladies' rooms. A snack vending machine and an old-style water fountain stood between those doors. Skye turned back to face Abraxas, who stood with a handful of zip ties.

"Simple courtesies," Abraxas said. "Water, and the machine works without coins. Now turn around and get on the floor so I can secure your feet."

"Hold up. Is that really necessary? How the hell am I supposed to get to the food machine and water if I'm tied hand and foot?"

"Oh that's right." Abraxas gave a short chuckle. "I'm sure you'll find a way but you *will* be bound. Consider it an expression of respect. You may be the second most dangerous woman alive."

Skye tipped her head in recognition of the compliment, sighed and began to turn. But the turn became a lightning-fast spin, a low spinning back kick. Even with her hands locked behind her, she packed enough power into that kick to dislocate a knee.

Abraxas' eyes widened in surprise, but she caught Skye's ankle on her palm and kicked Skye's other leg out from under her. Skye twisted to land on her shoulder instead of hands. Abraxas dropped on her, straddling her with a hand at Skye's throat.

"You're damned fast," Abraxas said. "Almost fast enough."

Skye looked up into her eyes. "I had to try."

Abraxas nodded and slammed a fist into Skye's jaw. Stars exploded over Skye's head. She could see them, even with her eyes closed. Then the stars went out.

Someone was shouting her name, over and over. It was an annoying repetitive chant that was piercing the thick warm blanket of sleep she was hiding under. It was making her head hurt, or maybe something else was causing that. As her mind rose up out of the darkness, she realized it was annoying because it was Carter's voice. Would he never get tired of calling her? She just wanted to rest for a minute. Could she just have a minute? Maybe he would stop if she opened her eyes.

The stark light cast the world into black and white. The windows to her right made her, and the desk she was seated behind, throw long shadows to her left. The desk she was facing did the same. Carter sat behind that one, repeating her name like a mantra.

"I'm here," she muttered, "I'm awake, all right?"

"Thank God," he said. "I was afraid you'd never wake up."

"How long?"

"Hard to say," Carter said. "Can't see my watch with my hands tied behind me. Seemed like forever but probably not more than a couple minutes. You okay?"

"The usual," Skye said, pushing back from the desk. "Headache, nausea, a little dizziness, ringing in my ear. Won't last. You ever been knocked out?"

"No, thank goodness."

"You're lucky," she said. She looked down at her legs and frowned. Her ankles were wrapped in several layers of duct tape, and she thought she could feel straps beneath that. Probably the zip ties Abraxas had been carrying. She imagined her wrists were similarly secured. Abraxas was taking no chances with her.

"You tied like me?" she asked. "Hands and feet, duct tape over zip ties?"

"No, just my hands behind me," Carter said.

"I guess we ought to be thankful for small favors. You been out of that chair?"

Carter shook his head. "No reason to."

Well now there is," Skye said. "Abraxas said you don't need money to work the vending machine. Hop over there and get me a candy bar and a bag of chips."

"Maybe."

"What?"

"I've been thinking about all that's happened the last couple of days," Carter said. "You weren't really drunk in that hotel room, were you? And you purposely let me go off into danger with a gun that wasn't loaded. You lied to me. You tricked me."

"Are you serious?" Skye asked. "You knew this anagram thing and didn't say a word. Then you sneak off to meet with the people we were after. You lied to me. You tricked me. And you double-crossed me. Now drag your ass over to that machine. I'll need a blood sugar boost if I'm going to figure a way out of this. Unless of course you got a plan."

Carter huffed like a chastised child, then went to the machine and scanned the touch pad. He would have to match the letter-number combinations with the snack locations behind the glass since he would be pushing buttons with his back to their only food source.

"I'll take potato chips and whatever kind of chocolate you can pull out of that thing," Skye called.

A gruff male voice said, "I could do with a Baby Ruth."

Carter froze and Skye snapped to her feet, shoving the wheeled chair backward. She stared at the file cabinets, the source of the surprise announcement. A figure wiggled out from behind them, head first. He was clearly bound too, moving forward on his left side until he was exposed from the waist up. Skye hopped across the floor toward him. Halfway there she stopped. His injuries looked superficial but still bad. One eye puffed out, blood under his nose and a split lip spoke of a recent, serious beating. The injuries made him harder to identify but she knew that dark face, the dental veneers and stringy black hair. When Skye recognized him, she began to grin.

"Hey Carter! It's that asshole who tried to kill us on the road when we was driving down here. Still wearing that cheap ass suit he had on in the Borgata."

"For real?" Carter asked. "Put here to spy on us?"

"Don't think so," she said. "I don't think the damage I see is from a car flipping." She looked down at the bruised face. "I take it your Arab boss wasn't too happy that you failed to take us out. Of course, I can't blame him. If my feet weren't tied together, I'd kick you right in the teeth myself."

"I'm hoping you'll accept my sincere apology for that misjudgment in the car," he said in a strong New York accent. "I'm getting an idea who you are and believe me, I'm glad I missed you on the road. Not so glad about totaling my Bullitt Mustang though. I loved that car."

Skye dropped to her knees beside the man who, she could see, was bound like her, hand and foot with duct tape over zip ties. "Shit happens to people who aim guns at me. But what you just said don't make no kind of sense. Who are you, and what's your story? You ready to turn on your boss?"

"Name's Larry Newman." He wrestled himself into a seated position leaning back against the wall. "And I don't work for the people who locked us up in here. Never have."

"Right. You tried to shoot me just for laughs. And your failure has nothing to do with them beating your face in."

Newman shook his head. "I get why you think what you think. I take it you know about Rajul al-Baghdadi. I thought you were working for him. I saw enough to know you're responsible for at least two of the deaths in the Hotel Borgata a couple days ago. We had intel that Baghdadi had hired a female killer. Figured it had to be you. But clearly that's wrong."

Carter approached the two on the floor, turned and dropped his two handfuls of junk food near them. "That's all I could carry at once. And I wasn't paying attention and kind of missed the start of this conversation. How'd your face get like that?"

"Abraxas' pals pulled me out of my car," Newman said. "I think the beating was partially because I'm Jewish. But mostly because they know I'm Homeland Security."

Chapter 28

Carter turned to face the other two on his knees, the third point of a human triangle. "Okay, you're law enforcement, and Skye, he seems to know what you do for a living. Two trained survivors, right? So we're all hungry. We have food. You guys got an idea how we eat with our hands tied behind our backs?"

"Sure," Newman said. "Just calls for a bit of teamwork."

At Newman's direction, Carter sat with his back to the snacks that would constitute a late supper. He tore a candy bar open and held it as high as he could. Skye inched over and took a bite, chewed and continued until it was gone. He repeated the process for Newman. Then Skye turned and helped Carter eat. For the next half hour, they rotated in relative silence, feeding each other. By then they all agreed it was tiring and they would wait a bit before trying chips.

"Well, that was what I'd call an awkward bonding experience," Newman said, leaning back against the wall again.

With her back against the end filing cabinet, Skye asked, "Why was you hiding back there?"

"Not hiding, just trying to catch some sleep," Newman said. "It's a safe place to nap. These things are close enough to the wall that it makes it hard to kick you. When I heard Carter come in, I wasn't sure if he was friend or foe, so I just stayed quiet. After Abraxas put you down hard I was pretty sure you were on the side of the angels but still couldn't be sure. When I heard the two of you talking, that's when I knew you weren't with the terrorists."

"Yeah, well stand by for the rematch," Skye said. "Abraxas ain't just a competitor now, she's unfinished business."

"What the hell kind of a name is Abraxas anyway," Newman asked. "She an old school Santana fan or something?"

Carter lay on his back, knees up, hands clasped just under his behind. "It is an odd choice for a Japanese woman," he said to the ceiling. "It's a word of mystic meaning in the religious system created by a gnostic called Basilides in the second century."

"Well, what does it mean, college boy?" Skye asked. "And what the hell's a gnostic?"

"You really want to know?" Carter smiled and turned to face her, warming to his subject. "The gnostics were an early religious group, kind of halfway between Judaism and Christianity. Gnosticism is a loose corruption of the Greek word for knowledge. Basilides was Greek and in his teachings, Abraxas was the supreme deity, the source of divine power."

"Uh-huh," Skye said. "So it's an ego thing. Or maybe she picked a code name she figured would scare people around the world."

"Yeah, well I'm not scared of her," Newman said. "I'm scared of al-Baghdadi and what he can do with that satellite tech."

Skye eyed a Snickers bar with true longing, but she wasn't ready to ask Carter to feed her again. "So what's the big deal? Everybody loses cell phone reception and can't get the news for a few hours. It ain't like crashing into the Twin Towers."

"You're missing the point." Newman shook his head in evident exasperation. "No phones means no 9-1-1 calls, no fire alarms, no way to reach emergency services of any kind. No way to even send the codes inside most hospitals.

Beyond that, no GPS which is based on signals bounced off satellites."

"Okay," Skye said. "So people will have to use maps for one day."

Newman banged his head back against the wall. "Don't you get it? No way for aircraft to navigate. At the same time, no contact with a tower or other planes. At any given minute there's probably about ten thousand planes in the air over the U.S. carrying well over a million people. Blind and with no guidance from the ground for… God knows how long…."

"The Arab told me six hours."

Carter sat up. "Seriously? Think how many crashes would there be in that time? How many deaths?"

"Plus, the sheer panic," Newman said. "At first they'd figure it was a short term communications issue. They'd stay in the air trying to wait it out."

"Yeah," Newman said, "but most domestic flights carry just enough fuel to get to their destination, with a little extra for surprises, but not much."

Carter stared at the floor. "Imagine it's raining airplanes, many of them coming down into major cities, and you're getting nothing from your government or even local news about how or why it's happening."

Skye closed her eyes. She called up memories of the video she had seen of the 9/11 attack on New York's Twin Towers. It might be like that, only several times worse, spread over five or six states. That level of fear would lead to total chaos. This al-Baghdadi might be right.

"The greatest terrorist attack in history," she whispered. "Newman, you said you're Homeland Security. So it's your job to stop this shit, right?"

He nodded. "Kim, the genius who wrote the satellite disruption program, was terrified when he realized what it could actually do. He didn't share it with his bosses, but he confided in a few close friends, looking for advice. Finally, he reached out to the FBI. After some stupid turf crap, they handed off to us. We made arrangements to take him and his product into protective custody but before we could…"

"Abraxas killed him," Skye said. "And Quinn got the goods."

"After that we were a step behind. Somehow one of Oneida's competitors found out about it and got the magician, Brown to steal it."

"That was Gagnon. He wanted it, but he lied to me about what the program could do. And I'm feeling some kinda way about that."

Newman stopped talking, his eyes shifting back and forth in thought. "Damn. Is that who you're working for? If he got hold of this tech, he'd own the whole telecommunications industry. Anyway, we managed to track them down. We didn't know about you and the guy you were working with. So there we were, positioned to take Brown and Quinn, but then somebody put a bullet through Brown, youse guys showed up, and everything went to hell."

"Maybe you can bring the feds in after I eliminate Abraxas," Skye said. "But step one is get free."

"Could be a challenge," Newman said, "I did manage to check the desk drawers. "Empty. Nothing in this room that we could use to cut ourselves free."

"Yeah there is," Skye said, "but to get at it I'd have to get my left boot off."

"Is that your attempt at irony?" Carter asked.

"Don't even know what that means," Skye said. "Push that chair over here."

"I like your confidence," Newman said, "but what you got in mind?"

Carter turned the chair with his knees and sat in it. Pushing with his feet he maneuvered the wheeled chair over beside Skye. She glared at him until he realized he was supposed to get up. Once he moved Skye leaned back against the wall and pushed herself into a standing position. Then she turned and plopped down on the seat.

"Pretty sure I can get my boot out from under the zip tie," she said. "The duct tape's the problem. I think you can get it off with your teeth."

Carter looked up, distressed. "My teeth? You want me to put my mouth…?"

"What's the matter college boy?" Skye asked with a smirk. "Not one of your kinks?"

"Give it a shot, Carter," Newman said. "If you don't get through it all I'll take a turn."

"Oh, hell," Carter said. Newman squirmed farther back behind the filing cabinets to give Carter space. Carter lowered to his knees in front of Skye. She raised her legs to make Carter's task easier.

The click of the door lock opening hit her like a gun shot.

Chapter 29

With eyes on the door Skye stood. Straightening her legs sent the chair rolling back across the floor and into a desk. She leaned toward Carter and said, "Distract her" in a soft voice. Then she dropped to her knees and rolled to her right side. She pushed her body back until her lower legs were hidden behind the filing cabinets.

The door swung in. She expected Abraxas to be checking on them or moving them to an even less inviting location. But no. Instead, *she* walked in. Harmony Knight. Faux target. Set up to draw fire for Abraxas and too stupid to know that job would get her killed.

Harmony wore a tight black dress slit to her mid-thigh on the left. Skye's shoulder bag seemed to fit the outfit, the gun not so much. She scanned the room behind a revolver that was way too big for her. Then she clicked toward the others on three-inch heels, barrel aimed at Skye.

"Face down. Let me see those bonds."

Skye rolled onto her stomach but craned her neck upward. "You ever fired that forty-four? I'm betting it put you on your ass."

Harmony showed her teeth. "That one behind you had a lot of mouth when he got here, too. Now he hides behind these files. Hey, fed! Let me see your hands."

Newman faced the floor and remained silent. That seemed to be enough for Harmony who then turned to Carter who had perched on the nearest desk.

"And what about you, blue eyes?" she asked. "You doing okay?"

"Like you care?" Carter said. "And don't call me that."

Harmony's smile never wavered. "You didn't seem to mind it when we were rolling between the sheets." She raised a hand to brush a finger along his cheek. He pulled away.

"Yeah, that was before you tried to kill me."

"Oh, honey, if I wanted you dead you would be," Harmony said. "I'll admit that back in the Borgata things got a bit confused. I thought you had deceived me. I was hurt."

"What? You thought I betrayed *you*?"

Harmony affectionately tapped his chest with the tip of her gun barrel. "We'll get back to that. I have a little business to take care of first."

Skye was juggling too much input, trying to get it all mentally in order. Harmony was even less stable than she thought, and apparently, she still wanted Carter. Or, after thinking he was an enemy, had decided she wanted him again. Maybe she just wanted to keep the blond and blue-eyed American as a trophy. And that might be fine until her next mood swing when she might stab him in his sleep.

At the same time, Skye could feel the movement on her legs. After Harmony saw Newman's bonds and turned her attention to Carter, Newman slid closer to Skye. Hidden by the filing cabinets, he was working on the duct tape around her ankles with his teeth. That gave her hope, even while she wondered if peeling tape off a woman with his teeth was one of Newman's fantasies. That almost prompted a smile, but she needed to keep her face composed. If Harmony sensed anything happening behind the cabinets, it would cost Newman his life. And here she was, marching back toward them, dropping Skye's bag on the nearest desk, motioning with her revolver for Carter to move to the next desk down.

"Let's talk about what's in here," Harmony said, resting one cheek on the desk and rummaging in the bag.

"You looking for makeup tips?"

Harmony fished around in Skye's bag. She was a couple of inches taller than Skye's five foot five – average by American standards but tall for a Japanese woman. Maybe she was Korean, or maybe she had some white blood in her. She was holding items up like they were exhibits at a trial.

"I'm keeping this bag, but I want to know what all this stuff is," Harmony said. "This is obviously just a one-handed folder. Nice knife but nothing special. And this one, the fixed blade fighter…"

"Careful with that," Skye said. "It's a ballistic knife."

"Oh." Harmony said. "Nice! Now this fidget tool, with the two finger loops…"

Skye sighed as she felt the pressure on her ankles relax. They were free of the duct tape. There was just enough play in the zip tie to shift her feet so that one was not on top of the other. She kept her eyes on Harmony.

"It's really a garrote. Stick your middle fingers in the loops, twist and pull."

Harmony tried it. "Oh, that is nice. Eight inches of wire. Just enough. Now what about this?" She held up the light.

"Nothing special there. It's just a flashlight."

"That's hard to believe," Harmony said, hopping down to her feet. Skye felt her pulse quicken. Newman had managed to get his head under her left foot. He had that boot's zipper pull between his teeth, slowly easing it down. If Harmony came any closer, she'd see him, see that the duct tape was pulled loose. Skye closed her eyes and shook her head.

"Seriously, you think everything I touch is a weapon?" Skye said. "It's just a real good flashlight. I swear." If only Carter would do something to distract her, just for a couple minutes. Clearly this crazy girl had a thing for him.

Harmony took one step closer to Skye, moving as if the gun was pulling her forward.

Behind her, Carter said, "Hey, you said you thought I betrayed you. What changed your mind?"

Harmony spun to face him. "Does it matter?"

Had he somehow heard Skye's thoughts? Or was he just trying to do his part to save them. He was trying to act brave, but his voice quivered a little too much.

"Well, I figure it might determine whether I live or die," Carter said. "Bad things happen to people you see as enemies. I want to stay off that list."

Harmony moved closer to Carter, and he pulled back just a bit, but she had the gun pointed away from him. That was a good sign. Skye felt the zipper of her left boot sliding down. She felt it stop at the bottom. Now she had to squirm it off.

"I just don't understand why you got involved with this," Harmony said.

"I kind of got pulled into it after you threw a knife at me."

"But then you switched sides," Harmony said, shaking the gun at him like an extended finger. "You were so hurt because that black bitch wouldn't give it up. You wanted her so badly."

Carter stuttered but managed to say, "No. No. I… I did it to save you. She was after you. I didn't want you to get hurt."

The pause was too long. Did she believe him? Surely she wanted to believe him. Skye wished she could see Harmony's face.

"Remember that moment when your father was shot," Harmony said. "We had been close for weeks. I needed to appear to be a constant threat to you to try to compel your father's compliance. But then I was told a man had turned up to take your father in from the cold. As it turned out, a man and this bitch," Harmony jerked her head back toward Skye. "I wasn't worried. We had a good team in place. But then you ran to your father when he fell and, in the moment,

I thought you must be part of the retrieval team, undercover. I thought you had been playing me all that time, all those nights we spent together."

"But now you know different, right?" Carter asked.

Skye freed herself from the boot and reached backward as far as she could, trying to reach her bare foot. Her position was cramped, and she needed to stay silent. She felt Newman's head against her instep, holding her foot in place so she could reach it. Her fingertips scrabbled against the strip of tape over her arch. He probably could have pulled the tape with his teeth but that was maybe too much to expect of a man who she just met. His face on her naked foot was bad enough.

Harmony said, "At a calmer moment I realized that you were simply reacting to your father's death. I got to know you well enough to see that you are no operative. You are too simple and shallow. It is what makes you so endearing."

Harmony licked at Carter's neck, and he shuddered at the contact. Her head snapped back in surprise."

"Sorry," Carter quickly said, "but, well, you did kill my father."

"Had him killed," Harmony said. "And it's not like you were close."

Skye mentally begged him to hold her attention for just a couple more minutes. She had managed to peel the tape away to grip the three-inch blade she kept taped to the bottom of her left foot. Only half of the steel's length was sharpened, but that would be plenty if she could just have another minute or two.

"He was still my father," Carter said. He sounded wounded, and Skye knew he wasn't faking that.

"Well, gee, I can't un-kill him, can I?" Harmony's voice dripped sarcasm. "What can I do to make it up to you?"

In her mind, Skye pleaded with Carter not to ask Harmony to let them go. If she turned and saw the tape removed from Skye's wrists, she would kill them all. She had cut that away without much effort and was now sawing away at the plastic zip tie but with her hand movement so restricted it was slow work. Agonizingly slow.

Carter said, "How about freeing my hands long enough for me to go to the bathroom? I've been holding it for a while now."

"Hmmmm. Well, I am not going to free your hands. I like you like this. But I will help you pee. I'll just unzip you and, well, I have held it before."

Lord, was she this kind of naughty when she was playing at being his girlfriend? Skye rolled to her side, putting her arms against the wall. Carter sighed, hung his head and walked toward the restrooms. Was his apparent disappointment real, or was this his plan all along? Harmony swung a quick, arrogant smile at Skye as she passed, the equivalent of a child sticking her tongue out at her. Skye shot dagger eyes in return. It was fine for Harmony to see her as the competitor who had been outdone. The second she was out of sight, Skye returned to sliding her blade against the zip tie.

A few seconds later when Skye grunted, Newman whispered, "You okay?"

"Got a cramp in my hand. But I think I'm close."

Her fingers fumbled, nearly dropping the blade. She heard a toilet flush. Then there was a subtle pop and her arms moved apart. On her stomach she stretched her arms overhead, flexing her hands to restore circulation. Her left hand had almost fallen asleep, and the tingling was maddening.

Harmony's heels clicked back toward them. No time to free her legs. If Carter and Harmony returned to the desk he was sitting on before, they would walk past Skye in seconds. Fighting to keep her breathing quiet she got up on her knees.

Mostly hidden by the file cabinets. She'd only get one chance. She'd have to make it count.

Carter walked past, head hanging. Harmony followed, swinging her gun in her right hand the way someone might swing a picnic basket.

Skye sprang forward, jamming her knife down into Harmony's left calf just below her knee, and yanked it out quickly. Startled and shocked by pain, Harmony lost half a second before spinning toward Skye, swinging the pistol forward as she stumbled back. Skye swung her blade for Harmony's arm, hoping to slash her wrist. She missed, but the gash in the heel of Harmony's palm was enough to make her drop the gun. As it hit the floor Skye slapped the gun away with her left hand.

Skye had hoped Harmony would bang her head on the edge of the desk as she fell backward, but instead her back was the point of impact. Skye slammed the knife into Harmony's body just above her hip and used it as a handle to pull herself forward. Skye's left hand gripped the neckline of Harmony's dress, letting her pull herself farther. She freed the knife and jammed it into Harmony's neck just above her shoulder. Arterial spray from her carotid geysered over Skye's knuckles and across the room. Up close she saw nothing but surprise in Harmony's eyes.

"For Al," she whispered through clenched teeth. "For Ike."

The action had taken no more than four seconds. Harmony probably didn't have time to register all the pain or even know that she was dying. Her final thought was probably something like, "this can't be happening."

That was probably the last thing they all thought. Those who had time for a last thought.

Then Skye looked up at Carter with his mouth hanging open, his eyes bulging, his hands quivering. Their eyes locked. She considered what she must look like, her right hand painted red with blood. Her body draped across Harmony who was bleeding out from three vicious wounds. Your first messy death affects you, and this was way nastier than what little he may have seen while they were escaping the Atlantic City hotel. What was there to say?

Newman broke the moment, "Hey, can a guy get cut loose?"

"I'll get to you," Skye said, turning onto her behind and cutting her legs free. She straddled Newman's legs to work on his wrist bonds, but he was watching Carter.

"Hey, kid, if you're going to be sick go back in the bathroom, huh?"

Skye stood, grabbed one of Carter's arms and cut his wrist bonds. Carter covered his mouth with a hand and made eye contact with Skye again before he sprinted for the bathroom. She didn't have time to think about that. She returned to Newman, straddling his legs to cut his ankle bonds. The little blade was slippery, but she kept to her task, already trying to figure out their next move.

Chapter 30

Skye shook her head listening to Carter retching. She wiped her hands on Harmony's dress, removing as much blood as she could. She put her left boot back on. Then she walked in aimless circles, flexing her hands, getting circulation back.

Newman had hustled into the ladies room. She would go when he came out. In the meantime, she considered her environment. It was one big room with one door facing the well-lit courtyard, as did the only windows. Outside, two guard towers looked down on that open courtyard and she had no idea what lay behind the three buildings, or even where she was except that she was out in the woods. She hated the woods.

Newman returned, looking relieved. She appreciated his calm demeanor and the fact that he didn't waste words. He squatted beside Harmony's body and frisked her with swift efficiency. When he found nothing of value, he picked up the revolver, opened it, spun the cylinder slowly, and handed it to Skye.

"I'm good with these, but I think you might be better."

"Thanks," Skye said. "The dragon lady didn't have a backup weapon?"

"Nothing else," Newman said. He perched on a desk and watched Skye pacing for a moment. She stopped to stare at the men's room door.

"Is he ever coming out of there?"

"Your boyfriend did good," Newman said. "Kept the girl distracted so you could get free. This obviously isn't his scene, but you should cut him some slack."

"He's not my…" In the dim light she caught Newman's smile and managed one herself. "Hey, find us a way out of this while I'm in the bathroom." She was at the restroom door when Carter came out. He looked at her like he had something to say so she waited a moment with one hand against the door.

"Skye," he began, then swallowed. "I'm glad you did that."

"Good," she said. "I might not have got her if not for you. You kept her off us just long enough. Turns out you're a pretty good sidekick." That got a smile out of him.

Inside she quickly washed her hands, used the toilet, and pulled up her sleeves to wash her hands more thoroughly. Splashing water on her face she reconsidered her situation. She had had more luck than she deserved. Harmony had not managed to fire a shot. The fact that no one had come to the door meant no one heard the fight, or the vomiting. No one knew Harmony was dead or that the prisoners' hands and feet were free. It was probably closing on dawn, which meant everyone would be asleep except maybe the two guards. Harmony had returned her bag with its weapons and tools and gifted her with a Colt Anaconda with excellent rubber grips, a six-inch barrel and a nice ramp front sight. It would kick like a mother but anybody she hit with it would stay hit. Still, she was not at all confident that she could shoot her way out of there with six bullets.

When she left the restroom, she nearly bumped into Newman filling his pockets from the vending machine. Carter was sitting at the same desk. She winked at him, then went to the door in a half crouch. Moving to one side, she looked out the window for movement. Seeing none, she checked out the other window. Nothing. No guard at the door might have been a little insulting, but it probably just meant that Abraxas didn't tell anyone who and what Skye really was, so they trusted their three securely bound captives to stay put.

Feeling a bit better she squared her shoulders, faced Carter and walked to him with maximum swagger. Of course, just carrying the Anaconda made her feel bigger.

"Okay, what's the plan, Newman," Skye asked.

His sly grin implied he had anticipated her question. "All quiet outside. No roaming guards or anything. I see six vehicles parked side by side in front of one of the barracks. I'd guess the blue sportscar is yours. There's a Mercedes and four Jeep or Range Rover type vehicles."

"It looked like the only way in or out was that one road we came in on," Skye said. She put one foot up on the desk, leaning on her knee with an elbow. The smell of blood pulled her attention to the legs in her peripheral vision, all she could see of the body leaning against the end of the desk. Damn. She needed to focus. "How strong you figure the opposition to be? Numbers, I mean."

"No clue, really," Newman said. "I haven't seen anybody except the two clowns that pulled me out of my Mustang and this dead broad." He hooked a thumb at Harmony's body. "Based on the size of the two buildings I'd guess they couldn't sleep more than ten each. So I'd say the max is twenty."

Skye nodded and walked back over to the door. The lever moved freely. She pushed it forward a fraction of an inch. Not locked. She dropped to her knees to look up and out a window, scanning from one side to the other. She wished she knew more about the layout. Newman walked up behind her, and Carter followed.

"What you thinking?" Newman asked.

"I think decisions are easier when options are few. Do we all agree that we can't stay here?"

Newman looked to Carter, who had relapsed into his default confused expression. Newman rested a hand on Skye's shoulder.

"At some point they'll come in, to feed us or take us somewhere, or somebody will come looking for the dead girl. At that point, we're cornered, and they kill us. Leaving is the only option."

Skye nodded. "You wearing a watch?"

"It's 5:38," he said. "Maybe an hour of dark left."

Carter said, "Geez. The last time I pulled an all-nighter it was a lot more fun."

Skye walked toward him, forcing a smile. She shouldered her travel bag and retraced her steps to put her back to the door. "Here's how I see it. I crack this door open and take out the guy in the guard tower on the right. Then the other one. Then the three floodlights. In the darkness we run around and out the back between the two buildings into the woods. We don't know how many guys are here, but I figure by the time they get their shit together to come after us we can be lost out there in the trees. Then we just keep going until we bump into civilization. What do you think?"

Newman hesitated a moment. "Seriously? It's got to be 50 yards. Aiming up. You think you can do that with a handgun?"

"With this cannon I can hit a man size target at twice that distance,"

"If you say so," Newman said. "And if we do draw them all out into the woods, maybe I can double back and get the car."

Skye looked up, surprised. "I doubt they left the keys inside. Can you hot wire a car?"

"Not the cars they make today," Newman said. "But your vintage GTO? Yeah, I can hotwire that baby."

"Well then, I guess we got a plan," Skye said. "And we're running out of darkness, so I'm thinking the sooner we do this the better."

As she eased the door open just enough to push the gun barrel through, Carter asked, "What can I do?"

"Pray."

On one knee, Skye braced the gun's barrel against the doorjamb. Unasked, Newman held the door as close to closed as possible without touching her or her weapon. She stared up at the guard tower, slowing her breathing, searching for a good sight picture over the front sight. The guard sat behind a wide window that slid open to the side. The very tip of his rifle barrel rested on the windowsill. After three long slow breaths she muttered, "Damn."

"What?" Newman asked.

"I can't see him. I mean, I see where he is, nicely backlit up there. But he's sitting back. At this angle I can only see the top half of his face. Mighty small target with a handgun I haven't sighted in. I need him to come all the way to the window"

"Yeah, I see what you mean." Newman said. "He just needs something to get his attention. Like a target."

The door slammed open, and Skye watched Newman racing away from her, sprinting toward her car.

Chapter 31

Skye's heart leaped into overdrive with the unwanted adrenaline dump. Was he crazy? He was out in the open, racing across the brightly lit courtyard. Did he want to die?

No. He trusted her. Trusted her to be as good as she said she was. She returned her focus to the guard tower. Over the front sight she saw the guard lean forward, his rifle pushed out the window up to his left hand which supported the stock. He was tracking Newman across the yard.

Skye exhaled, stopped breathing, and fired. The roar of the shot reverberated through the room and against her ears. The barrel rose a foot. She brought it back down on target. The tower window was shattered but she knew the shot was a couple inches to the right. The rifleman jerked to the side, looking in every direction, then back at the impact point of Skye's bullet. Following an invisible line from there he turned to aim toward the source of the attack, but no way he could see her behind the door. Skye squeezed the trigger. Again, the sound hammered her ears and the gun tried to jump out of her hand. This time, the rifleman disappeared, and his weapon dropped from his nerveless fingers and out the window.

Before the rifle reached the ground Skye had spun to aim around the door at the second guard tower. He was forward as well. She had a good sight picture. But before she could fire, he did. Newman fell forward, first to his knees then prone.

Skye squeezed the trigger and once more the revolver punished her ears and her right arm. The gunman was slapped backward out of sight and a second rifle spun to the ground.

The door slammed open, and Carter darted out of the room running toward Newman. She didn't have time to ponder this new burst of insanity. She stood, stepped out the door and shot out the floodlight over one of the barracks, then the other. By then Carter had Newman over one shoulder and was moving back toward Skye. She looked up and put her last bullet into the light on the front of the building she had just left. The darkness outside the courtyard rushed in and swallowed them. Carter slowed but Skye had marked the location of the first dropped rifle in her mind. She rushed to snatch it up and side stepped toward their escape route.

"Carter," she said, pointing. "Straight through there, between these two buildings. I got your back."

Lights came on inside both barracks buildings and the office space atop the tower she just left. Carter managed a moderate gait with Newman, who moaned as they passed her. She followed but lay prone when she reached the alley between the buildings. She figured the boys inside had never planned for, or trained for, this eventuality. They were slow to react. When one did charge out of the second barracks, backlit with just his pants and a submachine gun, she put a bullet in his face. It was too easy. Her borrowed rifle had a nice, light-gathering scope. The first man out of the other building never figured out what direction to run in before she shot him in the chest.

Skye turned and sprinted into the woods behind the buildings, knowing that the darkness and the deaths would make any other pursuers hesitate. Less than six yards separated the back walls of the three buildings from a wall of old growth trees. She slipped between them, getting slapped by branches as she pushed forward. There was no way to go quietly, but she didn't hear anyone following her.

She'd be pretty hard to track in the dark and anyway she doubted the men in the compound considered her a threat. Abraxas would not have told them who she, Skye, really was. They probably assumed one of the men got lucky with a gun and got them away from the compound. Most likely they would expect the prisoners to run as far and fast as they could and never look back. Still, she kept moving until she was a good fifty yards into the forest. A big, fallen trunk offered a good place to settle. With the rifle laid across the trunk, pointing back the way she came, she allowed her body to relax while her mind stayed busy.

Visibility was limited but she didn't hear any activity from the compound. Maybe they'd wait for the morning to look for her. Even if some of them did consider the escapees a threat, those who saw the two corpses on their doorsteps would not be eager to follow her. Besides, maybe they were advised to stand down. If Abraxas thought like Skye, she'd realize that following a competent killer into the dense woods on foot was a losing proposition when fallen leaves signaled the slightest movement. Starlight was not nearly enough to navigate by.

Skye still had no idea where they were. She wondered how far Carter and Newman got. Was Newman even alive? And why did the world smell like Pine-sol when she was lying on a damp bed of leaves?

Then she heard rustling, off to her right and behind her. An animal? *Who knows what kind of things live out here.* She rolled very slowly, and swung the rifle barrel toward the sound. The next sound was definitely a footstep. So it was a human. Or maybe bears sound the same way stepping on leaves. Did they travel at night? Her pulse spiked again. *Oh God please don't let it be a bear.*

Out of the darkness, Carter's voice said, "Is someone there?"

Skye moved toward the sound. After a half dozen steps the man's form came into view. He was standing up straight with hands raised, as if he assumed anyone out there was a threat to him. She could hear him breathing before she could make out his face.

"You know if I was somebody else you'd be dead now." she whispered.

"Skye? About time something went our way!"

"You okay?" she asked when they were inches apart.

"Yeah, yeah, fine, but Newman, he's shot. I didn't know what to do. We settled over here behind some dead trees. He said no but I was going to go back for help."

Skye shook her head and just said, "Show me."

Carter led her to a small depression in the ground surrounded on three sides by large dead trees. The men hadn't gone much farther than she. The logs were arranged to overlap and present a fence of sorts about three feet high. Behind them, Newman was braced up against a low berm. His sport coat was folded under his right leg, held in place with his belt. Skye crouched beside him.

"That was a dumbass thing to do."

"Seemed like a good idea at the time," Newman said.

"Sorry I wasn't faster. I saw you go down."

Newman grunted with teeth bared, maybe in reaction to a wave of pain. "Yeah, I wouldn't have got out of there if not for Carter. He lugged me out here."

"How bad you hurt? Pretty sure the rifles are chambered for .308 Winchester. Too much kick for 7.62 rounds."

"That means you got some of them?" Newman asked. When Skye nodded, he said, "Glad you're a better shot than them guys. With a rifle and a scope, he managed to crease my thigh. Messy, a lot of blood but not much damage."

"Must hurt like hell," Skye said. "You need a doctor. We need to pack you out of here."

"Well I hope you're better in the outdoors than me," Newman said. "I wasn't a Boy Scout. I got no idea which way to go. We could wander out here for days. That's why the boy took off to get help. I tried to stop him."

Carter was sitting a couple feet away, just close enough to be visible. She reached out to slap him on the shoulder. "You done good, grabbing Newman up and getting him to safety. Now, are you all right?"

"Me? I'm fine. He's the one who got shot."

"I keep telling him it's minor," Newman said. "I'm fine, just not up to a lot of walking around."

"Be real with me," she said. "You be okay here for a couple of hours?"

"Sure," Newman said. "I figure we're a good half hour away from daylight and there's no point moving in the dark."

"Good," she said, standing. "I'll be back soon after sunrise."

"Back?" Carter said. "Where are you going?"

"Back to that compound," she said. "I've got some unfinished business to take care of."

The ground was uneven, every step was on something hard or mushy, and she could not walk in a straight line for trees whose placement was random. This was not her environment at all. Except the dark. She was comfortable in the dark. Her fatigue-dulled senses clung to that one familiar thing.

It all fell into place in her mind while she retraced her steps. There was only one road leading into the little settlement. The men in the compound were only worried about an attack force coming down that one road. They would figure the escaped prisoners would keep running, as fast and as far as they could. But considering the length of the drive in, they might well be several hours' walk to civilization, and that depended on them knowing which way to go. So even if some of the men in the compound did see the escapees as a threat, they would never guess one of them would return right away.

No one in the hidden encampment could know about Skye's self-assigned mission. She was there for Abraxas. If Skye didn't take care of Abraxas today, the Japanese assassin would disappear again. She'd find a new proxy to be her public face and Skye would never be able to hunt her down. She needed to kill Abraxas now while she would not expect an attack. According to Newman there might be twenty others in those three buildings – well, sixteen now – but they would not think of protecting the hired assassin. They would not think she would need help.

And what would Abraxas do? The crazy Arab Rajul al-Baghdadi would be as paranoid as every other megalomaniac. He would want to keep Abraxas close. It might take her a while to convince Rajul that he was in no danger. But before too long she'd be looking for her decoy protégé. Soon after sunrise, she'd go looking for Harmony. That would be Skye's chance to take her by surprise.

At the edge of the clearing Skye stopped to take a couple of deep, cleansing breaths. She was starting to feel the weight of the rifle and her small shoulder bag. Neither would be weighing on her soon. The encampment was still dark except for light coming from the second floor of the middle tower building. She thought there might be patrols of some kind, but no one was in sight. Crouching low, she sprinted across the open area to the alley between the tower where they had been held and the right-side barracks. Through her rifle sight she could see men in the guard towers again and a couple more outside the two barracks. They were all focused on that one road in.

Staying low, moving without a sound, Skye slipped across the front of the tower building, lost in the deep shadows. Once she was inside, she could relax for a while. She would simply take a seat and aim her rifle at the door. In an hour or so Abraxas would walk in that door, looking for Harmony. Skye would take her off the board with a single .308 round. The shot would raise chaos but by the time the soldiers figured out where the shot came from, she'd be back in the woods rejoining the men and working on finding the way to civilization. And the world would have one less master assassin.

Skye was aware of her own fatigue, physical and mental, but once she was settled in that space where she so recently was bound, she would have a chance to rest and pump up her blood sugar with a couple bags of M&Ms. She reached the door without incident. Checking over her shoulder, she turned the door handle. Still unlocked. These idiots didn't even think to secure the building. She stepped inside, into an even deeper darkness.

Something thumped the back of her head. Her forward ankle was hooked. She fell forward, rolling so she came up in a crouch facing back toward the door. Her rifle flew from her hand. That, she knew, was a kick. Then a light smacked her in the eyes. It moved away. As her eyes adjusted, she saw it was a lantern style flashlight now sitting on one of the front desks, pointed at the back wall. Abraxas stood beside it, relaxed, arms folded so her hands almost touched the two pistols in her double shoulder holster. That should have scared Skye, but that wasn't it. What really stirred fear in her heart was the smile. Abraxas was smiling down on her.

Yep. Shit just got real.

fit. The small pistols glimmered in the flashlight's beam, a pair of Colt Commanders.

"Chrome?" Skye asked. *Why surrender the obvious advantage? Was this a trick?*

"Yes," Abraxas said. "A vanity, I know."

"Okay," Skye said, dropping her shoulders to project vulnerability.

"You have a good knife in that bag?" Abraxas asked.

"Yeah."

"Good. Let's do it that way." Abraxas said. She reached back and slid the knife up from behind her head. It looked to be a throwing dagger, five or six inches of steel with a dimpled bone handle. She nodded to Skye who pushed her right hand into her bag and pulled out her fixed blade fighter, the one Carter had almost killed her with. She dropped into a low fighting stance, blade forward. Abraxas began to bob left to right. She held her blade in a reverse grip, the blade reaching down from her fist instead of up by her thumb.

"Have you a backup blade?"

"Yeah," Skye said. "Why?"

"I've lost count of the number of men I've sent to their final rest," Abraxas said. "Some kills were effortless, some required great effort. You offer the one thing I have not had in my entire career. A fair fight."

Skye shrugged and pulled her SOG folder from the bag with her left hand. She flipped it open with her thumb and shifted it to the reverse grip. Now she was able to separate herself from Abraxas mentally. This woman was not a mirror image of Skye. Abraxas wanted to prove her superiority on a level playing field. To Skye, finding herself in a fair fight just meant she had not planned her attack properly.

At that moment, Skye wanted to adjust the environment. Abraxas had circled so that the light was hitting Skye at the back and on her left. Abraxas was deeper in the shadows, her form hard to define and constantly shifting left to right. The woman was too fast to take a chance with. Skye wanted a clear target. Could she lure Abraxas forward, more into the light? She crouched lower, hoping to be a more tempting target.

"Well? I ain't got all day."

"No," Abraxas said in a low tone. "You have very little time left."

Skye lost her for a moment as Abraxas darted to her own left, running low behind one desk, then another. She suddenly appeared on Skye's right. Her high-pitched scream might have frozen a lesser opponent for an instant. Skye jerked backward, dodging a backhand slash. Abraxas followed with her left hand, and this time she made contact. The gash on Skye's right upper arm was shallow but the flash of pain slowed her own attack with that arm. But as Abraxas passed in front of her, she managed a snap kick into Abraxas' stomach. Abraxas grunted and rolled back into the darkness. Skye could feel her pulse pounding in her ears.

Knife fights are never long affairs. Skye knew that to survive she'd have to seize the initiative somehow. Maybe she was wrong about the advantage of being backlit. She shuffled to the other side of the room with her back to the desk on her left. She was sure she'd hear Abraxas getting behind her and fighting over the desk would limit any attack. Skye moved slowly forward, farther into the room, farther from the light. She kept her fixed blade forward, just in case she got a clear shot. As she moved deeper into the darkness Abraxas appeared on the other side of the room, her back to those desks, moving in the other direction. She wanted to be backlit. Good.

When she was even with Harmony's corpse, Skye moved into the center of the room and raised her folding knife in a defensive posture in front of her chest. The ache in her right upper arm made her breath catch when she held the fixed blade forward. The room was filled with the odor of their sweat. She couldn't hear Abraxas' breathing, but her blades caught bits of light as she moved more to the center of the room as well. In contrast, her face was lost in darkness. She was moving to be entirely in front of the lantern, casting a long shadow that fell just short of her opponent. Skye stepped forward, imagining Abraxas grinning as she appeared to be closing for an attack. And in fact, she was.

Now! Abraxas was directly in front of the only light source. Skye's left arm thrust forward, and she hit the hidden button. Abraxas had not guessed that Skye's fixed blade was a ballistic knife. The blade flew forward and Skye was already charging behind it.

Abraxas was blessed with incredible reflexes. Despite surprise she jerked to her right. Her left arm snapped up. The blade flew past her, not into her, and continued its journey to its real target.

There was a pop and a flash when the flying knife blade drove into the lens of the lantern flashlight. Skye had closed her eyes against the expected burst of light. When darkness flooded the room Skye was already airborne. Her left heel snapped forward, stamping into Abraxas' chest. The Japanese killer slammed backward on the floor. Skye heard at least one knife blade skitter across the floor. Which one had Abraxas lost?

A swoosh toward her face. Skye blocked with her knife and heard the second blade hit the floor. She must have slashed Abraxas' fingers in the block. Skye reached out, felt Abraxas' torso and landed a hard kidney punch, then scrambled to get an arm around the other woman's neck. She was behind Abraxas now, on the floor. Her left leg wrapped around Abraxas, feeling wetness. The ballistic knife must have sliced her on its way past. Gripping her opponent tightly, Skye caught the acrid smell of blood. Her own? Abraxas'? maybe Harmony's.

Skye was in position for a solid choke hold. With her legs she could limit Abraxas' breathing. Her own body ached, and fatigue threatened to burn up the adrenaline she was running on. But she had turned the tables on Abraxas. She only needed a couple of minutes to end this.

Abraxas twisted hard. One hand swung back, fingertips jabbing into Skye's face. Where did she get the energy? A claw hand dug hard into Skye's upper arm, into the knife wound she was trying so hard to ignore. With a guttural moan she yanked her right arm back pushing Abraxas' hand away. Abraxas reversed her twist, slamming her left elbow into Skye's ribs. Skye's grip loosened and Abraxas spun to face her, trying to straddle her. Skye managed to get a knee to her chest and kicked out, pushing Abraxas off.

Both women rolled away. Skye landed on fingertips, left knee and right toes. She was panting hard, but breathing through her mouth it was close to silent. Abraxas' breathing was louder. Skye had her position marked. She was ready to launch from the line of scrimmage and sack Abraxas. She tensed to drive forward but stopped when that voice came out of the darkness.

"I believe…" Abraxas' breathing was rough. Had Skye's flying kick cracked a rib? Abraxas started over, with a smile in her voice. "I believe you may have earned a draw."

Was she serious? "Bitch, you in my house now," Skye spat back. The dark was her element, much more than her opponent's. So, Abraxas had been wrong, and Gagnon got it right. Not a samurai but a ninja. A black, urban ninja with an attitude. She quietly shifted left a couple of feet. Abraxas would never know where the final attack came from. This was it.

And then the lights came on.

Skye's head whipped up to the windows. Outside, they got one of the floodlights working. Brightness poured into the room, Abraxas crouched low, fists in a defensive posture, facing thirty degrees in the wrong direction. Skye saw blood splotches on the floor, spots they had both contributed to. One knife lay in front of the door, another under the nearest desk. Then both pairs of eyes fell on the chair.

The chair Skye had rolled to the center of the room, hours ago that felt like days. The chair Abraxas had draped her double shoulder holster rig across. It sat there, a silent challenge, between the two combatants. To Skye's judgement they were exactly the same distance from those two guns. Skye was sure Abraxas would carry them cocked and locked.

Abraxas did truly smile now, shifting her position to match Skye's. Her eyes went from Skye to the guns and back again. Skye shifted her position as well. Again the fear tried to rise in her throat, and again she tamped it down. Without the advantage of darkness there was no way to win if Abraxas had a gun in her hand. Skye had no more hidden weapons, no more tricks to use.

Abraxas managed a deep breath. "You can't think you can reach a gun, draw, and fire faster than I can."

With that, Skye saw her one chance. "Only one way to find out."

Chapter 33

As if in response to some silent starter's pistol the two women leaped forward. Skye saw the action in agonizing slow motion. Four steps slapping the tiles at exactly the same time. Abraxas' hand wrapped around a gun butt a tenth of a second before Skye gripped the other. Abraxas smoothly pulled the gun from its holster, raising it toward Skye.

Skye did not draw. She swiveled the gun toward Abraxas and fired through the bottom of the holster. The bullet punched the center of Abraxas' chest a bare instant before she fired. Skye felt the heat of Abraxas' shot flying past her ear. Abraxas snapped backward as if yanked by some invisible wire. Her body thumped on the floor.

Skye collapsed on her knees, arms on the seat of the chair. She was gulping big, deep breaths, eyes wide. Only now did she realize how scared she was. That was the razor edge of death. She needed a minute. But she didn't have one. Now was the greatest danger.

The camp must have heard the two gunshots in there, and it was no longer dark outside. She was shaky, but she needed to move. She reached under the desk for the rifle and ran across the room for the magazine. No idea how many men were waiting out there. She'd know soon.

Two steps toward the door she looked back. Was it ego, or arrogance that made her consider a trophy at this moment? Didn't matter. She snatched the custom shoulder holsters off the chair. She had admired it from the minute she saw it and, damn it, she had earned it just now. She snatched the other gun from Abraxas' limp hand and holstered it. She slung the double rig across one shoulder, her bag on the other. She leaned against the door. They were out there, or they weren't. If they were, it was a target acquisition contest.

One more deep breath. She shouldered the door open and ran across the front of the building, keeping close to the wall. Four men walked toward the door she just ran through. Each had a rifle, but they weren't aiming. Holding her rifle at waist level she fired. Hit. Two men fired back. Both missed. She fired again. Another man fell. Two more bullets hit the building, not her. Thank God these fools were such lousy shots. When she reached the end of the wall she turned and disappeared between the buildings into the forest and kept running. Legs screaming, ribs aching, she kept running. No sounds of pursuit. She kept running. Her breathing was ragged and coarse in her throat. She kept running.

When her shoulder hit a tree she gritted her teeth against the pain, spun and kept going but slowed down. She tripped on a root. A quick flash of pain shot from her foot up her shin, but she didn't fall. The rifle felt twice as heavy as it did when she was walking into the compound. Unable to catch her breath, she stopped. She rested the rifle against a tree and put the double shoulder holster on the right way. When she put her right arm through, she winced as the leather slid across her shoulder. That ugly scab would become a nasty scar. She was lucky it wasn't worse.

"Over here."

Skye turned right toward Carter's stage whisper. The world was getting brighter, although trees spreading overhead made it impossible to see the sun. She staggered on for the longest three minutes of her life. Carter ran to her and took the rifle. Newman leaned against a tree, all but hidden in a natural depression in the earth. She dropped to her knees in front of him.

"If you're here I take it the dragon lady's history," Newman said.

Skye nodded. "How's the leg?"

"It'll do. You get al-Baghdadi?"

Skye shook her head. "I had one job. I did it. Now I hurt all over and I'm tired as fuck. Need to put my head down for a couple minutes."

She looked around at the leaf-covered ground. Not inviting, but she could feel her remaining energy draining out of her as if it were seeping into the ground. They should set a sentry. Show Carter how to work the rifle. But the gears up there, north of her neck, were grinding instead of meshing. Newman smiled and patted his good leg. Skye crumpled, resting her head on his thigh.

It was quiet, except for the sound of something small moving above her. The world smelled like garbage and sweat. The pillowcase under her cheek was rough and damp. *Where the hell am I?*

Skye's eyes snapped open. She registered the forest, the squirrels on limbs overhead, the dead leaves below the leg her head rested on. She sat up. She stared up through the branches, but nothing appeared to have changed. Carter stood beside her holding what looked like a soda can.

"How you feeling?" Newman asked. "Thirsty?"

She hadn't noticed how dry her mouth was. Carter handed her the can. She seized it, gulping greedily.

"I found that can out here in the woods," Carter said. "Ignored it at first, but then I found this little stream. Fresh, clean water but I didn't want Newman to walk that far so then I remembered seeing this can and I went back for it and then rinsed it out real good and…"

"Thanks," Skye said, cutting him off. Looking at Carter's puppy dog eyes, she softened her tone. "Really, Thank you.

Water is more important than food when you're stranded like this."

"Hungry?" Newman asked. "We saved a couple candy bars for you."

Newman tossed her two Hershey's with Almonds. She smiled her thanks, pushed one bar halfway up out of the paper wrapper and peeled the foil off the top inch of chocolate. "Good looking out, boys." She took a bite, and said, "How long did I sleep?"

"Nearly eight hours," Newman said. "You needed the rest, but we couldn't afford for you to sleep any longer." Skye looked at him in surprise. Eight hours? No wonder she was so hungry. She glanced heavenward again. Near dusk did look a lot like near dawn when you couldn't see the sun. She considered the shambles this job had become. Captured like an amateur. Betrayed, although Carter had made up for it and then some. Beaten. But she had fought her way out of it and they were all in one piece. Now if they could just find their way out of the woods, they'd be okay.

"Have you fellows figured out what direction we go in to get to civilization?"

"No clue," Carter said, picking up the empty soda can.

"Can't go yet anyway," Newman said. "Need to finish the business back at the compound."

"You're kidding, right?" Skye asked. "That leg will be getting infected pretty bad. We need to get you to a doctor."

Newman shook his head. "What we need to do is stop Rajul al-Baghdadi." He sucked a breath through his teeth, reaching for his wounded leg. "We can't let him commit such an extreme act of terrorism. Not right here on American soil."

"Fine," Skye said. "We find civilization, find a phone and call in the National Guard or whatever."

Newman pushed down with both hands to straighten his back against the tree. "I see you don't understand the situation here. We don't have time to go searching for the cavalry. Back at Wallops Island they launched a satellite into orbit today. Quinn Robinson messed with the programming. When Rajul triggers the stolen software, it will cause that satellite to block transmissions from everything in orbit. No phones. No news. No radio contact. No GPS."

"Yeah, yeah, you mansplained all that to me already. Planes in flight and shit."

"Yes. And he's planning to do that at 6 o'clock, about an hour after sundown. Less than two hours from right now."

Carter looked from one of them to the other. "Holy crap! Are we doing this?"

This was insane. She was sitting cross-legged on the ground facing a man in suit and tie whose left leg was probably creeping toward gangrene, looking up at a clueless child in a man's body. If she was ever going to take direction, it wasn't going to be from the likes of them. Not to be ganged up on, she handed Carter the empty soda can.

"Get us a refill, college boy."

Carter took the can, pouted, and loped off between the trees. Now she could talk sense to the grownup.

"Newman. You been shot. That makeshift bandage wasn't sterile. You're underfed and under hydrated. But if we get you to a hospital fast enough, you might keep that leg."

"Are you seriously talking about me when there are thousands of lives at stake?"

"Well, I don't know them," Skye said. "And I don't think you understand what you're asking me. To walk into an armed camp that I've already invaded once."

"I've seen you in action," Newman said. "I've known a few good operators, and I can see you're very good at this."

Skye got to her feet. "You don't even know what I do. I'm not some special forces op or a secret agent or something. What I do is kill people. That's what I do for a living." She expected a reaction from Newman: skepticism or surprise or even revulsion. Instead, she got a lopsided smile.

"Okay. All right. And that's what you need to do. Kill one man. One terrorist. We won't even see this as murder. And you'll be protecting your own family and friends. Doesn't that matter?"

If he only knew. Family? None. Friends? One. Well, maybe two. She stepped closer, to look down on him.

"What matters is that I've done what I was paid to do. Two women damn near killed me, but I got the job done. This anti-terrorist crap, this ain't my job."

Carter tapped her shoulder. She glanced at him, took the can, and gulped down half its contents. When her attention returned to Newman he sucked in a sharp breath, and she saw pain in his eyes. From his leg? Or something else.

"You're right," Newman said, not looking at her. "It's not your job. It's mine. But I can't do it, can I? There's nobody to even try to do this job except you."

She handed Newman the water. He seemed like a good man, but he had no idea. Generally, death was her tool. Sometimes she thought of death as her friend. But for the last couple of days that bastard had been looking over her shoulder, reaching for her, trying to let her taste what she had served to so many others. His cold hand had gripped her heart. No amount of training, no amount of skill could keep fear away in the still times. This job had taught her how much she didn't like being scared.

"You know who this terrorist is, right?" Carter asked. She just nodded. Of course she knew who he was. She had looked into his eyes.

"I mean, you get it, right?" Carter pressed. "He's evil. He's the bad guys."

Skye turned to press her face up close to his. "So? Have you met me? *I'm* the bad guys!"

She stepped away. Carter looked at Newman who just shook his head. She turned her back to the men, but felt Carter move up behind her. He was still speaking in a calm, soft manner.

"I know you think I'm the naïve one, and maybe I am, but I'm not stupid. And I think you're the one who doesn't get it this time. Don't you realize where we are?"

Skye turned to face him again, eyes alight with anger. "Where we are? If I knew where the fuck we are I'd be getting us back to civilization."

"No, no." Carter shook his head. What she saw in his clenched fists and bright eyes was frustration. "Where we are in this game. We've beaten every level so far and now we've made it to the top. This al-Baghdadi guy, he's the Big Bad. You got to beat him to win."

"Are you crazy? This ain't no game."

Carter shook his head again, looked up at the sky, then back at her. "Look at me. I've marched with Black Lives Matter. I've marched for women's reproductive rights. Know why I do that stuff? Because sometimes you've got to fight the fight that isn't your fight. You've got to fight the bad guy who isn't after you. That's how we get justice in this world."

Something about Carter's fervor was making her uncomfortable. Skye took a couple steps away. Carter followed.

"Now these terrorists. Do you understand why they do this stuff? Why they hate us? They are reacting to some slight, some insult they think we've done them. They're mad about something some Americans did years ago to offend their nationality or their religion or their culture. When they commit wholesale murder, they think they're just seeking justice for their people. Well, you know what? Pardon my

French, but that's kind of a fucked up view of justice if you ask me."

Skye froze and stared up into the infinite overhead. She didn't want to see it but he was right. And that was, after all, what people paid her for. To un-fuck it.

A deep breath. A second. She turned, brushed past Carter and dropped into a crouch beside Newman.

"Did they take your wallet?"

"What? What difference… no, they didn't even bother to take my ID. I think they wanted me to be easy to identify when people found my body. Why?"

"Give it to me," she said, hand out.

Carter said, "I'd do what this lady asks."

Newman winced with pain when he rolled to the side to pull his wallet out of a hip pocket. Skye opened it. Two 20-dollar bills. She pulled one out and dropped the wallet in Newman's lap. His brow wrinkled in confusion as she waved the bill in his face.

"My fee. The U.S. government just hired the best at one hell of a discount. I got just a couple of hours to plan and execute my next hit."

Chapter 34

Seated on a mossy log, Skye pushed her mind to fall into her usual pre-mission focus. She kept asking herself what the hell she was doing but none of the answers made sense. Like the log beneath her, this was where she had fallen so she had to move on from there. Unlike the log, she was not yet serving her purpose. She had more to do. She needed to concentrate on one thing. The job at hand. Step one was to inventory her assets.

She had a rifle. She dropped the magazine from the basic A-10. The 20-round magazine still held 16 shells. If Newman's guess was right that was more than the maximum number of soldiers remaining in the compound. If she had more time, she could win this battle through attrition. But that was not the case.

She drew the pistol from under her left arm. It was a Lightweight Colt Commander, the slightly scaled down M1911 with an aluminum frame and a four and a quarter inch barrel. These were built for concealed carry. The seven round magazine held six .45 ACP rounds. Abraxas must have loaded it with one in the chamber, as there was now. The pistols were twins and they felt good in her hands. She tried a road agent spin and slid them into their holsters, butt forward. If she got cornered at least she'd be able to make a hell of a mess of the opposition before she went down.

She dumped her shoulder bag in front of her. She hated having no knives. She had abandoned them back in the tower. There was no time to scoop them up after the fight with Abraxas. But here was her fidget toy that was really a garrote. She slipped that into the left front pocket of her jeans. And she had her Elite Tac flashlight. That she pushed into the right-side pocket. As she did, ideas began to form. She found a short stick and moved back to Newman. Crouching beside him she brushed dead leaves away to create an open smooth space on the ground. While Newman watched, and Carter looked over her shoulder, she scratched a square into the ground and a rectangle on either side of it to represent the compound buildings. Opposite the square, two lines represented the road in. Then she nudged Newman with an elbow.

"Last night you mentioned the vehicles at the compound," she said. "That got me thinking that maybe you were able to observe more about the place than I was."

Newman flicked an insect off his leg. "What do you want to know?"

"Where are the vehicles?"

Newman grunted as he leaned forward. He took the stick from Skye and scratched smaller rectangles in the dirt in front of the left rectangle. "Here," he said. "They're parked nose in to the building, the first one just to the right of the middle where the door is. That's the Mercedes. Then the 4 SUVs. Your car's on the end. I saw that just before some idiot shot me."

Skye nodded and stared at her diagram for a minute. She could probably just walk between two of the buildings and shoot her way in. She might even reach the crazy Arab and take him out. But if she survived that, then what? As is so often the case with an assault, the challenge wasn't getting in to reach the target, it was getting out.

"Can you shoot in through the tower windows?" Carter asked.

"Wrong angle," Newman said. "Unless he actually comes to the window to look out there's no way to hit him. And the man's not that stupid."

"Climb the wall?" Carter asked. "Once you got to the window…"

"Then I'd be the target," Skye said. "All right, fellows, we're going to have to move in close. I can see one way this might work. I'll need a whole lot of luck and one big ass distraction."

When you can't see the sun, days end rather abruptly. A solid cloud cover helped disguise the line between day and night. Insect chatter seemed to signal the shadows to lengthen. Then someone sucked the color out of the world. Darkness didn't fall as much as rise up out of the earth.

Skye saw all of this staring through the tops of tall grass six feet from the clearing behind the compound. She, Carter and Newman lay prone on the cold ground facing the left end of one of the barracks. The tower was to its right. Skye pulled Carter's shoulder, yanking his head closer to her face. She opened her mouth to speak but Carter held up his hand.

"Before you say anything, I just wanted to tell you how sorry I am. I know I'm the reason we're in this fix. If I hadn't listened to that fake hotel owner. If I hadn't let her talk me into walking you into a trap…"

"Not the time, college boy," Skye said. "And it ain't a thing. You fucked up, but then you made it right."

"I should have been a better partner," he said. "Or more like you said, a sidekick."

Skye couldn't help but smile. "You got that shit right. But you know, for a guy with no skills, no training and no sense you done okay, college boy. But now you gonna have a job to do. You gonna have one job and you got to do it right."

"Just tell me what I've got to do," Carter said. "Don't really see how I can help with all this, but give me a chance. I won't let you down."

"I'm getting ready to go back into that compound and put down a terrorist," she said. "You'll stay here with Newman.

But when you get the signal, it's going to be your job to get Newman in my car, race down that one road out of here, and get help. You understand?"

"You expect us to just abandon you?"

"I won't have time to watch out for you boys," Skye said. "I'll be too busy shooting my way up them stairs."

"But…" was all Carter could say before Skye pushed his face to the ground. There was movement in the clearing. That was a surprise. A big, broad-shouldered man carrying a rifle at port arms was walking slowly from the edge of the building. Those morons had posted a guard. She guessed that after they found their two hired killers dead they grasped the idea of how dangerous she was. One woman died messy, the other died neat, but both died ugly. It must have occurred to someone in there that the woman who killed them might come back.

Yet they still didn't understand the situation. That was clear from the fact that the sentry was alone. He was moving slowly. And he was not even looking out into the woods, where an attack would come from. Even better, he had a KA-BAR knife strapped to his leg.

When Skye first spotted the guard he was just about to pass her. She stayed low and moved quietly until she reached the clearing. She dashed toward the building. The sentry heard her but turned to his right, toward the woods. For her it was three long strides and a hop. Her left foot hit the wall and she burst away from it. She landed on the big man's back. Her left arm circled his throat. Her right hand yanked his knife out of its scabbard and rammed the point down into the base of his neck. He stiffened, then collapsed to his knees before falling backward. Skye rolled him over, grabbed his left arm and dragged him toward the tree line. Carter ran out to grip his other arm. They pulled him into the forest and dropped to their knees.

Carter looked down at the sentry. "Is he… is he…?"

"He better be," Skye said, gripping the knife's leather handle. She pulled it out and blood sprayed like a fountain. Okay, so maybe his heart kept pumping for a couple seconds. Carter looked a little green. Skye gave him a light slap. "I need you to focus, college boy. They'll miss this guy pretty quick so I need to move fast. Remember, you've got one job. When you see or hear the signal, you get Newman to the car. Okay?"

"Okay," Carter said as she moved toward the building. "But wait. What's the signal?"

Over her shoulder, Skye said, "Don't worry. You'll know."

Skye stayed low almost to the building's front corner, then dropped to her stomach. She wiped the sentry's fighting knife on her sleeve and grimaced before she took it between her teeth. She low crawled to the front of the building, grateful for luck she hadn't earned. The cloud cover meant no visible moon. The terrorists had only one light working, on the roof of the barracks across the square. Were the others irreparably damaged? Or did they decide that with one day to mission accomplishment it was too much work to fix the other two lights?

They had made other changes. Aside from the men in the two towers there was a rifleman on the porch around the second floor of the center tower building and another perched on the stairs. That left maybe nine men unseen. A gauntlet to be run on her way to Rajul al-Baghdadi.

This time the man in the opposite guard house was leaning forward. He was alert but probably scared. Skye was exposed but as long as she didn't move, she was all but invisible. She wished she could relax her body for what was to come but instead her muscles stayed tense and were beginning to ache. Her stomach growled and she mentally told it to shut up. She knew what only combat veterans and extreme athletes know. Sleep was not the same as rest.

Fatigue made her limbs feel like lead. But she could do this. Eyes on the prize.

Finally, the man in the tower scanned to his left, away from her. She crawled quickly, covering the ten feet between the corner and her car. Once she was under the GTO she was able to force a few deep breaths. Concealed and pushing her limbs to relax, she was ready for the next step.

The vehicles were parked close enough to each other that there was little danger of being seen while crawling under them. Even with her nose in the thin weeds below, her head brushed the GTO's exhaust pipe. The next four had more ground clearance. Her elbows were getting scraped and again her right shoulder was complaining but she tuned it out and focused on moving forward.

Her forehead bumped the Mercedes undercarriage. Lower than the four-wheel drive beast over her. Good thing she didn't need to crawl under it. That sentry had been a bit of luck. Her original plan called for her to fiddle around under the front of the car to find the gas line and work it loose. Instead, she turned toward the rear end of the car.

The Jeep, like almost all European vehicles, and most American cars, had a plastic gas tank. She took the knife in her right fist and jerked it upward, punching the blade into the gas tank. When she yanked it down, the slippery liquid poured out, along with its sharp, acrid stench. She pulled back, dragging the knife point along the ground, creating a narrow channel for some of the gasoline to follow. She paused under the next SUV and slid to her right, toward the front of the vehicle, to slide the edge of her blade across the gas line. Not cut all the way through, it dripped slowly.

She continued her backward motion, scraping the ground to continue the original channel that led to the Mercedes. She stopped when her head was under the second vehicles, the one next to her GTO. She didn't want her feet exposed yet. She stabbed the knife into the inside sidewall of the right rear tire. Whether a Jeep or Range Rover or whatever, it was not equipped with run-flat tires. The Mercedes probably was. Not that it mattered now.

It took some wiggling to get her hand down to her right front pocket, but she managed to free her flashlight. She kept it aimed at the ground and flipped it on. She adjusted it for maximum output and found the thin trail of clear liquid.

The Tac flashlight's halogen beam was kicking out a whopping 2,300 lumens. In the sales demonstration she had seen this beam burn through plastic. Once when he took her caving, Papa Maddox had cracked an egg into his tin canteen mug and fried it using this flashlight.

She wished life was more like the movies, where you could fire a gun into a car's gas tank and cause an explosion. Sadly, bullets aren't that hot on impact and anyway, it was the fumes that created combustion, not liquid gasoline. But poured on the ground, gasoline immediately started to evaporate. If she could smell it, she could use it.

She only saw the tiny blue flame for an instant. She clamped her eyes shut and started squirming backward. The deafening roar slammed her ears, and she imagined the Mercedes Benz doing a handstand before slamming back down onto the ground. By the time she was clear of the car and getting to her feet the movement was past. The Mercedes had decided to flip forward, its rear bumper leaning against the front of the building, its belly exposed to the night. She drew her two pistols and sprinted toward the tower.

The rooftop guards must have been thrown into shock. She heard four or five shots fired but none came anywhere near her. Men poured out of both barracks buildings behind her, many not armed at all. Those that were must have been shooting at shadows because nothing came close while she was running. She looked up. The fool on the second floor porch moved to the top of the stairs, but he was aiming at the burning car. Skye reached the bottom of the outside stairs before the men standing on it realized she was there. She blew them off the stairs, one with her left gun, one with her right. In her mind, .45 ACP meant never having to shoot anyone twice.

A bullet splintered the railing a couple of inches from her. She spun to face her attackers, almost sitting on the stairs as she fired. Three more shots, three more dead men. They were rushing toward her now, screams of rage or hate or fear blending with the roar of the fire behind them. A dense column of black smoke rose from the inverted car, blinding one of the rooftop guards. Skye kept shooting, her heart pounding in her chest, feeling exposed and vulnerable. Each bright flash launched a bullet meant for her. Both her arms were swinging to catch the next target, the man closest to her. A dozen shot and she was running out of time and ammo. Despite the cool evening breeze sweat broke out on her forehead and dripped down her neck. Was this where they'd find her in the morning? Well, she had made a hell of a mess of the opposition before she went down.

Chapter 35

In timed competitive shooting events Skye tracked her shots as she made them. To get the best score she had to know when to reload. Thanks to that mental reflex she knew she had one round in each gun when the second explosion rocked the courtyard. The Range Rover beside the inverted Mercedes leaped into the air, balanced on a bright red ball of fire. Men fell, either thrown off balance by the blast, diving to the ground in fear or slapped down by flying pieces of debris. A wave of heat washed over her face. She turned, ran up the last three steps, and kicked the door in.

Skye dived into the room, clinging to the ground, her left arm already extended, aiming where she figured the last line of defense would be. The lone terrorist guard fired his rifle over her head. She put the last bullet from her left hand gun into his throat. Then she got to one knee facing what she figured was her final target.

Sitting at a control panel, Rajul al-Baghdadi turned to face her. His face moved a lot, anguished and distorted as if a rush of words was pouring out, but all he really said was "No! No! No!"

"Yes, yes, mother fucker," Skye said. "Time to collect your 72 virgins or whatever the hell you get for dying for your screwed up cause."

Skye raised her pistol toward Rajul but something yanked at her attention. Instinct or peripheral vision. She jerked her head to her left in time to see the blade arcing down toward her. Her body spun and she fired at her attacker.

Abraxas' face was just inches away. Skye's shot slammed into Abraxas' chest a little right of center, shoving her away, but the swinging knife caught Skye's arm, slashing her left triceps.

Damn that hurt. A cut to match the one Abraxas gave me on the other arm yesterday. And what the hell? Abraxas alive? Well, not anymore. But there Skye sat on her knees holding two pistols. The slides of both were locked back showing that they were empty. And Rajul al-Baghdadi had the nerve to laugh at her.

"You Americans are arrogant, but arrogance alone will not defeat the Islamic State," Rajul al-Baghdadi bellowed. "With two more simple commands I shall bring your condescending nation to its knees."

"Well then," Skye said, dropping the pistols and fighting to stand., "Guess I'll just have to do this the hard way."

She cursed the unsteadiness in her legs. Rajul was ignoring her, his focus on the control panel. He pushed one lever upward. Skye fell forward, leaning on the computer-laden table. She pulled her fidget tool from her pocket, slipped her middle fingers into the two rings and yanked. Rajul was reaching to push a button near the top of the panel. When she whipped the wire around his neck and pulled back, he missed. He tried to get his hands on her, his big beefy arms flailing, but her face was pressed against his back.

Her fists crossed at the back of his neck and slowly moved away from each other. Pain raced down both of Skye's arms from the cuts on both sides. Her eyes were clenched shut, leaking tears that she didn't care about. Like so many past targets, this bastard needed killing.

Wire garrotes aren't designed to just strangle a target. As she squeezed, the wire cut into his flesh, slicing his throat. She cried out with the effort. The big man thrashed and struggled against her. He gurgled as blood poured into his lungs. More blood came from the sides of his neck. There was that familiar metallic smell again. Had she cut deeply enough to sever his carotid artery? Or maybe his jugular vein? More blood dripped from her left elbow, but that was probably from her most recent knife wound.

When Rajul's body was still Skye released the garrote, leaving it deep in the terrorist's throat. Dropping to her knees again, she recovered the twin automatics, thumbed the levers to let the slides snap forward, and slipped them into their holsters. She pulled open the cabinet under the control panel. She wasn't sure the whole satellite issue was solved so she reached inside and found a wire panel. She pulled wires at random, disconnecting whatever cables and cords her hand hit until there was nothing left to pull on and the control panel itself was dark. She had already earned her fee. This was just a little extra.

She heard no more gunshots from outside. The fires still crackled. She figured Carter and Newman would be long gone in the GTO, raising the alarm and bringing the posse. Whatever terrorist gunmen survived had probably scattered into the woods or piled into one of the undamaged Range Rovers and run for cover. She wanted to check one thing before she did the same.

Fatigue left Skye a little shaky on her feet. Her jaw dropped when she saw Abraxas on the other side of the room, sitting up. She was leaning against the wall. No part of her moved except her eyes. Her hands lay empty and limp at her sides. A few steps closer Skye could see the answer to her unasked question. Her 45-caliber wad-cutter slug was flattened and clinging to the thick fabric encasing Abraxas' chest.

"Your leotard," Skye said. "It's Kevlar."

"Of course," Abraxas croaked.

She lived but was certainly no threat. The Kevlar vest had prevented penetration but two .45 slugs at such close range would still do a lot of damage. Most likely her sternum was cracked by the first shot. The second probably broke a rib or two. And she was unarmed. Skye looked over her shoulder at the knife on the floor.

"So," Abraxas said. "What? You kill me now?"

"Yep."

Abraxas smiled. "Ego, yes? You get to say you beat the best. Is that it?"

"Not really."

Abraxas squinted in confusion. "Then why? You've killed your target, right? Rajul al-Baghdadi will serve as a warning to any future terrorist foolish enough to set up on American soil. Am I then what you call a freebie?"

"Oh, no, bitch, don't get it twisted," Skye said. "I was paid to eliminate you. The client, that idiot, he thought Harmony was Abraxas. He'd have paid to have her smoked. But I knew she wasn't the real deal. And he really wanted you. If anything, that Arab asshole was the freebie. Well, not quite, but more like collateral damage."

Abraxas nodded. "Your client, he wanted me dead? But why?"

Did it matter? "You remember Quincy Page, right? Vacation home in Nevada? Wife and kids with him?"

"Oh yes." Abraxas' breathing was rough, as if something was pushing into one of her lungs. "I was instructed to make it messy. I think they planned to throw the blame at the North Koreans. But yes, I remember."

"Well Page worked for my client," Skye said. "So did Alan Brown. And Ike Thomas. Harmony was responsible for them, but she was working for you, so…"

"So, he wanted revenge," Abraxas said in a calm, thoughtful voice. "I guess I didn't ask the right questions when I captured you. Had I known all that, I would have killed you right away." A small chuckle made her face clamp down with pain. "But it is good to know I am not just collateral damage or an incidental death."

Skye had heard enough. She picked up the knife that had slashed her arm. She'd place the point at the notch of Abraxas' collarbone and push. Then she'd walk down the dirt road out of there. Maybe she'd meet Newman's cleanup team on their way in.

As Skye approached, Abraxas sought eye contact. "If I may ask one favor."

"You're kidding right? What, like, don't kill me?"

Abraxas shook her head. "Not here. Not in the room with that… that…" she pointed at al-Baghdadi, dripping into the scarlet pool spreading beneath his chair. "That Gesu yarō"

Skye had no idea what that meant but she guessed it wasn't a compliment. Still, why should it matter to her? What did she owe this woman who captured, tortured and tried to kill her?

Maybe, some respect.

With a heavy sigh, she slipped the knife into the empty scabbard on her back between the two shoulder holsters. She bent to grab Abraxas' ankles and dragged her across the floor and out the door onto the wraparound deck. Then Skye punched her once in the stomach. Abraxas moaned in pain. Skye gripped her leotard and hoisted her to slam her back against the railing. Abraxas grunted, clenched her teeth and fought to catch her breath.

"Thank you. I will pay you for this favor," she wheezed. "You should not die by surprise."

"What?"

"al-Baghdadi planned to erase the evidence of this terrorist act as soon as it was done. Once all the satellites were blacked out, he allowed just enough time for him to gather his captives and escape the area before pre-set explosives in each of the buildings totally erased this compound. You do not have time to escape the explosions on foot, but at least your death will not be a surprise to you. You will be able to make your peace with your Western God." She forced a smile. "So you see, you are doomed too. I will meet you in the other world."

"Yeah, well I'll kick your ass there too."

One sharp push and Abraxas flipped backward over the railing. She did not scream, or flail about. She landed solidly on her head, the weight of her body snapping her neck.

Skye expected a rush of emotion, a burst of triumph, the sense of victory she didn't have time to get the first time she thought she killed Abraxas. Celebration seemed to be in order. She had beaten the best. Maybe Abraxas' calm acceptance had robbed her of that feeling. Whatever, she had more important things to think about.

Skye moved down the stairs as quickly as she could. How much time did she have? Five minutes? Ten? Under ideal conditions, she could push a mile or two into the woods in that time. But she was beaten and wounded. Just swinging her arms hurt. How could she run? Injuries aside she was on the downside of a flood of Adrenalin and exhaustion was setting in. Plus, pain aside, she could not outrun hunger and thirst with sheer force of will.

She tried to jog but actually stumbled across the courtyard toward the door to one of the barracks. The whole world smelled like burning oil and plastic. The cars had burned themselves out and some moron had killed the one working floodlight. It was dark as a tomb and damned near as quiet. Could she defuse the bombs? Defuse not one but three unfamiliar devices, when she didn't even know their locations in the buildings? Unlikely. What else.

She found herself walking toward the smoldering vehicles. The Mercedes was upside down. One Land Rover was gutted from underneath. The next one was missing. Survivors must have driven it away. She had flattened a tire of the remaining SUV. But if she could get it running it would still be faster than she could move on foot right then. But it seemed unlikely the fleeing terrorists would leave the key behind.

God, she was drained. Tears of frustration crawled down her cheeks as she dragged herself through the darkness. Her tank was on E and she knew damned well she couldn't hot wire that vehicle. She couldn't run fast enough, and she couldn't stop the bombs. But with grim determination she knew there was one other thing she could not do. She could not give up.

Skye could not remember the last time she prayed. Maybe she was pre-school age. It was way before her father left. Before her mother left. Before drugs took her brother. Before her first kill. She didn't think she would do it now, but she did raise her eyes to the dark skies for a moment.

"Hey. Little help?"

She kept trudging forward. She was almost within reach of the remaining Range Rover when the light burst in her face from directly ahead of her. Momentarily blinded, she heard movement ahead and a hand touched her arm. She brushed it way and tried to get into a defensive stance.

"What the hell?" Carter asked. "Are you okay?"

Her eyes came into focus. There he stood with that same dumb look on his face.

"Carter? What the fuck are you doing here, college boy?" She squinted past him, seeing that her own vehicle was the source of the blinding light.

Carter gripped her arm. "I'm sorry. We couldn't go."

"Couldn't? You mean Newman couldn't start the car?"

"Oh, he got it started okay," Carter said. *Was he... blushing?* "But his leg hurt too much for him to drive. And then he passed out. And I, well, geez, it's a manual transmission and I don't know how to drive it. I tried but..."

It all rushed in on her at once. Surprise, anger, even fear were washed away by the absurdity of the situation. This ridiculous set of circumstances had given her a chance. She grabbed Carter's arm and half-ran, half-staggered to her car.

"Get in the back," she shouted, jumping into the driver's seat. Beside her, Newman was pale and still, his breathing rough. The improvised bandage on his right leg was soaked and dripping. Exhaustion, hunger, the walk to the car, blood loss had all teamed up to slap him down. But how fast? She reached under the dash, relieved to feel wires pulled loose.

"Buckle up," she said. She needed only to depress the clutch and touch one wire to the others already twisted together. The engine roared to life, sounding as impatient as she. She shoved it into reverse. The car jerked back from the building. She shifted into first gear, pointed the car toward the single lane out of there and punched the accelerator.

Carter slammed back into his seat, bounced forward and grabbed the driver's seat. "Whoa! What's the hurry? I looked around a little back there and it looked like everybody in the place was dead."

"Yeah, and I ain't trying to join them," Skye said. "The whole place is rigged to…"

First, the flash of light in her rearview mirror blinded her. The deafening roar and shock wave came right behind it. The rear of the GTO lifted from the ground. She was floating for an instant, tossed like a cork in the surf. Leafless trees stood shoulder to shoulder, an impressive defensive line they were rushing toward. She clamped her eyes shut.

Chapter 36

"Can you hear me?"

Vibrations but not feeling much else.

"Can you hear me?

Air never smells this sweet, this pure. Where do you get air like this?

"Miss are you with us?"

The copper taste of blood and, damn it, a loose tooth. Eyes open but all there is, is white. *Can't turn my head. I can't turn my head. What the hell?*

"Miss, can you…"

"Yes!" Skye screamed. "Yes! Yes, God damn it I can hear you. Why can't I move my head?"

"That's the purpose of the brace and collar," she said. The woman's face came into view, smiling down at Skye. A white girl, young, pretty, with clear brown eyes. A nurse.

"Why the nurse got to be a wise ass?"

The woman breathed a sigh of relief. "I guess we don't need to worry about the effects of the concussion. You were in and out there for a while. Bad blow to the head. Concerned about a neck injury too so until we get you to the hospital, you're stuck with the ceiling as your view. Oh, and thanks for the compliment, but I'm an EMT, not a nurse."

Only then did Skye notice the woman was squeezing her hand. It hurt to move her eyes, but she had to see more. The inside of the ambulance looked just like they do on television. An IV ran into her right arm. Tubes were pushing oxygen into her nose. She was starting to feel sleepy again.

"The boys?"

"We found two men in the car with you," The nurse said. "They're riding behind us. Can you tell me your name?"

"Call me Skye."

"Skye…." The nurse left space for a last name.

"Just Skye. How'd you find us? We were way out in the boonies."

The nurse responded but Skye had trouble getting meaning from the words. The movement was oddly soothing. The black curtain was coming down again and she couldn't fight it.

When the sun returned it flowed through Venetian blind slats that laid black lines across her bed. Hospital beds have crappy mattresses but this one was raised at just the right angle so Skye wasn't complaining. She hurt everywhere but she could move. She made fists and wiggled her toes. She was pretty sure nothing was broken, and she was breathing okay. Despite the pain she was full of energy. Good drugs, she assumed. Were there any clothes in that closet area? If so, she could get out of there before anyone came back to ask questions she was not prepared to answer.

As she flipped the covers back, the door eased open. Larry Newman walked in, leaning on a cane. His right leg wasn't bending, the left side of his face was black and blue and he grunted with the effort of taking each step. Two fingers on his left hand stuck out at a bad angle.

"Don't get up," he said, "and don't worry. We got you covered."

"You look like you been through a meat grinder," Skye said, pulling the covers back over her legs.

"Have you seen you?"

"Fair enough," she said with a smirk. "I can't even tell where it's bad, cause it hurts the same amount all over me. But it's under control. Now, I hate to sound all cliché and shit but where am I?"

"McCready Memorial Hospital," Newman said. "There ain't much to it, kind of an independent emergency room, but the folks have been really nice and easy to deal with once my friends showed up and started flashing badges."

Skye nodded. Her neck was a little stiff, but not bad. "How's Carter doing?"

Newman pulled a chair over close to the bed and slowly lowered himself into it. "Carter's on his way to surgery. I think he broke his hip. No damage to internal organs. In fact, that goes for all of us. We were damned lucky."

Pressing her hands down on the bed she was able sit up straighter, but her arms and shoulders hurt like hell. She didn't feel lucky. "Glad he's alive. But he'll probably be running his mouth, which means I need to get in the wind before people show up asking all the wrong questions."

"Don't worry," Newman said. "Nobody's coming in here until after I leave. I've got a man on the door. I needed time to talk to you. Trust me, okay? My people will cover you."

Skye's eyes narrowed. "Your people?"

"Homeland Security," Newman said.

"Oh, so I'm trapped here," she said, collapsing back on the bed, "They the ones found us out there in the woods? You got a tracker in you or something?"

Newman leaned back, unconsciously rubbing his right thigh. "Afraid not. It was the blast. Those Islamic State boys went a little overboard, planting an Oklahoma City style explosive in each of the three buildings. Must have been a hell of a lot of fertilizer and fuel oil. Visible from miles away. It was a race between police and news helicopters to get there and see what happened. They spotted the car from the air. Or what was left of it."

"That explains the ambulance rides," Skye said. The beeping of the machines attached to her was becoming annoying. "So can I get back to my private security gig? I work for Eric Gagnon you know. I was supposed to be protecting this Carter Brown dude when I got sucked into your crazy espionage shit."

Newman was shaking his head but didn't interrupt. When she stopped, he said, "Skye, we know who you are. We're not sure how you got involved in this case, but we know who you are and we know what you do. I hired you, remember?"

Skye's face fell, although her eyes shifted from side to side. She had told this fed way too much. What could she do with no tools, no weapons, and federal agents at the door? She didn't even know what floor she was on. She could take Newman out if she had to but what then?

She could feel Newman's hard stare, as if he was reading her face, seeing all that was going on behind it. His brows lowered and his mouth opened as if he had heard her say something that surprised him.

Finally, he said, "Oh." And after another second, "Relax. Please. You're not being detained or anything. Hey, you saved my life. At least twice. Did you think I'd come after you?"

"You a dedicated G man," Skye said. "And you've seen me work."

Newman actually smiled. "I've seen your skills, but I haven't seen you do anything criminal. Even if I did, Homeland Security is focused on threats to our country, not individual felons. Besides, your nation owes you a great debt."

"Not looking for no medals, pal, just want to be left alone."

"No headlines for this one," Newman said. "Just one more in a long line of terrorist threats that the public will never know about. We've already made up a silly explanation for that explosion that nobody will really believe. The conspiracy theorists will push three or four even sillier explanations, but the confusion will put off any mass panic."

Skye sat forward and squinted hard at him. "So that's it? You just lie to everybody and let me go?"

Newman pushed to his feet, walked to the table beside her bed and poured himself a cup of water. "That can be it. Unless you know where the rest of this terrorist cell was based. We don't like these people being so close to Wallops Island." He took a long slow drink while she thought. He put his cup down and held her eyes while she considered her options.

"Where's my stuff?" She thought that would throw him, but nothing seemed to.

"I have your stuff."

"All my stuff?" she asked.

"Well, your clothes are here in the room closet," he said. "I have all the fun stuff."

Skye nodded. "Okay, look, they got some property in the area. It's all listed under the name Abraxas was using."

"You have addresses? Locations?"

"I won't tell you where," Skye said. "But, if you're nice I will show you. I got some unfinished business at one of these places. Assuming you can get me out of here."

"You got me out of a death trap. I think I can get you out of a hospital ward."

Two hours later Skye sat in the back seat of a black Chevy Suburban beside Newman, grateful to whomever washed her jeans, her blouse and her denim jacket. As they rolled into the parking lot of the Mahelona Inn she remembered her first meeting with Abraxas and winced at her own stupidity.

"Don't look much like a terrorist headquarters, do it?"

"That's precisely the point," Newman said. "Of course, we must assume the guests are real. And for all we know, the staff is all local hires for cover."

"Yeah, but you can bet the management is all Islamic State, or working for them," Skye said. "You let me go in alone and I'll tell you how many you got to deal with."

"Well, that sounds like a pretty stupid idea," Newman said, "but I'm not the guy who's going to try to stop you. Your business is on the second floor, right? I'll watch the window for your signal."

"So you're good with this? I mean, you know why I'm here, right?"

Newman took a big breath and blew it out slowly. "I know what my boss would say. I know what *his* boss would say. But I agree with you on this one."

Skye climbed out of the vehicle as two more Suburbans moved in behind them. It was good to have backup, but she knew she was putting her foot squarely into a bear trap. If things went sideways in there, she was not at all sure she could handle it. She took a deep breath, pushed her hands into her jacket pockets and headed for the door.

The eclectic décor, the mix of Eastern shore, Polynesian and rocket ornaments, felt even more disjointed with a Middle Eastern man standing behind the registration desk. This time there were three others in the lobby. Two guys played cards at a small table, one white, one black. The woman on the other side reading her book looked Indian or Pakistani. It was the freaking United Nations in there. She walked straight to the desk.

"Good morning," the manager said. "I am Farid. How may I help you?"

Skye made a show of looking around. "Considering the name of this place you'd expect the owner to be Hawaiian or something."

Farid's smile almost swallowed his face. "We are under new management. The previous owner…"

"Disappeared suddenly," Skye said. "I know. Did you know her?" One of the card players looked toward her.

Farid's smile dimmed a little. "We had met."

"Let me ask you something," Skye said. "Did you ever see her when she wasn't dressed up as a fat Hawaiian woman?"

Now both card players stopped and stared at her. The other woman in the room didn't react. Farid's smile disappeared entirely.

"Who are you?" he asked.

Skye leaned in, hands still in her pockets. "Answer the question."

Farid stood a little taller. "I knew her that well. How did you know her?"

Skye pulled up her danger face, lips barely parted showing clenched teeth. "Did you ever see her with these on?" She spread her jacket open, giving him a good look at the holsters hanging under each of her arms. Farid's eyes sprang open wide. She heard chairs move behind her.

"Who are you?" Farid said again. "What makes you think you can walk in here and question me? I think you should leave now."

"Really?" Skye asked. "How you think I got these?" Then she waited. Whoever blinked first was the loser.

Farid blinked and took a step back.

"I got some business upstairs," Skye said in a soft voice. "You don't follow. Neither do your two friends behind me. I finish my business. I leave. Nobody has to die today. We good?"

Farid looked over her at the men behind her. Then his smile limped back onto his face. "Of course, Miss."

"Cool. Is room 202 empty?"

"Why yes. Yes it is." Farid handed over the key card. Skye smiled and thanked him.

Skye headed up the stairs. As she stepped into the hallway she fell against the wall. Her shoulders dropped. Her knees felt weak.

Breathe girl. You're past the bad stuff.

She went into her old room and opened the sliding glass door. On the little balcony she held up three fingers. Then she went back inside. She pulled a drawer open and felt under it. She clawed the dried chewing gum off the wood and the small flash drive with it. Now that she knew what the program could do, she understood why everyone wanted it. No business could resist that kind of power. No nation would pass up a chance to weaponize such a capability. The flash drive only held half of the program, but she suspected that the right team of programmers could complete it given this head start.

She felt lighter once she had dropped the drive into the toilet and flushed it down. She jogged back down the stairs. She found Newman standing behind the registration desk. Now two new men sat at the little card table. Their suits looked like they came from the same place Newman got his. She dropped the key card on the desk.

"What happened to my friend Farid?"

Newman smiled. "We are under new management."

Chapter 37

Alan Brown's funeral was on a bright and blazing hot Saturday morning. In Las Vegas, September meant it might not reach 100 degrees that day. Skye suffered like all the other women in black dresses. To her left, the sun was a lonely yellow disc in a clear and open sky. To her right, the moon was still visible over the distant trees. Two objects in the vast, otherwise empty sky within sight of each other but forever forbidden to keep each other company.

A dozen feet from the tight-knit group of mourners clustered around Carter Brown, Skye felt as lonely as the fading moon. She knew she didn't belong there. Yet she had to say her final goodbyes to the man she had known for a few weeks after high school, the man she couldn't save. Carter would be out of that wheelchair in a couple weeks, but his physical hurt would heal faster than the emotional anguish he felt. His friends and family shared his pain as well as memories of his father. They knew how to comfort him. They knew what to say. She had no idea.

The other person who didn't belong there approached her. The man who paid for the plot in the well-tended cemetery, the ostentatious coffin, the grand memorial stone. The man who had invited Alan Brown's old friends with names like Blaine, Copperfield and Angel. He had done all he should do, but she could see in his eyes that he had no idea what to say either. Eric Gagnon stood beside her, his hands thrust into the pockets of the only black seersucker suit she had ever seen.

"You cost me a great deal," he said, not turning from the grave.

"I did what you paid me to do. I should have charged you double for taking those two women out of the game."

"You might have recovered that computer program," he said. "Or at least the part that was on the flash drive I foolishly let you leave with. That bit of code could have made me…"

"What? Rich? Ain't you got enough paper already?"

"Is there such a thing as enough?" When she didn't respond, he said, "And I do believe I did pay you double. You know, you could live better. Would you consider employment, rather than being a freelance?"

Skye looked up into Gagnon's cold dead eyes. "Let me tell you a couple things a man like you should not ever have. That program that got blown to hell in the Virginia woods and control over somebody like me. Our business is done. And with all your money, trust and believe you don't ever want to get on the wrong side of me."

The small knot of mourners was breaking up. Carter was rolling toward the limo Gagnon provided. It looked like he was leaving alone. Heading home, wherever that was. Skye trotted toward him, slowing to a walk when she got within a few feet. He looked up, holding a neutral expression. Holding it all in, Skye thought. He wouldn't want to break down in front of her.

"Carter, I just wanted to say I'm so sorry I couldn't save your father," she said. "He was a good man."

Carter stopped and faced her. "I don't blame you, Skye. For a while I blamed Gagnon for getting my father involved in that mess. But I realize now that everything my father did was his choice. He was a master of illusions, but he chose to do some things that are riskier than a trick if it goes wrong."

"You right," Skye said, lowering her head. "He knew there were risks, but he never shied away from them. In that way, he was like my adopted father. One thing we have in common."

"Yeah, you never stop mourning your parents, do you?" Carter rolled toward the car with Skye following closely. When he got close the driver opened the door for him and held out a hand to help him in.

"Listen, you and me we been through some stuff," Skye said. "The kind of stuff you don't forget fast."

"That's the truth," Carter said. "Some of the things I saw you do, well, I'll never be able to forget."

Skye smiled and leaned against the car. "Looks like you're kind of on your own. So am I. How about you tell the driver to take you to your favorite hangout spot. I can follow in my rental. We can get a meal and talk about stuff. This ain't no time to be all on your own. Besides," she tilted her head and smiled, "you're my sidekick, right?"

Carter took a deep breath. "I guess I was there for a while." He seemed to be staring off at some memory, but she didn't know if they were exciting, frightening or just confusing to him.

"So, where's your favorite watering hole around here?"

It looked like Carter shivered a bit, as if a chilly breeze had cut through the heat. He looked down at his own lap, then looked up at her. His face didn't change, although his brow seemed tighter.

"Look, Skye." He looked away, then turned back to her. "There's no nice way to say this. I appreciate that you saved my life, I really do. And I regret betraying you like I did. That was wrong. But I know who you are, I know what you do. Hell, I've seen you do it."

"But still… the adventure of a lifetime, right?"

"A lot of that was the stuff of nightmares. You are just not the kind of person I want in my life. Can you understand that? I'd like to get back to a normal life and the truth is… I'm sorry, but I really hope I never see you again."

Skye stood beside the limo while the driver helped Carter inside. She stayed silent while the driver got in and the big black vehicle pulled away. The moon was gone. There was not a cloud in the sky. The sun had floated up farther away from the horizon. That single yellow orb ruled the vast openness above, bright, powerful, and alone.

Skye looked around to realize she was last to leave. She strode back to the only remaining car and climbed into the seat. Her flight wasn't until late that night, but she wouldn't spend the day exploring Sin City.

She lurched into her room and dropped onto the bed. She was spent, every which way: Physically, mentally, emotionally. She would lay there in that hotel room until it was time to get to the airport. She was ready to be home.

He was waiting at the curb when she stepped through the arrival doors of Ronald Reagan Washington National Airport. This time it was an ordinary suitcase she wheeled to the trunk. After closing the lid, she took a moment to look around and breath in the local atmosphere. Despite its name, the airport was in Virginia, but it still felt like she was back in the city where she belonged. She slid into the back seat.

Mo looked at her in the rearview mirror. "You ready to go home now?"

"Yeah," she said. But when they reached the George Washington Parkway and were pointed toward The District, she was shaking her head. "You know what? I don't think so."

"Let me guess," Mo said. "You want to talk about your stuff?"

"What? No. Well, maybe. I will ask you to make one more stop, but not where you think."

Skye walked toward the modest building from two blocks away. This time she thought she was at least dressed appropriately. The long black dress and pumps she wore wouldn't draw any stares. With luck she would blend in and go unnoticed at the back of the room.

Those hopes disappeared when she saw the tall, light-skinned black woman standing at the door. Chalondra wasn't Skye's idea of a church lady but then, she didn't have a lot of experience in that area. Hoping for the best she kept walking until she stood in front of the white painted door. Chalondra gasped but didn't look away.

"Child you look like you been down ten miles of rough road. What in the world happened to you?"

How did one explain the nasty gash across her forehead. The nearly healed bruises on her cheeks. The thin red line where her lip had been split?

"I fell."

"Yeah, right," Chalondra said. "I seen a lot of sisters fell down them same stairs and walked into a doorknob or two. Is that what brings you to the Lord's house?"

"Look, I'm not…" Skye clenched her lips and shook her head. She didn't think it would be this hard. "It's been a difficult week. Believe me, the person who did this to my face won't do it again, not to nobody. That's not it. I just needed a place to be still, to get some peace. And this morning, I just didn't want to be alone."

Chalondra nodded and put a hand on Skye's shoulder. "Well, you did right. This is a place of fellowship, not judgement." She turned and pulled the door open.

"I got to be honest," Skye said. "I'm not a believer."

Chalondra smiled and placed a soft hand on the small of Skye's back. "Don't matter if you believe in Him. He believes in you. Come on in, sister Skye. Maybe your spirit can find some peace for a while."

Skye stepped in out of the cold. She knew her life would not change, but as she settled into the back pew, she thought she was already starting to heal.

AUTHOR BIO

Austin S. Camacho is the author of eight novels about Washington DC-based private eye Hannibal Jones, five in the Stark and O'Brien international adventure-thriller series, and the detective novel Beyond Blue. His short stories have been featured in several anthologies and he is featured in the Edgar nominated African American Mystery Writers: A Historical and Thematic Study by Frankie Y. Bailey. He is a past president of the Maryland Writers Association, past Vice President of the Virginia Writers Club, and one of the creators of the Creatures, Crimes & Creativity (C^3) literary conference.

To My Readers…

First, THANK YOU for going on this thrilling ride with my action character Skye. She has a lot more exciting adventures ahead and I hope you follow her through them.

I love to hear from my readers! After you've read my novel please do send me some feedback. Your opinions and reactions will help me with shaping future novels. You can write to me at ascamacho@hotmail.com and I will always respond. You can also reach me through my website– www.ascamacho.com–see my latest news on Facebook https://www.facebook.com/austin.camacho.author and follow my random meanderings on my blog https://ascamacho.blogspot.com

The only thing better than hearing from my readers is meeting them! So, if you're a member of a book club, I would love to see you. If your group decides to read one of my books I would be most happy to attend the meeting when you talk about it. That way I can answer any questions you have and fill you in on the background of how that particular book came to be (and bring along some special gifts.)

Thanks again for reading my work, and I hope I get the chance to meet you or hear from you in the future.

Ciao, for niao,
Austin